Show M

A Masters of the Shadowlands Novella

By Cherise Sinclair

1001 Dark Nights

Show Me, Baby
A Master of the Shadowlands Novella
By Cherise Sinclair

1001 Dark Nights

ISBN: 978-1-940887-07-4

Published by Evil Eye Concepts, Incorporated

Author's Note

To my readers,

The books I write are fiction, not reality, and as in most romantic fiction, the romance is compressed into a very, very short time period.

You, my darlings, live in the real world, and I want you to take a little more time in your relationships. Good Doms don't grow on trees, and there are some strange people out there. So while you're looking for that special Dom, please, be careful.

When you find him, realize he can't read your mind. Yes, frightening as it might be, you're going to have to open up and talk to him. And you listen to him in return. Share your hopes and fears, what you want from him, what scares you spitless. Okay, he may try to push your boundaries a little—he's a Dom, after all—but you will have your safe word. You will have a safe word, am I clear? Use protection. Have a backup person. Communicate.

Remember: safe, sane, and consensual.

Know that I'm hoping you find that special, loving person who will understand your needs and hold you close.

And while you're looking or even if you've already found your dearheart, come and hang out with the Masters of the Shadowlands.

Love,
Cherise

Sign up for the 1001 Dark Nights Newsletter
and be entered to win a Tiffany Key necklace.

There's a contest every month!

Go to http://www.1001darknights.com to subscribe.

As a bonus, all subscribers will receive a free
1001 Dark Nights story on 1/1/15.
The First Night
by Shayla Black, Lexi Blake & M.J. Rose

One Thousand and One Dark Nights

Once upon a time, in the future…

I was a student fascinated with stories and learning. I studied philosophy, poetry, history, the occult, and the art and science of love and magic. I had a vast library at my father's home and collected thousands of volumes of fantastic tales.

I learned all about ancient races and bygone times. About myths and legends and dreams of all people through the millennium. And the more I read the stronger my imagination grew until I discovered that I was able to travel into the stories... to actually become part of them.

I wish I could say that I listened to my teacher and respected my gift, as I ought to have. If I had, I would not be telling you this tale now.
But I was foolhardy and confused, showing off with bravery.

One afternoon, curious about the myth of the Arabian Nights, I traveled back to ancient Persia to see for myself if it was true that every day Shahryar (Persian: شهریار, "king") married a new virgin, and then sent yesterday's wife to be beheaded. It was written and I had read, that by the time he met Scheherazade, the vizier's daughter, he'd killed one thousand women.

Something went wrong with my efforts. I arrived in the midst of the story and somehow exchanged places with Scheherazade – a phenomena that had never occurred before and that still to this day, I cannot explain.

Now I am trapped in that ancient past. I have taken on Scheherazade's life and the only way I can protect myself and stay alive is to do what she did to protect herself and stay alive.

Every night the King calls for me and listens as I spin tales. And when the evening ends and dawn breaks, I stop at a point that leaves him breathless and yearning for more. And so the King spares my life for one more day, so that he might hear the rest of my dark tale.

As soon as I finish a story... I begin a new one... like the one that you, dear reader, have before you now.

Chapter One

"He's going to fire me," Rainie Kuras muttered. The noise of hammering rain on the car roof drowned out her voice as she peered through her streaked windshield. The streets were filled with standing water in a special Florida trap for the unwary. She glanced up at the heavens where indubitably lived a whole slew of annoying gods. "Do you think I have extra time to waste? Really?"

Her grip on the steering wheel dented the faded blue padding. She mustn't be late to her job at the towing company. Not now, thanks to dear Cory, the owner's jerk of a son who'd taken over the business last week. What an excruciating beginning to the new year.

Since then, each day had been a misery. Rainie's sigh sounded bitter, even to her own ears.

But she couldn't afford to quit. Not after wiping out the last of her savings. She didn't regret spending the money. Miss Lily had been as comfortable as possible before she'd "gone home"—as the fragile old woman termed death.

Rainie blinked back tears. Why did it seem as if it had been raining every day since her passing, as if the world itself mourned?

A horn blared behind the Civic, startling Rainie into the present. After a glance in the rearview mirror, she veered toward the curb to let the *let-me-drive-up-your-ass* BMW with Boston plates zip past. Cell phone in one hand, the driver used his other to hit the horn again.

"Idiotic, irritating ignoramus." Rainie rolled her eyes. *Better slow down, dude.*

The speeding car reached the flooded intersection. Alas, no passage miraculously opened for Moses. As water sprayed outward, the vehicle hydroplaned, fishtailing violently.

"Foot off the gas, don't panic," Rainie whispered, cringing inwardly.

As the Boston car's tires caught traction, the rear pendulumed to the other side. A high yelp sounded. A brown animal was flung to the curb. The BMW kept going.

Oh no, no, no. Rainie's already clammy hands slid on the steering wheel. She didn't know how to fix injuries, especially non-people ones. *Move, dog. Move.* The little body lay motionless.

God, please let the dog be okay. Carefully, she drove across the flooded intersection, turned on the hazard flashers, and jumped out. The heavy rain flattened her hair and soaked her suit.

Blinking through damp eyelashes, she saw the dog was breathing. "God, you poor thing." With its fur matted down, the dog wasn't much bigger than a cat. Terrified. Panting. Trembling.

"I'm so not good with animals." How could she be? She'd lived in apartments. Never had a pet. She squatted awkwardly, trying to check for bleeding and broken bones.

Brushing aside the fur, she scowled at the blood oozing from a scraped shoulder, but kept her voice smooth and easy. "Jessica's cat likes me. Does that help? Is there an animal letter of recommendation I should get?"

The dog's tail beat once against the pavement.

"I need to take you to a vet." She couldn't really determine if anything was wrong—not in the rain. "Okay, baby, if you don't want a doctor exam, you have to tell me you're all right. Can you—can't you get up?" Tears blurred her vision. *Don't die, little dog. Please.*

It whined, looked up at her with pain-filled, dark brown eyes, and sealed her doom.

* * * *

Exhaustion sat heavy on Jake Sheffield's shoulders as he stared at the impossible schedule...and considered the merits of murder. He'd start with his partner, Saxon, for taking a scuba diving vacation in Cozumel.

After disposing of his best friend's body, he'd execute the so-called office manager of their veterinary clinic. Yes, most definitely—Lynette had to die. He studied the schedule a second longer.

Or maybe he'd kill himself instead.

"You knew a month ago that Sax would be gone, and you still scheduled surgeries for him?" Jake asked in a low tone. He was thirty-one, a veteran, a veterinarian, and a sexual Dominant since his first year in vet school; he'd had ample practice throttling back anger. "I have a full load of exams. Sax isn't here. Who exactly is going to perform those surgeries, Lynette?" The first appointments would start arriving in a few minutes.

"I...guess I messed up, huh?" Lynette's blue eyes shimmered with tears.

Amateur hour in the damp eyes arena wouldn't cut it with him. In the dungeon, women were always crying. He'd caused more than a few appealing sobbing fits himself. Deliberately.

Lynette could save herself the trouble of squeezing out some salt water.

And now he knew why Saxon had been pressured to give Lynette a job—and why her sole job reference had been so noncommittal. Because she couldn't spell, forgot assignments, and took garbled messages. Even basic receptionist tasks were beyond her. The slender blonde was about as useful as dewclaws on a Chihuahua.

It'd be the last time he let Saxon hire anyone.

"Yes. You messed up," Jake said evenly. "Now call and shift some appointments to later in the week." They had a substitute vet who might be willing to pitch in on such short notice. Or maybe he could—

The clinic's entrance door hissed open.

Jake looked up, and his mood lightened. The woman in the doorway was Rainie, a submissive in his and Saxon's favorite BDSM club, the Shadowlands. "Come on in."

When he and Saxon opened the clinic over two years ago, they'd been surprised and delighted when the owner of the club had trusted them with his cat. Since then, many of the Shadowlands members had brought their pets to the clinic.

Considering how the trainee avoided him at the club, her presence here was a surprise.

And he'd never seen her in street clothing, let alone a tailored suit. Her streaky brown hair was in an intricate coil at her nape. Even drenched and mud-streaked, she looked amazing. Saxon had once commented she could be a model for a BBW—big, beautiful woman. And that was only the beginning of her appeal.

"I don't know what to do." Her carefully even voice couldn't conceal the underlying panic. The blanket wrapped around the animal showed a growing bloodstain.

Ignoring the office manager's hissed, "She doesn't have an appointment," he motioned to an exam room. "Let's have a look."

After Rainie set the animal on the stainless steel table, Jake carefully unwrapped the bundle.

Dark brown eyes, wavy filthy fur. A small dog with an equally small growl.

"He bite?" Jake asked.

"Uh…"

"Never mind." She might not know, especially if her pet hadn't been seriously injured before. Jake would simply be careful, as always. Nothing obviously broken. Alert, eyes slightly glazed—probably with pain. Breathing fast. Where was the blood coming from? "What happened?"

"A car. Off Highway 19." Her wide-set, hazel eyes sparked with anger. "The driver didn't even stop."

"Happens more often than you'd think." Jake moved slowly, letting the dog smell him. A quick glance ascertained gender. "Easy, boy. I see you're battered and sore, so I'm going to go nice and slow. You're being a good dog. Your mama will be proud of you."

Under the measured rhythm of the words, Rainie relaxed. Dr. Jake Sheffield's smooth baritone projected utter confidence. That he was there to help. That he *could* help.

She studied him for a moment. Some of the Shadowlands Masters had the bulky musculature of powerlifters. Not Master Jake. He was a couple of inches over six feet with a lean, muscular build. Not too lean, though. The shoulders under his white polo shirt were broad, and the sleeves strained to fit around rock-hard biceps. The man was drop-dead gorgeous, with the chiseled features of a model. Shadowy designer stubble added a dangerous cast to a hard jawline.

Every instinct told her to flee.

A sizzling hot guy she could handle. But not this one. The first time she'd seen Jake had been over a decade ago, and she'd turned so starry-eyed her high school classmates had made fun of her. And…her entire life had been flushed down the toilet that day because of him.

Not his fault, certainly. He'd never even known she existed.

He sure wouldn't have been her choice of a veterinarian today. But on the phone, Linda had insisted Jake was the best vet in the area. Master Sam, Marcus, and Master Z took their pets to his clinic.

Maybe Linda was right. Dr. Sheffield seemed very competent, carefully checking every inch of the little dog while murmuring reassurances. The ball of fur was shaking less.

Then Jake touched something painful, and the dog yelped.

"Dammit." Rainie glared at him. "If you hurt him again, I'm going to hit you."

The sun lines at the corners of his eyes deepened. His warm hand closed on hers. "Let me look under there. Just for a minute."

Rainie realized her fingers lay on the dog's neck. She'd been trying to comfort the poor thing, even if she hadn't a clue what she was doing. "Right. Sorry." She stepped away.

The dog on the metal table scrabbled in an attempt to stand.

"Get back here." Iron edged Jake's quiet order. His voice gentled as he said, "Easy, boy. She's not going anywhere. See?"

Mouth open in surprise, Rainie resumed her place. When Jake set her hand on the dog's shoulder, the small body relaxed. Eyes the color of dark chocolate watched her anxiously. Was the tiny dog fearful she'd move away again?

She could feel the tug, as if a string had been tied to her heart.

"There you go, little guy. She loves you, see?" As Jake palpated the dog's stomach, his brows drew together. "Has he been off his feed? He's way underweight. And full of burrs. Do you live in the country?"

"What?" She massaged the wet fur lightly and felt gritty dirt. "He's not mine—I mean I picked him up when the Boston butt-head hit him."

"Boston's your boyfriend?"

"No. A car in front of me with Boston plates. I just got stuck with damage control." And speaking of damage, she was totally screwed. "Oh Go—goodness, I have to get to work."

When she looked at her watch, her heart sank. She was horrendously late. And her suit was wet and muddy and covered with dog fur. "I need to leave. Or I'll be fired."

"I see." Jake's dark brown hair fell over his forehead as he watched her with green eyes the color of leaves in midsummer. "I don't think any bones are broken, but I'd like to take some X-rays and check for internal damage. You can pick him up tonight on your way home."

"Pick him up? But he's not my dog."

"Maybe. Maybe not. Our tech will check if anyone's looking for him." He stroked his hand down the dog's side, flattening the curly fur. Rainie could see the hollowing below the ribs. "I'd say he's been living on the streets. Might've been dumped."

"Seriously? A little dog?" That was just wrong. A warm wave of kinship to the animal ran through her. She knew how it felt to be abandoned. Alone and not wanted. Surviving on the streets. "Poor baby." She gently ruffled the dog's ears and heard his soft whine of...gratitude? Longing?

Oh heavens, what was she thinking? Brows pulling together, she scowled at Jake. "You are *not* going to coerce me into keeping this dog. I don't do animals."

"All things change, subbie," he said softly, for her ears alone. The light amusement of an utterly confident Dom made her insides shiver. His voice returned to a normal level. "You pick up the dog tonight, and I won't charge you for his care."

Her mouth dropped open. *Charge me?* But...but... This day kept getting worse. She hadn't even thought about a vet bill, and from the professional appearance of the office, the clinic probably charged a whack of a lot.

But, to be fair, it was Jake's living.

Unfortunately, she didn't have the cost of a vet visit in her savings. If he'd take care of the little dog for free...

In return, she'd be stuck finding the little guy a good home. She drew herself up and gave him the iciest look she could muster. "Fine. I'll be in around five-thirty."

"Mmmhmm." His firm lips quirked. "That works."

* * * *

Half an hour later, Rainie's new boss sneered at her. "You think to work in *my* place looking like you got screwed by every long-hauler at the truck stop? Haven't changed much, have you?"

Her jaw tightened at his ugly allusion to when she'd been a teenager, but she didn't dignify his rudeness by checking her ruined suit. "A dog was hit by a car. I took it to the vet."

"Nice to know you have priorities," he said. "It's a shame your job doesn't head up the list."

"Listen, I—"

"No, you listen." He walked over, close enough that her breasts almost touched his chest. "You want to keep working here, you got to give me your all."

She knew what he was implying—that he wanted more than office work from her. Disgust held its own taste—a foul one. “I work harder than anyone else you’d find for this job. That’s why your father made me manager.”

And Cory’d never worked hard a day in his life.

“Excuse me. I need to get the payroll started.” She sidestepped him and moved toward her desk.

The phone rang. Rainie glanced that direction, but, as always, Mrs. Fitzhugh had things under control. After dispatching a truck, the gray-haired woman gave Rainie her usual good morning smile and returned to record keeping. Not a chatterbox, Mrs. Fitzhugh.

But thank goodness she was here.

Since Cory took over, Rainie had made sure she was never in the office alone with him. He *probably* wouldn’t be stupid enough to get physical, but she’d discovered early in her life how a boner could shut down every cell in a man’s brain.

And, although the company’s owner, Bart, liked her, he wasn’t here, and he might not believe her against Cory. He thought his boy was all pure and wonderful.

A burst of thunder shook the squatty building as sheets of rain slammed into the concrete outside. A wrecking truck drove by. The twisted mess of a brand-new pickup on the trailer was a pointed reminder that life could be fleeting.

She’d worked for Thompson Towing and Recovery since starting grad school. Apparently, in the last few years, she’d forgotten that nothing lasts forever.

Not that she planned to stay, now that she had her MBA. No, she planned to leave the Tampa/St. Pete area—and her white-trash background—far behind. She’d settle in a different state, find an established, distinguished corporation, and take a position doing something that would garner admiration and respect.

But Miss Lily’s illness had wiped out Rainie’s savings, and moving required funds. By the time her apartment lease expired in mid-February, she should have enough money to relocate.

At the sight of the mess on her desk, Rainie came to a halt. She turned to Cory. “What were you doing in my desk?”

He smirked. “Looking for a file.”

Rainie growled under her breath. Her “personal” drawer was open, and he’d rummaged through her stuff—makeup, breath mints, even tampons. The sense of being violated was keen. Unfortunately, after her years in foster care, this was not an unfamiliar feeling.

Cory was such a bastard. Her jaw clamped to keep from spitting out her fury.

Bart was an honest, good ol’ boy, like the truckers he employed. His son, however, was all show and no substance and never kept a job longer than a few months. Yet, Bart was convinced Cory could manage the company. *Parents can be so blind.*

A handsome thirty-year-old with carefully styled flaxen hair, a golden tan, and blue eyes, Cory figured if he wanted something, he should have it.

And to think he'd implied she hadn't changed much. She huffed a laugh. He hadn't changed at all. At sixteen, she'd run away from her foster home and a drug dealer took her in. Cory'd shown up to buy coke for a frat party…then tried to buy her too. For a *quickie*. When Shiz refused, Cory'd thrown his weight around…and gotten the crap beat out of him. They'd dumped him in a garbage bin.

One nasty night. One nasty memory. Shaking her head, Rainie straightened up her personal drawer. Soon after Bart'd hired her, she'd run into Cory—but he'd wisely pretended not to know her. She'd returned the favor. Just went to show St. Petersburg, Florida, really was too small of a city.

Now Cory was her boss, and his father was in Europe. Talk about an occupational nightmare.

Yesterday, when Mrs. Fitzhugh had taken lunch, Cory'd sneaked up behind Rainie and groped her. Her outraged shove had caught him by surprise—and he'd fallen over a chair.

Rainie smiled slightly. She might surrender to a Dom she liked, but when it came to physically protecting herself from slimeballs? She didn't have a single submissive cell in her body. As she finished her tidying, she caught Cory staring at her.

"Were you looking for a particular file?" she asked. Her desk contained all her current projects. And she had a lot. She'd put her MBA coursework to work by taking on the business's payroll, scheduling, and advertising. Last month, she'd started on the arcane arena of insurance. God, she loved juggling the multitude of tasks, and Bart'd been delighted to designate her the "office manager" and hand over the reins.

Unfortunately, now Cory ran the company.

Face flushed, Cory stopped beside her desk, crowding her. When a file drawer slammed louder than the thunder outside, he realized Mrs. Fitzhugh was watching. He took a step back. "I'll do the trucker's schedules this month."

Hopefully he wouldn't screw it up too badly. Rainie gave him a polite smile. "How nice." With his history, he'd be bored with the company even before she quit. *Be patient.*

"Here are the requests for days off." She handed him the correct folder and couldn't resist adding, "The schedule is due up on Monday."

Cory made a noise like a mouse flattened by a golf cart—lovely sound. But then he leaned forward and lowered his voice. "You might consider being friendlier…assuming you want to keep this job."

"I don't need to be friendlier to manage the taxes, the advertising, the software, or the payroll," she assured him in a kind voice. "And since the truckers get irritable if not paid on time, I'd better start."

His gaze swept over her and lingered on her breasts.

With the soaking she'd gotten, her shirt was almost translucent. The perverted prick. Turning away, she buttoned up her suit coat, then pulled up the payroll on her monitor. Finally…he moved away.

She breathed out. God, how long could she put up with him? But he wouldn't do anything. After all, he couldn't run the place without her.

And she couldn't leave. Rent was due. Her savings were gone. She needed the job.

Chapter Two

Aching with misery, Jake entered the main room of the still quiet Shadowlands BDSM club. As the mansion's air-conditioning struggled against the evening heat, the humidity added to his weariness.

Pretty sad to be decades older than a two-year-old and to be craving a nap. But because of the clinic's messed-up schedule, he'd put in twelve-hour days the entire week. And his last furry patient today had been…bad.

At the long, oval bar in the room's center, Cullen and his submissive, Andrea, were concocting pitchers of drinks.

Jake eyed the water condensing on the outside of the crystal glass. The way he felt, a drink would be more satisfying than a scene. He slid onto a barstool. "You're adding vodka to an energy drink?"

"A special for tonight's glow party theme." Cullen grinned. "The liquid shines under the black lights." He patted the white T-shirt covering his massive chest. "And so will this. People need to be able to find the bartender."

"Hate to say this, but no one'll notice you with your gorgeous submissive around," Jake noted.

Andrea wore a cut-off, white shirt that barely covered her full breasts. Her boy briefs curved delightfully over her round ass.

"This is true," Cullen said in open agreement. "She is gorgeous, isn't she?"

At her Master's ready compliment, Andrea's face brightened as if a ray of sunlight had caught it.

"So, buddy, Z wondered where you were." Cullen put a few drops of blue food coloring into cne pitcher. "You missed the Masters' briefing."

"I had an emergency surgery." Jake's gut tightened. "A puppy chased a cat onto the highway. The driver of the car tried to stop. Cat got across okay. Dog didn't."

Andrea turned, a stricken look on her face. "Is the puppy all right?"

"His hind leg is fractured, and he has internal injuries." Jake sighed and ran his fingers through his hair. "He might recover." *Or not.* The wife had been in tears, and her husband pretty damn close.

"At least the dog had you to take care of him." Andrea patted his hand.

Jake straightened, uncomfortable with her sympathy. A Dom should comfort submissives, not the other way around.

Obviously, his exhaustion had turned him into a wimp, or so his BDSM mentor would have said. Even in his sixties, the Marine Gunnery Sergeant had never admitted to tiredness…let alone depression over an injured pet.

Andrea put a bottle of water in front of him. "If you were in surgery, you probably didn't get supper, did you?" An experienced submissive, she read the answer from his expression. "I thought not."

She glanced at her Master and got a nod before heading for the munchie corner.

With an effort, Jake suppressed a surge of loneliness. Last year, he and Heather had been close enough to communicate without speaking. But when she'd dumped him for her career, he'd wondered if they'd truly communicated at all. She'd left so quickly that sometimes he felt as if he could still hear the door swing shut behind her.

Well, lesson learned. He'd be more careful next time.

"What was in the briefing?" he asked Cullen.

"The black lights stay on all night, and Z suggests light scenes. The theme rooms have normal lighting for those playing harder. He has some special floggers and paddles, too."

"What's special about them?"

Cullen snorted as he mixed tonic water with juice. "Sprayed with neon paint. Should make for interesting scenes." He pointed to the white-linen-covered tables. "Also, there are glow paints. Submissives are to be decorated by Doms—can't do it themselves. The trainees are wearing black underwear or the equivalent."

Submissive painting. Glowing floggers. "Sounds like fun."

"Could be. Trouble is, we're short on Masters tonight. Dan's vacationing with Kari and the baby. Marcus is stuck at the courthouse, waiting on a jury verdict. Raoul is flying back tonight from a construction job in Panama." Cullen swiped up the few drops he'd spilled.

"Need an extra dungeon monitor?" He wasn't scheduled, but he could handle it. He'd just shift gears from his expectation of a lazy evening to an active one.

"Yep." Cullen thumped a gold-trimmed black leather monitor vest on top of the bar. "If you can cover the main room for an hour now and then again at midnight, I'd appreciate it. There's no Trainee Master tonight, so we're all watching out for them."

"Got it." With only three trainees left, keeping an eye on them wasn't a problem.

When Z had set up the program for submissives needing increased immersion in the lifestyle, most of the Shadowlands Masters and Mistresses were single. Now, since only Mistress Anne, Jake, and Holt were unattached, the program was ending once the last trainee found a Dom. "Was there anything Z required them to work on?"

"Nope. Tonight is for fun and light play. They're even to do their own scene negotiations. Good practice for them, actually."

Jake pulled on the vest, amusement lightening his mood. "But since Z's a mother hen, he asked us to check on them anyway."

"Bingo."

"Here, Master Jake." Andrea placed a small plate piled with finger foods in front of him. "This should keep your furnace stoked for a while."

Cullen is one lucky Dom. "Thank you, sweetheart."

The sincerity of his gratitude made her smile.

He popped a mini-quiche into his mouth and considered his next bite.

"Master Cullen, I'm here." The liltingly melodic voice came from beside him.

Jake glanced down to see Rainie at his shoulder, one beautifully curvy woman, about five-seven. Not too short, not too tall.

Unlike earlier in the week when she'd brought in the injured dog, she wasn't dressed conservatively. In leather wrist cuffs, a black halter bra, and barely-there, black skirt, she was an explosion of light and color and softness, from her shoulder-length, brown hair streaked with bright gold and red, to the fountain-and-blossom tattoos that flowed upward beside her spine, over one shoulder, and down between her magnificent breasts.

Cullen poured a glass of juice and handed it to her. "Good to see you, sweetheart. Did you bring in cookies for the munchie corner?"

"Already there, Sir. I used Kari's recipe, in fact."

"Perfect. The caterers are good, but their sweets never taste like homemade."

"Hello, Rainie," Jake said, watching her closely. Considering she'd brought him her dog, would she still avoid him?

"Master Jake." She took a step away from him, then her gaze fell on the plate in front of him. She frowned. "I didn't think you liked crab cakes."

"I don't, but—"

She picked the mini crab cake from his plate and replaced it with the chocolate chip cookie in her hand. As she looked up at him, her hazel eyes were more brown than green in the dim light of the room. "I bet you'd prefer this."

A cookie. His day brightened. "I've never met a cookie I didn't like. How'd you know?"

"Master Z says we're supposed to keep track of everyone's preferences." Rainie popped the crab cake in her mouth.

Her lips were as lush as the rest of her, and he tried not to imagine other things he'd like to feed her…like his cock. He'd managed to ignore the craving before this week, but after seeing her with the pup—well, women with soft hearts were irresistible.

However, a Master wasn't worth much if he didn't master himself. "Good job of paying attention, then."

He studied her and decided not to ask about the dog he'd treated. He didn't mind blending his two personas, but others tended to be more cautious, especially submissives. And from the classic-cut suit she'd worn in his clinic, he'd guess Rainie held down a good, conventional job.

In contrast, when relaxed in the Shadowlands, she had a warm earthiness to her, much like a vivid hearth goddess.

"Hey, everybody." Jessica, the club owner's pregnant wife, appeared on Rainie's other side and beamed at Andrea. "Andrea, I love your outfit."

"Gracias, Jessica."

The little blonde turned her attention to Rainie and wrinkled her nose. "Boy, Z didn't do you trainees any favors."

"Boring, all right." Rainie tugged on the black halter top, then her brow creased. "You look tired, girlfriend."

"Nothing new." Jessica cupped her big belly. "I carry a lead basketball around all day."

"Then stop walking for a while." With a snort, Rainie walked away.

She returned with a folding chair, set it behind the bar, and patted the seat. "Plant your butt."

Jessica scowled. Stalled.

Jake had to agree with the trainee. "Jessica, sit," he said quietly, knowing the effect the command would have on a trained submissive.

The blonde sat and pouted at him. "You're as dictatorial as Z." Then she glared at Rainie. "And you're supposed to be submissive."

"True, I submit to Doms. Aside from them, I'm the alpha-female in this place and don't you forget it." Rainie exchanged a high-five with Andrea before returning to sit on a barstool beside Jake. Turned away from him, she picked up her drink and asked Andrea how work was going.

Stubborn and *caring*. How had he missed seeing that facet of her personality?

As Jake ate and traded greetings with incoming members, he kept an ear turned to Andrea's chat with Rainie and Jessica about the underprivileged youngsters she'd hired for her cleaning service. Sounded as if the kids were a handful and needed instruction in not only housekeeping, but also manners and attire.

"Watch out for pilfering," Rainie commented. "I know you're keeping them away from your residential clients, but even in offices, people leave easily pocketed valuables on their desks."

Odd. He hadn't thought Rainie would be prejudiced against the poor. Then again, her matter-of-fact tone lacked scorn.

"This is true." Andrea frowned. "I'll be observant." The two women exchanged looks with undertones of...something shared?

As Jake studied them, his gaze focused on Rainie's yellow and red streaked hair. A few stiffer strands were green as well. "Did you get something in your hair?"

"Oh, did I. Master Galen brought in neon hairspray and wanted to be artistic." She rolled her eyes. "Crazy Fed."

Jake turned slightly. Unfortunately, he couldn't let her impertinence pass. "Rainie." Fisting her hair, he pulled her smoothly to her feet.

"Hey!" She grabbed his wrist.

"Whether you have a problem with the FBI agents or not, you're going to be respectful." He paused and added, *"Trainee."*

Her arm lowered. "I…I'm sorry, Sir."

The instinctive yielding of her body sent a frisson of pleasure up his spine. Be a delight to push her further. "There are lines a submissive shouldn't cross. *You* shouldn't cross. Not only for a Dom's comfort, but yours as well. I'll enforce those limits, Rainie." He didn't bother to add she wouldn't enjoy coming up against his will. Either she was smart enough to know it or she'd learn.

"I'll keep that in mind," she said. When he twisted her hair, increasing the pull, she added a hasty, "Sir. I'll remember, Sir."

He eyed her. Was she going to cause trouble tonight? She and Uzuri were known pranksters. Only two other submissives in the Shadowlands were more mischievous. He smothered a smile. Gabi's mouthiness kept Marcus on top of the D/s game, and little Sally was such a handful it took both Galen and Vance to keep her playfulness within bounds.

He had to admit he envied the other Masters their spirited submissives.

Keeping Rainie quiet with his hand in her hair, he regarded her clothing. Completely black… He glanced at Cullen. "Let me guess—Z's using the trainees as walking canvases?"

"That's affirmative, buddy. And all submissives—trainee or not—get their lips painted so they glow." Cullen tapped Rainie's mouth and barked a laugh when she snapped her teeth at him.

Jake studied the sumptuous female feast he held and zeroed in on her very fuckable mouth. She had softly pink lips with a crease in the center of the lower one. "Were your lips glow-painted?"

Rainie looked up through a stray lock of hair. "Uh. No." When he didn't respond, she added a hasty, "Sir."

"Let's get the task out of the way then." He put a hand on her nape, and her thick, silky hair tickled his fingers as he guided her toward a table. With an effort, he ignored the effect she had on him. The woman was too damned appealing for his good.

The reverse wasn't true. For whatever reason, she didn't want anything to do with him—and he figured that was a submissive's choice to make. Even if it left him feeling fucking disgruntled.

Master Jake had big hands. Rainie felt the power in the fingers curled around the back of her neck. She barely managed to suppress a shiver and wanted to scold her body for getting worked up. *Burned once, twice shy.*

But that thought kept slipping away when she was close enough to see the laugh lines fanning from the corners of his eyes.

He was known as a fun Master. Friendly. Easy-going…to a point. She liked that kind of Dominant.

But even without the past between them—although he knew nothing about that day—she wouldn't want to be with him. Last winter, when a date had taken her to the super-expensive restaurant, Caretta on the Gulf, Jake had been there with a gorgeous, thin, designer-clad woman. His suit had said money. His manners had said polish and class. Everything about him reaffirmed he was out of her league.

And yet his grip did funny things to her insides.

When they reached the table, he released her.

Silently, she looked up at him. He was more than a half-foot taller than her five-seven, and totally lean and muscled. His cheekbones were defined. His jaw, strong. His nose, a work of art.

And here she stood. A fluffy, plus-sized woman from the slums. They had nothing in common.

"Z wanted scenes to be lightweight. Will his dictate put a crimp in your plans tonight?" Jake's voice was as flowing and flawless as the black silk shirt he wore.

"Not really. Hitting the dance floor is at the top of my agenda." Dancing was far more fun than sex—and tonight, it would be awesome under the black lights.

One sharply angled, masculine eyebrow rose. In all his perfection, he reminded her of a slightly younger Master Marcus. Jake must be…about thirty or thirty-one, right?

"Aren't you interested in doing scenes? Finding the ideal Dom?" he asked.

At one time when she'd joined, she'd wanted to score the perfect Dom. Now? Not so much. "Of course," she lied.

She crossed her arms over her chest as the heavy weight of a Dom's scrutiny landed on her—Jake's scrutiny—and her spine turned to water. How did he do that?

"Hey, Jake." Kendall—known in the club as Barge—strolled over. The Dom wore a skin-tight, black vinyl shirt and pants. Sometimes she wondered if he'd joined the Shadowlands just to dress up.

"Barge. Good to see you." As the wall sconces dimmed and the black lights came on, Jake dipped his finger into the glowing red pot and outlined her lips with the body paint.

Why did the simple glide of his finger seem like sexual overture? Why did his touch have to feel right? She knew better. *No perving on the sophisticated, classy Dom.*

When Master Jake stepped back, she stifled her urge to get closer. Instead, she turned her attention to Barge.

"Want to do an easy flogging scene?" Barge asked her. "Z lent me a flogger, and I'd like to see the falls in the black light."

Rainie considered. Last month, Barge had talked her into seeing him outside the club. Although their two dates had been pleasant enough, he reminded her of other "nice" men she'd known, possessing a personality more willow tree than oak. When push came to shove, Barge would bend—much as her previous boyfriends had when confronted with peer or family pressures over dating her.

However, even though she didn't want to date Barge, his scenes were fun. She wasn't looking for anything more intense—not after her horrible week.

"Sure." After a warning look from Jake, she amended her answer to, "I'd like that, Sir."

"Okay then. Let's go, subbie."

"Yes, Sir." She followed Barge across the room and managed to check over her shoulder only once…to see Jake watching her thoughtfully.

* * * *

Jake's hour of serving as a dungeon monitor was over. After handing off the gold-trimmed vest and getting a bottled water, he dropped down in a leather chair between two scenes to admire the light show. In the shadowy room, the glow-painted floggers, canes, and paddles were mesmerizing.

There were also some enthusiastic body-paint jobs, especially on submissives' breasts and pussies. Stripes, circles, dots. In one shadowy section, a pair of glowing green breasts seemed to float in the air without a supporting body.

Z had developed a great theme, as usual. During Jake's travels in the Army Veterinary Corps, he'd appraised several BDSM clubs and none suited him as well as here.

Being voted in as a Shadowlands "Master" had been an honor he hadn't expected. He didn't mind putting in the extra time Z requested of the Masters. He figured mentoring new Doms, supervising scenes, and protecting submissives were all activities any experienced Dom should perform without being asked.

Of course, Z did have his favorite project. And during the past hour, Jake had made a point of checking on the trainees. Uzuri had gone upstairs with Holt, one of her favorite Doms. In the far corner, Tanner waited in a dog kennel while a married couple—a Mistress and a switch—prepared for the scene they'd do.

And here was the third trainee.

In the scene area to Jake's left, Barge and Rainie finished cleaning the equipment and sat down to talk. She had her back turned to Jake, and he spotted a few light pink areas on the untattooed parts of her shoulders, but no welts. She hadn't cried, hadn't reached subspace, didn't appear stressed. Then again, not much frazzled Rainie.

She definitely had an interesting personality—and a confusing one. Damned if he could figure out why she had such an aversion to him.

He turned away to observe the other scene where Mistress Anne was caning a male submissive. The sub groaned with each smack of the cane and yelped at the lightest touch to his genitalia. The lack of expression on Anne's face conveyed her displeasure. The Mistress liked to dispense pain, and she didn't play with lightweights. As often happened, the submissive had probably tried to impress her by claiming to have a high pain tolerance.

Now they both knew the truth.

Barge's lifted voice drew Jake's attention.

"C'mon, Rainie. I'm willing to work around your schedule," Barge said. "Surely you've got a night free next week."

"I really don't. It's a busy time at my company, and I'm sorry, but my career comes first."

She didn't sound particularly sorry, Jake thought. She sounded like a woman flicking an impertinent bug off her arm. His jaw clenched as memories rained down on him. *"I'm sorry, Jake. I have my future to think about. I can't turn down an opportunity like this."* At least, Heather hadn't been cold. No, she'd cried. Told him she loved him.

And then she'd moved to the West Coast the very next day.

Fair enough. He'd picked himself up and worked through the defeat. *Live and learn, right?* He still wanted a wife. Children. Damn straight. He just needed to fall for a woman whose priorities matched his own—and someone who would at least *talk* about compromise.

Feeling as if his presence was an intrusion, he rose. Their argument was polite enough. No need to intervene…although he'd keep an eye on them from farther away.

As he retreated, he noticed Z and Sam also within hearing range. Sam had on a gold-trimmed dungeon monitor's vest, so he was on duty.

Z wore his usual tailored black clothing, right down to the black leather, black-faced watch. He tilted his head in an invitation to join them. "Jacob, did anything of interest occur this evening?"

"No disasters." Jake smiled. "I think you'll lose Tanner from the trainees shortly. The Coltons plan to ask him to become a third in their relationship."

"That would be a good match for all three," Z said.

"Agreed." Sam glanced behind them with displeasure. "Barge and Rainie, though. Not a match."

"Not even close." Jake's brows drew together. On a different night, he wouldn't have permitted the scene with Barge. She didn't need lightweight play. "I'd say she's in a rut. Doesn't want to be pushed. Doesn't want anything heavy."

"Indeed." The lines bracketing Z's mouth deepened. "I need to carve out more time for the trainees."

Jake shook his head, seeing the guilt drop onto the Dom's shoulders. The owner considered the trainees—hell, all the members—to be his responsibility. "I don't think you *have* more time available, Zachary." He deliberately used Z's full name. "And you have new obligations, like a pregnant wife. Time to lighten the load and learn to delegate."

Sam's sandpapery chuckle held approval.

To Jake's relief, Z gave him a wry smile. The best Doms saw themselves clearly—and had a sense of humor. "Perhaps so, Jacob. In fact, I think *you* should take over the trainees."

"Me? I don't—"

Gray eyes alight with amusement, Z squeezed his shoulder. "You're not only equal to the challenge, but you would also enjoy it."

"Maybe." *Probably*. Jake held up his hand to stall. To think. After a minute, he said, "I might like being the Trainee Master, but I need to refuse."

"What the hell?" Sam growled.

"The responsibility isn't a concern." Jake's gaze drifted to Rainie. Since she'd come into his clinic, he'd had an...urge that grew stronger each day. Time to ante up. "I believe a Trainee Master shouldn't meet a trainee outside of the Shadowlands. Which is why I'd prefer to avoid the job."

Z followed his gaze, and a faint smile appeared. "I see. And respect your honesty. Will you have a problem working with her as a Master?"

"Not at all," Jake said.

"Excellent," Z said.

Sam shifted his weight. "Got a chore for you then. The girl has trouble refusing a Dom's orders. Maybe she's intimidated, maybe wants to please too badly, maybe both. I figured she'd conquered the problem, but"—he nodded toward the couch—"she's lying instead of just saying no."

Work with Rainie? Hell, yes. "I'll take that project."

"Very good," Z said. "Thank you, Jacob."

As the two men continued their rounds, Jake stayed in place, considering. "*...trouble refusing.*" Not good.

As a veterinarian, Jake was skilled in reading body language—although admittedly, humans were vastly more difficult. He'd never exceeded a submissive's boundaries, spoken or not. But not every Dom had learned to read a submissive.

And even in a pick-up scene, a submissive and Dominant performed an intricate dance. To be fulfilled, the sub *needed* to give up control. Yet, a Dom had to trust that a sub would say *stop* if he pushed too far.

Sam, being a sadist, certainly knew the danger of a bottom lying to a top. Was he right about Rainie having a problem?

As he drank his water, Jake considered. When she'd agreed to scene with Barge, her body had been relaxed. No conflict between her body language and her words. But later, she'd refused a date and insisted she had to work. At that time, her head had jerked sideways in unspoken contradiction. She'd widened her eyes and fixed her gaze on Barge, a technique often used by liars to show their honesty.

Yes, she'd lied to Barge. If Sam was correct, she'd been uncomfortable saying "no" to a Dom.

The thought of Rainie caving in and doing something she didn't like sent a trickle of anger through him. Knowing she'd lied didn't make him happy either. His job—tonight—would be to change that behavior.

Jake tipped his head back and studied the ceiling. How best to achieve that goal?

She'd have to practice saying no...but in a realistically intimidating setting. One where she'd find refusing difficult.

He'd have to find more than one Dom to assist. She might find it easy to decline a stranger's orders, so he'd create a tenuous bond between her and the Dom—and punish her for anything other than a firm *no.*

Plan forming in his head, Jake looked around and picked out the Doms he'd trust to follow instructions.

* * * *

This is ridiculous. Rainie couldn't put up with more of Barge's bullshit. With some effort—stupid low-slung couch—she struggled to her feet. "I'm going to clean up."

To her relief, Barge remained sitting.

She gave him a token bow. "Thank you for the scene, Sir."

Brows drawn down in anger, he didn't answer.

She turned away, annoyed more with herself than him. She was totally a sniveling, spineless slug. Why hadn't she simply said she wasn't interested in dating him? That he did nice scenes, but she didn't want anything else from him? But no-o-o, instead, she invented excuses. With a disgusted grunt, she shoved her hair back.

Thank goodness, Master Sam hadn't been around. When he'd caught her waffling rather than giving a straight refusal, the sadist had given her a "lesson" by smacking her ass until she'd managed to spit out a resolute "no."

She thought she'd learned that day. Apparently not.

Let's not mention the backsliding to Master Sam, okay?

After a leisurely trip to the restroom—to give Barge a chance to leave—Rainie headed for the bar. Since Master Z'd started hiring waitresses, she didn't have any official duties. Right now, she wanted to go home. A quick word to Master Cullen, and she'd be free to leave.

Midevening, several club members had finished playing and sat at the bar socializing. Jessica perched on a barstool. Beside her, Master Z was talking to Mistress Olivia.

"Rainie. C'mere." Jessica had always been curvy, but her pregnancy made her even rounder. A while back, she'd abandoned her pretty corsets. Tonight, she wore a low-cut green tank top with a loose-waisted vinyl skirt held up by suspenders. Trust Master Z to attire his submissive in an outfit that would make even pregnancy sexy. "Did you have a bad session? You seem unhappy."

"Nah, the scene was fun. The glowing strands on the cat-o'-nine-tails were spectacular." As she'd hoped, the flogging had been mostly a massage. If only Barge hadn't been a putz afterward.

"The paddles flash pretty good too." Jessica shifted her weight on the stool as if her bottom hurt. "I can testify to that."

"Oh really?" Rainie glared at Master Z. He'd hit a pregnant woman?

"Don't look like that." Jessica wrinkled her nose. "He'd told me to stay put and I didn't, so I got a few good swats."

A few swats with a paddle wouldn't hurt her. "Well, you actually do look better. Not so tired."

"Nope. I'm good. Andrea made me sit longer after you left. And when I tried to restock the munchie tables, Z swatted my ass and planted me here." With a pout, Jessica stroked a hand over her rotund stomach. "Yeah, *planted.* I swear, I feel more like a potato than a woman."

Obviously hearing her, Master Z curved his arm around her waist so his palm rested on her baby bump. "If you want to compare yourself to a food, I'd say a peach. Ripe. Succulent." He kissed the curve of her shoulder and neck, and his resonant voice deepened. "You're beautiful, kitten, and I love you more every single day."

As Jessica's eyes filled with tears, her hand covered her husband's. Her Dom's.

A disconcerting yearning shook Rainie.

I want that. Want it all.

But no. She wanted no husband or babies, at least not here in the Tampa/St. Pete area where her past would rise up and bite her in the butt.

She retreated a step and bumped into a body that was totally bone and muscle. Honestly, hadn't men ever heard of padding?

Lean fingers gripped her shoulders, steadying her. "Just the person I was looking for," Master Jake said.

Oh, this is just craptastic. Green eyes. Carved features. And a trimmed five-o'clock shadow on his strong jaw. She realized she was breathless. "Can I help you with something, Sir?"

"Mmmhmm. I've got some time, so we're going to work together tonight"—he added the final word as if to let her know she was screwed—"trainee."

"But I thought the trainees weren't… No. We're free to make our own choices tonight."

To her dismay, Master Z turned to contemplate her for a long, long moment. "You haven't the appearance of a satisfied submissive. Go with Master Jacob."

Oh hellfire and hissyfit hyena shoes. "Of course, Sir," she said obediently and looked at Master Jake. "Sir, do you have an assignment for me?"

"Let's talk a bit." He curled his hand around her arm, firmly enough that she felt controlled, carefully enough that she knew he wouldn't hurt her by accident. On purpose, though…

Despite her avoidance of him, she'd observed him play, something he did frequently and well and with a variety of submissives. His BDSM skills appeared exhaustive. He well deserved the "Master" title he'd been voted into last summer.

And, from the way just his touch had melted her insides into liquid goo, she'd still underestimated him. Unlike the in-your-face authority of other Doms, Master Jake's power was a lazy riptide, drawing a submissive under his command before she even realized she'd surrendered.

He steered her to a secluded area and pointed to a chair. As she settled onto the leather cushion, he drew the other chair around so they sat face–to–face.

When his long legs bumped into hers, she pulled her feet up onto the chair.

A corner of his mouth tipped up and then he leaned forward to rest his forearms on his thighs, shifting right into her personal space.

"What did you want to discuss, Master Jake?" Considering her lack of attire, her manager's voice proved ineffective. Actually, she rather doubted the "voice" would daunt Jake no matter what she wore.

"Couple of things. I'm curious—your papers show only 'Rainie.' Is it your given name?"

"'Fraid so." He'd checked out her trainee forms. Why? "My mother liked names to convey something. Her name was Carol, but she called herself Sunny."

"And?" He was too close, his gaze too intent.

She turned her head. At a nearby scene, someone's single-tail flashed under the UV lights. The thrum of the bass from the dance floor speakers struck her skin almost like impact play. "*Sunny* didn't want a baby and cried all the way through her pregnancy. So she christened me Rainie for rainy."

His snort held disgust.

"Yeah, that's pretty much how I felt." Her mother had often ranted about her unwanted pregnancy, the ghastly labor, and the amount of work raising a child required.

When younger, Rainie had fled in tears from the cruel words. She was a tougher bitch now. *Oh yeah.*

"Here, I thought Rainie might be an abbreviation for Lorraine or something," Jake mused.

"Nope. It must frustrate Master Z not to have a 'real' name to call me." Master Z disliked nicknames. Sam was Samuel. Dan was Daniel. Jake, Jacob.

Amusement lit Jake's eyes. "I bet."

He kneaded her calf in an absent-minded act she didn't believe for a second. That friendly, casual attitude of his disguised a very controlled Dom.

The sensation of being touched without permission—and dammit, wanting to be touched—hit a sonorous note deep inside her. *Behave, body, or no chocolate for a week.*

"Rainie's a pretty name." His baritone held a hint of smokiness at the edges. "However, I've never met anyone less like rainfall."

A compliment? Had he just given her a compliment? Her gaze swung back.

His eyes were straightforward…and his long, tapered fingers traced a pattern on her leg.

She swallowed. "You didn't drag me here to talk about my name."

"Now, Rainie, I didn't force you here." His lips curved up slightly. "But I can arrange to drag you if it's something you'd like."

Being *dragged.*

By Jake. The surge of sheer desire made her stiffen, even as she wanted to melt. But no. *No, no, no. No Jake.* She shook her head. "I don't think I'd like that."

He cocked a brow and made a sound, showing how little he believed her answer.

She tried to steady her breathing. Jake Sheffield had been a gorgeous twenty-one-year-old college student. As a confident, virile Dominant, he was lethal. She'd been right to avoid him.

"I noticed something odd in your files," he said. "Tell me, when did you last have a serious scene?"

"I—" Even with her gaze on the leather cuffs circling her wrists, she sensed his gaze never wavered. "A few months, maybe."

"I see. Sweetling, what is it you want from being a trainee?"

The endearment made her heart flutter until she remembered whom she was talking to. *Jake.*

Why did some memories turn to shadows…and others corrode into rawness? Even after a decade, she could hear her classmates. *"Did you see how she stared at Jennifer's brother?" "The fatty wants Jake Sheffield." "God, I think I'm going to throw up."*

She shook her head, hoping to fling the thoughts away.

Concentrate on the present, girl. He'd asked a question. *"What is it you want?"* She didn't have a ready answer. Her goals had changed. As irritation bubbled up, she glared at him and tried to tug her leg from his grip. "Excuse me, but when did this turn into a job interview?"

His deeply masculine voice held a note of steel. "When I decided it did."

He pulled her legs off the chair, placing them on the outside of his knees. His downward glance reminded her she wore nothing under the short skirt. At least her large thighs hid her pussy. Mostly.

His hands opened, palms up. "Give me your breasts."

"What?"

"Now."

From the raging heat in her face, she knew her cheeks were redder than the lotus flowers in her tattoos. With a hand under each heavy breast, she hesitated. He didn't move. Well, at least he hadn't told her to remove her top. She inched forward on the chair. Her legs slid alongside his until her inner thighs aligned with his knees, and his jeans scraped against her tender skin.

Cool air touched the flesh of her labia. Now, she was completely exposed before him. And somehow, with the physical nakedness, the barricades protecting her emotions were splintering.

Leaning forward slightly, she set her breasts onto his cupped palms. Giving him her body. Giving him her soul.

"Very good." His fingers gripped her breasts over the fabric.

He angled his knees outward, spreading her legs farther apart. Opening her. Her instinctive jerk back was countered by his hold on her top half. She wouldn't be permitted to retreat.

At the amused look in his forest green eyes, she growled under her breath. The flames streaming up and down her spine, made her want to…to kneel. To beg. To submit.

"You like being controlled. Do you know how much your surrender pleases a Dom?" he asked softly, his gaze on her face, then her breasts. "Lace your fingers together behind your neck."

How did he know the common hands-behind-the-back position was one she couldn't easily achieve? Her hair spilled over her wrists as she complied. Her breasts lifted with the movement.

"Very nice." His resonant voice was as firm as the hands holding her breasts. "I enjoy seeing you in this position, sweetling. Giving me your breasts. Offering your cunt."

And, oh God, she was. She wanted him to take her, to control her, to have her in any way he chose. As if she knelt on the beach in a heavy surf, the ground beneath her was being swept away, leaving her unbalanced. And she was being pushed right to him. She swallowed, her voice coming out husky. "I didn't offer. Sir."

On top of the fabric, his thumbs circled her jutting nipples, making them bunch so tightly they ached. "When a woman's nipples are this hard, Rainie, I'd say you're an offering ready to be taken."

The way her lower half turned into a heated pool, her body agreed. She stared at the silk of his shirt, knowing she was wet. *Please, please, please, don't let him notice how he turns me on.*

"As a trainee, you're supposed to learn about new kinks. Meet and work with different Doms, searching for the one with whom you fit. Why aren't you doing that?" While he talked, he used one hand on her left breast as a restraint, and the other slid under her halter bra to roll her right nipple. The skin-to-skin sensation grew more intense with each second. Her toes curled.

What had he asked?

"I—" She shouldn't have looked up. Tanned skin. Green eyes. Sun streaked hair the beautiful brown of chocolate, falling over his forehead, luring her to touch. She closed her eyes.

A light pinch on her breast made her gasp.

"Eyes on me, trainee."

Between his unyielding grip and his resolute focus on her, she couldn't seem to concentrate. "I've tried out new things. It's just… I-I don't know." *I've given up. There's no one out there for me.*

"I think you're not giving me the complete story, sweetling." His focus had locked on her in a way that had her very bones trembling. "It's time your reasons were examined."

His grip gentled. "Right now, make me a mental list of which Doms you've decided against and the ones you'd like to play with."

She stared, mouth open, unable to find a reply.

He actually grinned. "You sit here and think until I return."

Chapter Three

As Jake moved away from Rainie, he saw her pretty face scrunch into a scowl.

What a cutie. And more. She'd responded like a dream to his hands, his will. Even as he'd watched her mind and emotions war, her body had been sweetly compliant. God, she was beautiful.

But something was going on with her, and it was more than her difficulties in honest refusals.

Whenever a trainee was unsettled by a scene—whether performed by a Master or another Dom—her file got a note, so a follow-up could be performed. Jake had found no notes for months.

On her own, she requested scenes with lightweight Dominants, which wasn't necessarily wrong. However, he doubted she'd be content with a Dom who didn't push her.

Yes, a Master needed to have a long talk with her. Jake planned that Master would be him.

He picked up the short length of chain from behind the bar and returned.

Curled in the chair, Rainie felt her anxiety increase as Jake approached. The seriousness of his expression made her rub her sweaty palms against her skirt.

"Thinking done?" he asked. He stood over her, arms crossed over his chest, legs braced apart. His black jeans clung to his muscular thighs and cupped his bat and balls.

Bad Rainie. Pay attention.

With some effort, she lifted her gaze back to his face. "Started, but not concluded."

"Not a problem. This week, write everything out. Handwritten, not typed. In addition to the Dom lists, make another of your strengths and weaknesses as both a submissive and a person. Next weekend, we'll read over your homework together."

The thought was completely unnerving. *Put her thoughts and emotions down on paper for him to read? To discuss?* She'd rather have a root canal.

He held his hand out. "Let's walk, and you can tell me which Doms you know. Which ones you've rejected."

His nonchalant strength when he pulled her to her feet sent a dizzying desire through her. "I haven't played with everyone, but I've met most. I haven't—haven't rejected anyone."

Although a muscle flexed in his jaw, he merely nodded. When he put his arm around her and ran the knuckles of his other hand over the tops of her breasts, the casual intimacy of the touch blanked her mind.

"Since you haven't said no to anyone, should I assume any Dom here would make you a good *permanent* Dom?" he asked.

"Not permanent. I mean—"

"Mmmhmm."

She got the uncomfortable impression he saw right through her.

After pulling a short length of chain from his pocket, he secured her arms behind her back. The chain between her wrist cuffs was only about twelve inches, but long enough to prevent her shoulders from feeling dislocated.

On the way across the room, he picked up two tubes of body paint and a rag from a table.

She glanced at the tubes with a twinge of anxiety. Why did he need paint?

He guided her to a sitting area containing four Doms. "Gents, the trainee here needs to be decorated. Anyone up for the task?"

"Sure."

"Why not?"

"You bet."

All three single Doms indicated interest.

Jake turned Rainie toward the first, and she tensed. She'd hated her single experience with Donald. Some tops were deliberately sexually rough—which was hot. Earlier, when Jake had hurt her nipples, he'd done so with awareness of exactly what he was doing. He wasn't so self-absorbed to have missed her response.

Although Donald never overstepped the club boundaries, he was rough, because he was careless and selfish.

Rainie forced herself not to step back, and then realized Master Jake was watching her face. He arched a brow and directed her to stand in front of the other two. Although she hadn't played with them, neither had a bad reputation with the submissives.

"Brand, Casey," Jake said, ignoring Donald's annoyed grunt. "Show us your artistic talents."

Brand had silver at the temples and in his mustache, but his latex body shirt showed rippling muscles. His sweeping gaze took her in, and he smiled. "Who could resist painting those tits?" He glanced at Casey. "I'll take the outsides of her breasts and leave the nipples for you."

After tossing them the paint tubes and terrycloth rag, Master Jake wove his fingers into her hair and immobilized her. Her arms were already restrained behind her back. His other hand gripped her upper arm, ensuring she'd remain in place.

She looked at him from the corner of her eye. "You don't have to hold me," she muttered.

"But I like to," he murmured.

His woodsy masculine scent wrapped around her—which was just wrong. Anything that smelled that temping should be licensed. Regulated. Dispensed in very small amounts.

A touch on her chest startled her. She forced herself to hold still.

In front of her, Brand ran his finger over her halter top to circle her breast. Her breasts were sensitive. Responsive. And being touched there together with Jake's merciless control slid her body straight into a flustered arousal.

"Gorgeous breasts," Casey commented as he watched his friend paint. He glanced at Jake. "She's fair-skinned. Bet her nipples are a pretty pink."

"Be fun to find out, wouldn't it?" Still holding her hair, Master Jake undid the halter ties at her back and neck and pulled the top off. Her nipples contracted at the cool wash of air...and the heat of the men's assessing stares.

Jake's warm breath brushed her ear as he whispered, "You've got gorgeous breasts, trainee."

His hands. She wanted his hands on her so badly her knees wobbled.

"Magnificent," Brand said. "Guess I need to start over." After squeezing out some red paint, he drew filigree patterns on her bare right breast. The paint was cool over her heated skin.

He handed the second tube to Casey.

The younger Dom circled her left nipple with a bright yellow streak, then used one finger to massage in the paint.

God, having Jake standing so close, restraining her, watching her...somehow turned everything the others did into a type of foreplay. By the time the two men finished, her breasts were swollen and throbbing and sending urgent messages to her pussy.

Trying not to rub her thighs together, she shifted her weight.

Brand chuckled. "Your trainee is aroused, Jake. We'd be happy to co-top her in a private scene upstairs."

Dismay ran through Rainie like a whip of icy rain. *I don't do threesomes.*

Jake's steady gaze provided the only warmth in the suddenly cold, shadowy room. "Rainie, what do you say?"

Hadn't Jake read her papers? "I-I..."

Brand and Casey watched her with open anticipation, obviously expecting her consent.

She faltered out, "I—I have other things to—"

"Yes, you do have a problem, don't you?" Jake didn't release her hair as he stepped completely behind her. His hand smacked her bottom far, far harder than a fun swat.

Pain burst like fire across her buttocks. She bit back a yelp.

A second and third stinging spank followed. *Ow! God, what had she done?* Tears hazed her vision. She exhaled, trying to chase away the pain. "Why?

Why, Sir?"

Jake straightened and turned her to face him. His palm cupped her chin, forcing her to meet his grim gaze. "Sam said you'd already received a lesson on this."

"Master Sam?"

"Rainie, when you don't want to play with a Dom—or date a Dom—what is the proper answer?"

Her thoughts whirled in her head, but all she could think of was how her bottom hurt. A tear escaped.

Jake's eyes softened, although his jaw remained stern as he positioned her to face the two Doms. "What do you say to them, Rainie?"

Master Sam had told her to say *no.*

She cleared the thickness from her throat. "I-I—" When Jake's hand squeezed her shoulder in warning, the memory of the pain he could wield impelled her words. "I'm really sorry, Sirs, but I—No. No, thank you. I'm sorry."

"So are we," Brand said. "But you gave us a courteous refusal. Well done, pet."

"Gentlemen," Jake said politely and steered her away.

"I…I don't like threesomes," she told Jake. And she didn't want to be with him any longer, either. "I'm sure the restriction is on my limits list."

"Perhaps, but that's why I asked you to think about your limits again. A submissive's wants and needs change over time. Reassessment is needed."

I don't want to be reassessed.

The lack of a dedicated Trainee Master meant she'd escaped a re-evaluation for quite a while. But Jake's very posture held determination. He planned to be stubborn about this.

He turned her to face him, and his gaze dropped to her chest.

Brand had painted a Celtic-style knot band around the outside of her breasts. At the centers of each pattern, her areolas glowed yellow.

"Artwork like that is an open invitation to squeeze." Jake's fingers closed on one nipple, pinching and smearing the yellow paint. His green eyes stayed on her face as he squeezed firmly enough to hit the threshold of hurting—and made everything inside her tighten and pool. "Legs far apart and bend forward."

"What?" She stared up at him, seeing the matter-of-fact resolve in his expression.

He picked up a paper towel and wiped the paint from his fingers…and waited.

Well, God. She set her bare feet shoulder-width apart.

"More."

Fussy bastard.

After widening her stance, she bent forward, grateful his grip on her arm helped her balance. Her loose breasts hung down, swaying. Even worse, her very short skirt no longer covered her ass. As members of the club walked around her, her face flared with embarrassment.

And yet, her core rapidly filled with another kind of heat. No Master had driven her or controlled her so thoroughly in a long, long time. Her whole body seethed with excitement.

Jake ran his palm over the bare skin of her buttocks and squeezed, wakening the tender skin he'd spanked. Slowly, he slid his hand between her legs.

At the intimate touch, she jolted and tried to straighten.

His unyielding grip on her arm held her still. His fingers traced her labia, her entrance. "Nice and wet, baby. Good to know."

After helping her straighten, he tugged her skirt back down.

Her breathing was fast, and desire was a hammering pulse beat between her legs. With every command, every firm touch of his hand, she wanted to beg for more.

But not from Jake. No, not Jake. Tears pricked her eyes. She blinked, dredging up anger to burn away her weakness. "You could've just asked."

His brows lifted.

Even that miniscule movement made her knees try to buckle. "You could've just asked, *Sir*."

"Did I miss where your limits list noted 'no touching' or 'no touching intimately?'" he asked mildly.

Oh, he was the spawn of Satan. Why had she wanted him for so many years? "No."

"In fact, according to your lists and cuff colors, I could use my cock instead of my hand and fuck you, here and now. True?"

Her mouth twisted around the answer. "True." And she totally hated the surge of edgy excitement.

Instead, he tugged her forward. "Let's introduce you to more Doms, trainee."

Enjoying Rainie's mounting frustration, Jake steered his trainee through the room, visiting the Doms whom he'd prepped about the "scene." With his hand on her nape, he easily read her responsive body to determine how far he could push her.

Each time she attempted to defy him and failed, her trembling increased. Damn, but he wanted to comfort her and control her and explore the depths of her personality.

This wasn't the time.

Stay on task, Sheffield. Next lesson.

After he supervised her belly being painted, he checked her arousal. Nope, these two Doms didn't do it for her, although she was still wet.

One asked her to go upstairs to fuck.

She earned another two hard spanks before managing to refuse.

In preparation for the next group, he removed her skirt. She had a beautifully bare pussy, with the inner lips poking out between the plump outer labia. Damned tempting.

Stay on task, Sheffield. Next lesson.

Under his supervision, Adam and Carter painted her mound, ass cheeks, and upper thighs.

"I'd love to take that pretty asshole," Adam said. "Want to let me have some time with her?"

"Rainie, what do you say?"

She looked from him to Adam and back, and her cheeks pinkened with her dawning anger. Although Jake had made his expectations clear, she'd apparently not realized how thoroughly she'd been set up. "You-you…"

Smothering his grin, he tilted his head toward Adam. "Show me how you answer him, baby."

Despite now knowing the entire scenario was preplanned, she struggled. "I'm s-sorry, but I don't…" Her gaze dropped, and she swallowed hard.

"Rainie," Jake said quietly. "It's not difficult. Try this: *I'm afraid not, but thank you for the offer, Sir.*"

The gratitude in her eyes made him want to cuddle her. "I'm afraid n-not, but thank you for the offer, Sir," she parroted to Adam.

"Nicely done." The young Dom grinned. "Come and find me if you change your mind."

Chuckling over Rainie's disgruntled expression, Jake led her away. Her refusals would improve with practice. The physical memory of pain would provide impetus.

Being she was a smart woman, she'd probably study her past to figure out why she had so much trouble saying no. If necessary, he and the other Masters would help her explore.

He was pleased with the evening's work. And he'd gained some knowledge.

She didn't particularly like pain, but definitely got off on control, subtle or overt. She could tell the poser Doms from the real ones. Sexual submission was her gig, although she had a nice helping of service submissive in her personality, enough to create a need to please others. Especially Doms. Her smart-mouthed, independent personality tended to vie with the submissive side.

She was definitely an intriguing woman.

"Maybe I should do some painting, too," he murmured, catching the subtle scent of her body—a light spicy fragrance that mingled with the musk of her hunger. "Or, I could just play with you."

A flush of excitement darkened her lips and cheeks.

Interesting. She might avoid him—but she also wanted him. His cock swelled in response, although he'd been half-hard all evening as he'd hauled her around. Touching her lit him up as if he'd clasped a live wire.

She was everything he enjoyed in a woman, from her scent to her lush body to her sassy mouth. Trouble was, since he'd spent the evening as a

Master giving a lesson, he had to step back now. They each needed to be clear on what they wanted before moving on to fucking. Dominance and submission could definitely confuse matters.

So, to divert them both, he smacked her pretty painted ass hard enough to make her hiss. "That was a reminder to be truthful in relationships, whether you've known the Dom for one minute or one year. I want to see you honest in your emotions, your thoughts—and your refusals."

"Yes, Sir." She held still as he unfastened her wrist cuffs and the chain.

Once freed, she pulled in a breath and rubbed her ass, which probably hurt like hell. She'd have trouble sitting for a day or so. "If you want the truth…I'd really like to punch your face right now. Sir."

He grinned.

She pushed some hair back and faced him straight on. "Nonetheless, I'm grateful for the lesson."

And her honesty was even sexier than her gorgeous body. "Good night then, baby."

"Good night, Sir."

Chapter Four

"Well, Master Fuzzy-butt, I wish I felt like partying." The next night, Rainie stood in the bathroom, her makeup arrayed on the counter like a pre-battle army. Depressed and tired, she'd resorted to the heavy artillery: thicker foundation, darker eyes, and eyelashes long enough to reach her eyebrows.

She checked the mirror. Not quite slutty, but close. Perfect for tonight's bachelorette party and the "exotic dancers on the loose" theme. *God, what a theme.* Uncomfortable with looking like a hooker—outside of the Shadowlands—she'd tried to talk the other women out of the idea and been outvoted. *So…just get over it, Rainie.*

With a snort, she glanced at the fluffy little dog at her feet. "It's kind of dumb going to so much effort, really. I mean, a bachelorette party means all women."

Rhage obviously agreed since his fluffy, wagging tail whipped over the glittering blue nail polish on her toes.

She beamed at him. He was such a good conversationalist. "I can't believe the clinic didn't find someone looking for you, but thank God they didn't." Because losing Rhage would break her heart.

He felt that he owned her now, she knew. She grinned. The fifteen-pound fluff-ball had snarled at her neighbor's dog—and returned to her, totally convinced he'd saved her from the huge pit bull.

So she'd named him after her favorite fictional boyfriend. "You're my hero, Rhage."

Ears pricked up, Rhage watched her closely. Anything she said was important to him, and how lovely was that?

"I always thought I'd grow up and find my own hero." Rainie grimaced at herself in the mirror. Obviously, she shouldn't have wasted her youth on reading and daydreaming. "But I gave up; I'm not holding out for a hero anymore."

Rhage whined. Did that mean he agreed?

"I don't think heroes exist anymore, puppy." Her ex-fiancé, Geoffrey Hollingsworth, sure didn't qualify as a knight in shining armor. Or, maybe he hadn't considered her a prize worth fighting for. The memory was an unhealed bruise on her heart.

She'd been thrilled when he'd taken her up north to finally meet his family. "This is Rainie Kuras," he'd said.

But when his mother and sister looked down their noses at Rainie's painfully purchased college clothing, her hopes shriveled. Then Geoffrey's sister had whispered in her mother's ear, "…foster care…drugs…"

Mrs. Hollingsworth's lips had compressed tightly. Her gaze, not warm to start, chilled further. She'd straightened her thin frame. "How do you do?"

Obviously, Rainie wasn't "suitable," being a woman abundant in everything except money, respectability, and high-class ancestors. But then came the moment that really hurt. Despite past experiences, she'd foolishly expected Geoffrey to put his arm around her and show his family what she meant to him.

Nope.

Thus, she had learned a romance book was *fiction.* A hero who truly cared for the heroine was called a *fantasy.*

And *reality* was the way Geoffrey had sidled sideways to put distance between them. The way he'd avoided any discussion of that night. The way cold had oozed into the empty space where love and trust should lodge.

After a painful breath, Rainie slowly straightened the mess on her counter.

A paw placed on her foot said Rhage wanted the rest of the story.

"Sorry, honey. Nothing more to the tale. My so-called fiancé slithered out of my life with a ton of excuses. The putz. I'd respect him more if he'd been upfront about dumping me."

Upfront.

She froze, staring at her excuse-making, equivocating face in the mirror. Was she really belittling Geoffrey for not being honest after spending last night getting smacked for doing exactly the same thing herself? She was always making up excuses to avoid sex or dating or whatever.

Master Jake had been more right than he knew—and didn't that just suck?

Okay. No more lying. She was better than that. True, she intended to climb the corporate ladder, rung-by-rung, which meant using…tact...rather than unvarnished honesty. But she wouldn't abandon her character as she rose in status.

She scooped up the dog, cuddling him. "Don't worry, puppy. I'll never lie to you. Promise."

Her chin got a quick lick, and she rubbed her cheek on the top of his fuzzy head. The perfect hero. He didn't judge her by her clothing or her past mistakes or her horrible childhood. He loved her for who she was now. How rare was that? "How did I ever live all these years without you?"

After she finished dressing, she opened the huge, black suitcase containing *her* special stock.

Rhage bounced on his front paws, assuming the contents were new tug-of-war or chase-the-ball toys.

"'Fraid not, honey." Her lips curved as she studied a cock ring. It could be considered a type of chase the ball, right? "These are sex toys."

Was that an appalled look in Rhage's chocolate-brown eyes? "Sorry, dude." She ruffled his ears. "Arranging parties brings in extra money and lets me hang out with girls instead of truckers." And provided great prizes for bachelorette parties.

"Hopefully tonight won't run too late." She needed to work tomorrow—Sunday—to finish the payroll. Because of Cory. She scowled. "That man—all liabilities, no assets."

First, her "boss" had screwed up the schedule, ignoring a trucker's requested hours off. Then when the trucker threw a fit, Cory'd fired him and wouldn't let her mail off a final paycheck. She'd been stomping-mad furious—which was a trick to pull off in high heels.

And now she had to work tomorrow if anyone was going to be paid. "And it's all because Cory is one period short of a write-off. No, worse than that. He's a putrid, piss-drinking, pustule with a pin-sized prick."

Rainie winced. Had she really said that out loud?

Miss Lily had continually tried to mold her into someone with class. And Rainie'd curtailed her swearing—at least the true profanity. Did name-calling fall under the "*genteel women don't do that*" rules? Unfortunately, she couldn't ask Miss Lily. Not ever again.

Grief hit her so brutally, she held her chest, trying to pull in a breath. "Why'd you leave me?" *Like everyone else had.*

In a pale peach blouse, pearl necklace, and earrings, Miss Lily looked out of the picture frame. Her gaze was steady, her head high. Even in a photo, she displayed dignity. But she'd also known how to lay out the honesty.

At seventeen, Rainie'd been left for dead after a drug deal gone bad. Her upcoming destination was juvenile hall, but the judge had seen something in her. "*Would you like to meet Miss Lily?*" he'd asked, referring to his executive assistant from when he'd been some fancy lawyer. The person who'd helped him become the man—the judge—he was.

Rainie knew his question wasn't about choosing between juvvie and another foster home—it was about who she wanted to be when she grew up.

At the courthouse, Miss Lily had looked Rainie over and given her a thin smile. "You can continue on your bobsled ride into hell, young lady, or you can come home with me and become a lady in truth. Your decision."

Though one eye was swollen shut, Rainie had stared at the woman and tried not to whimper. Her life was in chaos and Jesus fucking God, she hurt. Shiz lay in the morgue. She didn't want to be herself any longer.

Years later, Miss Lily shared that she'd planned to turn the judge down, but she'd seen the longing in Rainie's eyes to be…more.

"I'm still trying, Miss Lily," Rainie told the woman in the photo. "I'll make you proud."

As she fought the tears, she knew what Miss Lily's response would be. *Then get moving. Do the next thing. Nothing is accomplished by tears or moping.*

"Yes, ma'am." Rainie returned to the bathroom and fixed the streaking mascara under her eyes. Enough with the past. This evening wasn't about her, but about the two bachelorettes, and she'd bust her ass to ensure Sally and

Gabi had fun.

Setting her bag of toys on the tiny dining table, she scowled at the notebook that was supposed to have Master Jake's *homework.* She'd started…and stopped. Like she'd ever share her weaknesses with a man? Or her disgusting past? *Never, never, never.*

And the list of what she wanted in a Dom only pointed out her nonexistent love life. Since Geoffrey, no "relationship" had lasted past a few dates.

He'd been the one to teach her about BDSM and, although he didn't like clubs, he'd taken her to the Shadowlands during a visitor's night. With him, she'd learned she liked bedroom domination. Because of her past, she kept a tight control over her life, but letting someone else take charge for scenes and sex was amazing.

Her smile faded. But because she'd trusted Geoffrey that much—enough to let go—his abandonment had ripped her apart.

A while after they broke up, she'd joined the Shadowlands, hoping to meet someone wonderful. Those dreams had died because investing all her trust and love in a man was simply an invitation to get hurt.

She bent over to tug lightly on Rhage's silky ears. "Are you cruel too, buddy? Since you're a male?"

His tail thumped the carpet.

"See, with humans, once a man conquers, he examines his prize and immediately begins picking her apart." She slapped her ample stomach. "I've got a lot to pick apart here. And my background provides even more."

Rhage waved a little paw in the air.

"You too, huh? Both of us with scummy backgrounds." Rainie smiled down at him. "Guess we'll just keep it to you and me." *No one else.*

She shoved the homework right off the table. Damn Master Jake anyway. After getting home last night, she'd dreamed of him, over and over. Even worse, she craved seeing him again—as though he was dark chocolate and she'd just come off a yearlong diet. She *wanted.*

But she could have dealt with dreams. Really. But the dreams had slowly twisted into nightmares of how she'd fled his sister's birthday party back to her foster care house—where she *should* have been safe.

Jake wasn't to blame. Nonetheless, he was a walking, talking reminder of why her life had descended straight into the sewer.

Her head lifted as she heard footsteps on the sidewalk. Probably the limousine driver.

"Okay, dog, I have to go party." She picked up an encompassing shawl and swirled it around her body. "You guard the house, okay?"

Rhage gave a small yip of agreement.

Who needed men? Rainie grinned. She had her own hero—an incredibly smart, cuddly, four-footed hero.

* * * *

As the others in the bachelor party settled in, Jake shed his suit coat, rolled up his shirtsleeves, and stuffed his tie into his slacks pocket. Comfortable, he leaned back and stretched out his legs. For bar furniture, the burgundy-red, well-cushioned chair was fairly comfortable.

Around the table, the others followed suit. Marcus removed his silvery-gray pinstripe jacket. Galen hung his black suit coat as well as Vance's over the back of a nearby chair. Holt dumped his behind him. Neither Raoul nor Nolan wore coats. But after assessing the size of the two men, doormen tended to ignore their less formal attire.

Jake was enjoying himself more than he'd anticipated. Well, aside from dying twice during the laser tag game earlier. Since the Shadowlands Masters were quite accustomed to exotic kink, the party hadn't bothered visiting strip clubs. Instead, they'd taken over a laser tag facility.

Jake gave two of the grooms, Vance and Galen, a respectful glance. The FBI agents had headed up the law enforcement team—and had shot him dead. Jake's team, consisting of ex-military men, had won by only one game.

After cleaning up and dining, the grooms and a few other Doms came here to check on the bachelorette party. Jake glanced around the crowded room. Supposedly, the women had picked this boutique nightclub for their last stop.

It was a good choice, actually. The DJ played music ranging from rock to metal designed to encourage dancing. Because Vance had selected a table in the elevated back section, the view of the ground floor was excellent—although Jake could hardly see his drink.

He glanced over at Marcus, one of the three grooms. "I didn't think bachelor parties were supposed to rendezvous with the corresponding bachelorette one."

"Be a shame to waste the opportunity." Marcus gave him an easy smile. "The ladies get drunk and revved up. Can't beat the sex."

"And the women encouraged you to butt into their party?"

"Hell, no. They don't know we're here." Galen's smile was evil. "But my company specializes in finding people—even when they're trying to hide." Galen's firm had a rep for delivering.

"I hear the trainees were on their own last night," Vance said to Jake. "You were lucky our Sally isn't one any longer."

"I'd have to agree with you," Jake said. The little brunette was adorable but a brat incarnate.

"It's a shame about the trainee program ending," Marcus said. "I found my Gabi. Maxie and Dara met their Doms through it."

"Speaking of trainees, do you hear from Heather?" Raoul asked Jake.

Heather. He braced for the pain of remembering her but found only a distant grief. "Now and then. She's doing well."

"Good. And you, my friend?"

Jake smiled slightly, thinking of the night before. "Guess I've recovered.

Women seem inviting again."

Nolan King snorted. "If the last months were you in mourning, I'd hate to see you at full strength."

At the chorus of agreement, Jake grinned ruefully. Okay, yes, he'd gone through a few submissives in an effort to forget the one lost. But the women had known he wasn't interested in more than a fun evening. He tilted his glass toward the tough contractor. "Watch and learn, old man."

Even as Nolan barked a laugh, Holt scowled at Jake. "When he rips your head off, it'll splatter blood all over my good suit."

"Beth will rescue me," Jake said, enjoying the way Nolan's eyes narrowed. "She likes me better anyway."

Laughing, Holt edged his chair farther from Jake. *Hell of a friend.*

"Doubtful." Nolan swirled his beer. "But since I like well-endowed women, I'll sample Rainie instead."

No. Fucking. Way. "You're married," Jake snapped. "Don't you fuck with Rainie."

As the men roared with laughter, Vance lifted his glass to Nolan. "And the King scores!"

Marcus grinned and told the others, "As a past Trainee Master, I do like the way Sheffield jumped to the trainee's defense."

And where the hell had his surge of possessiveness come from? Feeling like an idiot, Jake lifted his Kamikaze in a salute to Nolan. "I definitely jumped, you bastard."

The Dom's rare grin flashed. "Just so you know—if I strayed, Beth would wait until I was asleep, lop off my balls, and bury them in her garden. As fertilizer."

Jake grinned back. Nolan's little redhead was sweet, quiet, and had a spine of pure titanium. "I wonder what Rainie would do in a similar situation." Might be good to know.

The forthcoming suggestions were far too bloody for peace of mind.

Galen added, "Being the vindictive type, she'd probably stuff everything down the garbage disposal afterward."

Jesus. Jake could feel his balls draw up tight.

A second later, a commotion sounded at the door. Turning to look, Vance broke into laughter. "And there they are."

Jake stared. Those were Shadowlands submissives? The group of women strutting in would look at home on a stripper's stage. But, damn, they looked good. Hair out to there, eyelashes forever, deep red lips that made a man's cock stand up.

He'd seen less makeup on drag queens, but there was no doubt these were females, considering the amount of skin they were showing. Miniskirts, mesh stockings, cleavage to rival the Grand Canyon. And somehow, they made it all work.

After a minute, he spotted Rainie. She looked like sex, super-sized. A miniskirt of shiny black flirted with damn fine legs. Her dark blue bustier had almost no back, so her tattoo ran up and over her right shoulder, leading the eye straight down to those incredible breasts. God, he'd never wanted to touch someone so much in his life.

He smiled ruefully. A Dom should know himself...and he had to admit she was the reason he'd stayed with the grooms rather than peeling off like most of the others.

As the women formed a small group, Jake noticed Ben, the Shadowlands security guard, had accompanied them. The combination of his massive bulk, rough-hewn face, and fancy rags made him look like a lethal pimp.

As Jake watched, the women split into different directions. Beth headed for the DJ, Rainie and another women—"Is that Mistress Anne?" Jake choked out.

"It is." Raoul's smile was a flash of white in the darkness. "I've never seen her look so beautiful."

No lie. The sadistic Domme's attire usually held an edge of threat. What she wore tonight was complete and utter seduction, Penthouse style.

"Wonder what brave subbie talked the Mistress into that?" Marcus wondered.

Every Dom at the table answered, "Rainie."

Rainie hadn't expected to have so much fun. But her unhappiness about work had been erased by the amount of alcohol in her veins and her rowdy friends. Although the party had decreased from the original fifteen, the remaining few were serious partiers.

Even now, Kim was siccing Ben into intimidating a couple to move away from a large table to a smaller one.

Uzuri and Beth targeted the DJ to get the correct tune loaded up. Their private exotic dancing class at the start of the night had given them the moves to only one song.

Rainie and Anne had their own task. Rainie asked, "Is this bartender mine or yours?"

"I need to have a look at him," Anne said briskly.

Rainie grinned. The Mistress'd imbibed as heavily as everyone, but she sure didn't show it. Despite black vinyl boots that put her close to six feet, Anne never made a misstep.

In contrast, Rainie had to concentrate hard to walk in a straight line. Swaying her hips helped—and garnered appreciative whistles.

"Holy Mother of God," a man said as she and Mistress Anne wiggled their way through the throng around the bar. "Ladies, whatever you're asking, I'll pay."

Anne ignored him and leaned her forearms on the bar so she could watch the bartender. Rainie did likewise, assessing his interactions with the customers. "Straight," she judged.

"Agreed, but I think he's mine."

Rainie waited until the man's gaze met hers. She got no tingle from his quick look. Of course, there was no foolproof way to differentiate Doms from submissives, but his gaze held no punch. So if Anne thought he was submissive, then this one was hers to coax. "Go for it, sweetie-peach."

"*Sweetie-peach?*" Gripping the top edge of Rainie's stiff bustier, Anne yanked her forward until their faces were an inch apart. "This is a fun evening, but, little girl, watch the manners. I prefer cock torture, but I'll make an exception for pussy if annoyed."

Note to self: never call a sadist cutesy names. "Yes, Ma'am."

Although laughter lurked in Anne's eyes, the Mistress would undoubtedly be even more amused if wielding a pussy whip.

When Rainie swallowed, she heard at least three men around them do the same. "Sorry, Ma'am."

"Better." Anne released her as the bartender approached.

"Ladies, what can I get you?"

"We have a request," Rainie started with the familiar spiel. "We're with a bachelorette party and—"

"That's a relief," the bartender said. "Got two cops at the end of the bar figuring on busting some hookers."

Rainie concealed her flinch and the urge to flee, reminding herself she wasn't an underage kid living with a drug dealer. She managed a smile. "No soliciting in our group, just an upcoming double wedding. We wanted you to serve a special drink shot for the brides, Gabi and Sally. It's called the G and S Smackdown. If you agree to make it, we'll talk it up and get people to order it."

He shook his head. "I'm afraid not. See we have—"

And then Anne reached over the bar and wrapped the bartender's paisley tie around her slender hand. Rainie felt the blast of dominance accompanying the move, and when the bartender's gaze met the Domme's, his stubborn expression melted right off his face.

Anne slowly pulled him forward and said in her husky voice, "What is your name?"

"Lance." His voice was hoarse.

"That's a very nice name," Anne said, and the bartender actually quivered. "Lance, it would please me if you'd make the shooters."

"O-okay. Sure. I'd be happy to." His expression said he wished she'd ask him for something more so he could do that as well.

Rainie's smile faded as she remembered the night before and her absolute joy, right down to her toes, when she'd earned Master Jake's approval. Why, oh why, did Jake Sheffield have to be a Dom?

After ordering champagne drinks and handing over the recipe for the G and S Smackdowns, Rainie followed Anne back to the table, getting four requests to dance and two offers of a monetary nature. She grimaced and checked her bustier to make sure she hadn't popped out a nipple or something.

Nope. All good.

"Well, ladies." She settled in beside Kim. As her weight left the high-heeled sandals, her tortured feet throbbed in relief. "This is the last bar on the list, so let's give them a good show." She glanced around the table. Even without dancing, they made a colorful group.

Kim's short, short dress matched her icy blue eyes. Uzuri was in a skin-tight, red sheath that set off her chocolate-brown skin.

The brides-to-be had chosen white. Gabi wore a white leather miniskirt and sequined white corset. Her strawberry blonde hair now had a silver and blue streak to match the wedding colors. Sally was in a white leather minidress with cutouts that showed the sides of her breasts and hips.

Damn, she loved her girls. And so would the crowd. Smiling, Rainie edged back to survey the dance floor. Yes, there would be enough room for them to put on a show.

When she turned back, Gabi was lining up her prizes on the table…right next to the ones Uzuri had won. *Good God.*

Sensing a competition, Sally emptied her silver-striped party bag. A giant green dildo skidded across the table.

"Sally!" Kim hissed, a little too loudly.

Around them, conversations dimmed as eyeballs locked onto the array of sex toys.

"Hulkorama wanted out," Sally announced innocently. "He's too big to like being covered up."

"Well, that's true enough." Gabi wrinkled her nose at the green-veins bulging all over the dildo. "That's one ugly wanker. At least Iron Mania has some class." Picking up a sleek, dark-red-with-gold-stripes dildo, she waggled it at Sally.

"Personally, I've always preferred American military heroes," Rainie said, drawing her dildo like a sword. It was a gloriously garish red-white-and-blue, and dotted with stars. "The Captain here feels it's his patriotic duty to serve right up to his last brea—uh, vibration."

"Huh, good point." Gabi scowled. "I bet Iron Mania has a vile sense of humor. I'm not sure I can take an evil vibe as well as an evil Dom."

"Oooo, baby, that sounds like a story. What did Master Marcus do?" Uzuri asked.

"No wait—first tell us what you did to get in trouble?" Kim asked with a knowing smile.

Gabi pouted. "That stupid inflatable swan had a leak, so I was patching it, and I had the glue out, right?"

"Right. And?" As Uzuri absentmindedly toyed with the bulging veins on the green dildo, a man walking by spilled his drink.

"I just… Well, I glued together a bunch of the nipple clamps and gave the swan a pretty necklace."

As the shrieks of laughter burst around the table, Gabi started to giggle. "You should have seen Marcus's face when he saw the swan. Then when he couldn't get the tweezers clamps to open, his face got all…" Gabi pulled her brows together and set her mouth into a line.

Kim's head was planted in her hands, her shoulders shaking.

Uzuri was holding her sides. Sally leaned against her for support.

Mistress Anne shook her head in disapproval…but her lips were twitching.

Rainie managed to gasp, "What did he do?"

"Oh, you know how he is…" Gabi lowered her voice and added a southern accent, "Well, darlin', you got thayut swan all fancied up, *ah* do believe you should join it foah a party."

"Uh-oh," Uzuri muttered.

"E-zactilamente." Gabi gave a decidedly drunken nod. "The bastard tied a butterfly vibe right over my clit, put me on the swan, and chained my nipples to that damned necklace so tight I couldn't move."

"Oh, ow," Rainie muttered, folding her arms over her chest in sympathy. Nipple clamps were the worst.

"Yeah, right? Then he lounged by the pool, drinking his Grey Goose, and playing with the vibe's remote controls. Oh Lord, I'm sure the neighbors could hear me begging—and by the time he let me come, I *know* they heard me scream."

Rainie laughed so hard she had to push her thighs together to keep from peeing.

Next to her, Anne was grinning, but her expression was intrigued. *Uh-oh.* If the Mistress had a swimming pool, some poor submissive would be in for some rough pool sex.

"Ladies." Kim's attempt at sternness was ruined by her sputtering giggles. "Ladies, put your toys away before you get us evicted. Or before Ben blushes so much his face explodes."

To the poor security guard's horror, they all turned to look at him.

"Boy, you white people can really turn red," Uzuri said in awe.

Rainie tried to smother her snickers by drinking and ended up almost choking to death.

"No dying during a party." Mistress Anne gave her a well-placed whack between her shoulder blades.

The impact didn't clear her airways, but the pain definitely did. "God have mercy," Rainie wheezed. "I mean, Mistress, mercy."

After nodding a polite acceptance, Anne smiled as the bartender himself delivered their order.

He set the shots and drinks around the table, saving the last for Anne.

She held up one finger to him to wait and stood. "Ready, ladies?"

They rose and then hammered their hands on the table to create a thundering drumroll.

With the others, Rainie lifted her tiny glass high. After downing the shot, she slammed her glass onto the table. A chorus of thuds came from the others.

Hands lifted, a screech erupted. "G and S Smackdown!"

"That's for Gabi and me!" Sally yelled. She and Gabi leaned across the table and exchanged a lascivious kiss.

"Thank God, the grooms aren't here," Kim muttered to Rainie.

"No shi—kidding." Rainie glanced over to see Anne holding the bartender's face between her palms and saying, "You did very well, Lance. I'm pleased with you."

"God, if the guy possessed a tail, he'd wag it," Rainie said under her breath to Kim.

Kim huffed a laugh and touched the diamond-studded choker around her neck—the symbol of her relationship to her Master. "You know, when Master Raoul praises me, I'm exactly the same."

The edges of Rainie's happiness singed before she pushed her envy away. Kim had suffered, almost died before reaching safety with Raoul. Rainie planted a loud kiss on her friend's cheek. "That's good. You deserve every bit of the happiness you have."

When Kim's eyes filled, Rainie shook her head. "None of that, BFF." She lifted her glass of champagne. "Ladies."

The women looked up expectantly.

"To ex-trainees Gabi and Sally," Rainie said, "who left behind a matchless legacy of brattiness."

Under the cover of the clinking glasses and cheers, Anne resumed her seat. Her penetrating gaze settled on Rainie. "Speaking of brats, I still owe you a punishment for those bugs you put in my locker."

Rainie jerked, spilling her drink. "No, I'm sure you don't. Really."

"Oh, yes. I do. But perhaps I'll let Jake handle the matter."

"What?" Just his name made Rainie's heart rate increase. "Why?"

"I heard he enjoyed spanking you last night. I daresay he'd be delighted to get another chance."

"No. No way." The dismay—and excitement—was almost enough to drive the alcohol from Rainie's system. "He's… I don't even like him."

Anne's lips curved up. "I'll let him know you feel so strongly about him that you actually lied to me."

Rainie glared. "This conversation is under the bachelorette party seal. Silence is sacred."

Anne just smiled.

And then the DJ said, "Now we have a song dedicated to G and S."

Their music came on.

"Get your chairs, ladies," Rainie announced. "We're up."

Chapter Five

Jake's gut hurt from laughing as he sipped his drink and watched the bachelorette party. Sex toys all over the table. Girl on girl action. The women were totally blitzed and cuter than a room of kittens.

As the music changed to *Girls, Girls, Girls* by Mötley Crüe, they jumped to their feet. Holding their chairs in front like shields, they strutted their way to the dance section. The chairs hit the floor with a loud thump, and the women faced the room in one choreographed move.

Grinning, Jake leaned forward to watch.

To his amazement, the submissives—and Anne—proceeded to perform an incredible meld of pole and lap dancing, using some of the sexiest moves he'd ever seen.

"Where did Sally learn that shit?" Vance muttered to Galen.

Nolan frowned.

Marcus was tapping his fingers on the table in time with the beat, obviously enjoying the show.

Raoul, not so much. A low growl came from the Hispanic Master.

"Problem?" Jake asked him.

"She is showing off what is mine." With a glance at Jake, his frown lightened. "Do not look so worried. I will not punish her—much—for breaking a rule I hadn't mentioned. She will know better in the future."

Jake relaxed. Far be it from him to come between a Master and his slave, but Kim wouldn't knowingly upset her Master. Raoul knew it and would undoubtedly find his sense of humor once his woman was no longer being stared at.

Every guy in the place was definitely staring…with good reason. The women were mesmerizing as they danced. Wiggled. Shimmied. When their mesh-stockinged legs slid over the backs of chairs, all a man could think of was feeling a soft inner thigh against his shoulder.

Rainie straddled the chair seat, wiggling her hips, and Jake's cock pulsed with every beat of the music. The damned place had grown far too hot.

Needing to do something with his fingers—which had curved as if to grasp lush hips—he opened his dress shirt another button. Dammit, he wanted to be on that chair with Rainie rubbing those gorgeous breasts on his chest.

"If you'll excuse me, gentlemen." Marcus rose and tossed back the last of his drink. "I have a floozy to catch."

Everyone watched him stroll through the tables, then Vance and Galen stood. "Sorry, men," Vance said. "Bachelorette party will lose their second bride as well."

Jake grinned as the two walked away, discussing bondage and orgasms. Little Sally was in for a long hard night.

Marcus had reached the dance floor. When Gabi turned toward him, he hefted her over his shoulder. Her screech of surprise reached from wall to wall. The second scream was sheer anger. Given the mouth on that little submissive, Jake was pleased to be out of hearing range.

Sally had tripped when Gabi was carried away. After catching her balance, she managed to plant her ass on the chair rather than the floor and just sat there laughing.

Still dancing, the others were teasing her as she struggled to adjust her dress.

In a well-executed ambush, Galen picked up the back of Sally's chair and Vance yanked up on the front legs, tipping Sally back. As they bore their prize away, Sally was giggling too hard to protest.

Nolan rose. After a nod to the men, he strode to the dance floor and nabbed his Beth off the end of the line so quietly that none of the women noticed her disappearance.

Smooth. Jake grinned. Probably why the sneaky bastard had managed to get so many shots off in laser tag.

A moment later, Raoul slapped Jake's shoulder and nodded to Holt in farewell.

Kim was doing a hip-bump with Anne when Raoul stepped onto the floor. Anne noticed him, grinned, inclined her head politely, and moved away.

With a perplexed look, Kim turned to see what had attracted Anne's attention. She saw Raoul. Even as her eyes lit with delight, she bowed her head, sweetly acknowledging her Master.

Raoul's shoulders relaxed slightly.

Nice. Very nice. How could any Master not be pleased with such pretty and instant submission?

Raoul caressed his slave's cheek, spoke to her for a moment, and then swung her up into his arms and carried her away.

The music ended a couple of beats later, leaving Anne and Rainie and Uzuri exchanging high-fives. As the women returned to the table, taking the extra chairs with them, Ben walked over.

Probably to haul them home.

It would only be polite to help out the security guard—save him a drop off. Jake rose to his feet and glanced at Holt. "Guess I'll try to nab myself a subbie as well."

"Going for Rainie?" Holt grinned. "Good thing you have balls of steel."

"I do—so maybe she'll think twice before stuffing them in her garbage disposal."

Rainie settled into her chair with a pitiful sigh. Raoul's behavior with Kim had been so dominatingly romantic, it had hollowed out a place in her chest.

No one will ever love me like that.

She made herself smile at Uzuri and Anne. "Our poor group. Attacked and picked off one by one. We're the sole survivors."

"Were the Doms upset with the dancing?" Uzuri bit her lip. "Angry?"

Rainie patted her hand. She got the feeling Uzuri had experience with…disapproving men. Not getting dumped like Rainie, but more physical. "Girlfriend, the others might get fucked to death, but nothing worse."

As Uzuri shook off the past, her smile broke out. "It did look as if the guys were a bit…aroused."

Anne snorted and picked up the giant green dildo. "About to this degree, I'd say from my wealth of experience."

A throat cleared. Ben stood beside the table, staring at the green monster. His darkly red face clashed with his pink pimp shirt. "Are you ready for your transport home?"

"I believe so. Thank you, Ben." Anne stuffed the dildos into the correct party bags and handed them to the security guard, increasing his embarrassment.

As Anne rose, the bartender hurried over to offer his business card with obvious deference and embarrassment. Anne set her dainty foot on a chair and fisted the bartender's white shirt, pulling him closer. "You're a nice boy." She plucked the card from his fingers. "I'll think about it."

The guy didn't beg—although it was close. Rainie nodded approval.

As he headed back to his job, Anne watched, tapping the card on her palm.

"Will you call him?" Rainie asked.

"Probably not." Anne dropped the card in her bag—the one with a tiny flogger tied to the handle. "I'm not in the market for new boys."

Rainie exchanged a concerned glance with Uzuri. The Mistress hadn't been the same since breaking up with her submissive Joey months ago. Although she still played with random "boys" at the Shadowlands, she always left alone.

Someone needed to talk with her, but Rainie quailed at the thought. Anne wasn't the type who—

"I'll take this one home, Ben." The deeply masculine voice came from behind Rainie.

Jake? She twisted in her chair—not an easy move considering the snug fit of her bustier. "Uh, I don't need a ride."

A tailored suit enhanced his broad shoulders, and the open shirt collar framed his corded throat. Sensuality darkened his chiseled features as he smiled down at her. She could happily stare at him for hours, just taking in all that was Jake.

He slid her chair back from the table as if it held a feather pillow rather than a very ample woman. "I'm going to escort you home and check on your dog."

"My dog?" Her brains must have been overtaken by the alcohol...or something.

His smile disappeared. "Don't you still have the pup?"

"Rhage? Of course I do."

"Good. Let's go." He grasped her upper arms with strong hands and effortlessly lifted her to her feet.

Her heart fluttered as if buffeted by a gusting wind.

Uzuri handed Jake Rainie's bag. "So you were with the bachelor party?"

With his attention on Uzuri, Rainie managed to inhale.

"I was," Jake answered Uzuri. "By the way, when I checked the trainee records last night, I saw your goals haven't been updated recently. Do so before next weekend, please."

Blinking in surprise, Uzuri glanced at Rainie.

Oh yeah, he got me too. Rainie bugged out her eyes at her friend.

Jake turned in time to see. He bent down to whisper in Rainie's ear, "Be careful, subbie. I'd enjoy another excuse to turn that fine ass of yours bright red."

A shiver ran from the top of her spine right down to her toes...and he chuckled.

Turning, he nodded at the Mistress who stood at the other end of the table. "Anne, when you get some time, I'd—"

"Why, if it isn't Rainie." The shrill voice from nearby scraped away Rainie's composure like fingernails on a chalkboard.

Don't be real. Even the Gods wouldn't be so evil. Slowly, Rainie turned to see her old high school classmate. Life really wasn't fair sometimes.

Praying Jake and the others wouldn't notice, Rainie walked toward her. "Hello, Mandy."

"Fancy meeting you here." The brunette smirked. "I'm sure you remember Jefferson and Clay, don't you?"

The Gods of Cruelty were feeling lively that evening since the woman's two companions were also high school classmates. They'd ridiculed Rainie when she was poor, socially inept, and in dirty, ragged clothing. Their scorn had increased after they'd seen her on the streets with the drug dealer.

The two men looked her up and down as if assessing how much she'd charge for a blowjob.

Her mouth twisted. She'd never turned tricks. Ever.

Jefferson said, "I didn't realize they permitted your kind in nice clubs. How'd you get in the door?"

"How do you think, bro?" Clay made kissy noises. "Probably gave the bouncer a blowjob and—"

A second later, Jake moved right up into Clay's air space, his face set into hard lines of anger.

"Whoa, man." Clay stumbled back a step. "Hey, you're Jennifer's brother. Jake, right?"

"I take it you don't get out from under your rock often enough to recognize a bachelorette party?" Jake's raised voice carried to the surrounding tables.

He was defending her.

Rainie's skin went hot, went cold.

"Now listen—" Jefferson blustered.

"Perhaps your education is lacking in how a man should address a woman. I'll be happy to instruct you. Shall we move this outside, *gentlemen*?" Jake's voice held a fillet-sharp edge.

Clay and Jefferson flushed and retreated several more steps.

Mandy whined, "Jaaake, you don't—"

She received a look only a Shadowlands' Master could deliver, and her bright red lips shut so fast the lipstick smeared.

As Jake advanced on the two men, they glanced at each other, trying to decide how to withdraw without further loss of face. *Cowards.*

A second later, they backed away.

"Not going to fight over a piece of trash," Jefferson muttered once out of reach. They disappeared into the crowd.

Rainie let out the breath she'd been holding.

Mandy sneered at Rainie's low-cut bustier and short skirt before tilting her chin toward Jake. "I see you figured out how to get him, didn't you?" Her snide tone hadn't changed from a decade ago when her gang of mean girls spotted Rainie staring at Jake. Their cutting remarks still rotted in Rainie's memory, surfacing when her spirits were low.

As Jake walked back, Mandy sidled away.

Jake watched her leave, shaking his head. He glanced at Rainie, then over her shoulder, and his anger transformed to amusement. "No wonder the boys surrendered the field."

Rainie spun.

Ben stood nearby, his brawny arms folded over his huge chest. She was so used to his amiable grin that she'd forgotten how dangerous he could appear. While Jake was a razor-sharp blade, capable of slicing a man into thin strips, Ben was a cudgel designed to flatten them into the ground.

Like an elegant stiletto knife, Mistress Anne stood beside Ben, and the deadly glint in her eyes would make anyone afraid.

Warily, Rainie edged over to stand beside Uzuri.

"Scary, aren't they?" Uzuri said under her breath, visibly trembling.

"Yeah." In the Shadowlands, Rainie had viewed whippings, knife-play, needle-play—but the tops always had everything under control. They were careful, even when blood flowed. But here, the open threat of uncontrolled violence had turned her stomach.

After talking quietly for a minute, Jake, Anne, and Ben joined them.

"You okay?" Jake's gaze swept Uzuri and Rainie.

Although Uzuri nodded, her color was more gray than brown.

Ben set a big hand on her shoulder. "Nobody's going to hurt you, honey. Not while I'm here."

Jake stopped next to Rainie and lifted his brows. "And you, sweetling?"

Answering in the affirmative would be a lie, and annoying him right then would be unwise. So she dodged the question. "Thank you for the help."

Having him jump to defend her was… She couldn't even say how that made her feel. Was her shaking from her ex-classmates' cruelty or from the surprise of being protected?

How amazing. Really. She'd actually been rescued by a knight in shining armor. Rainie wrapped her arms around herself, wanting to cling to the sensation of being cared for.

If only Jake had saved her from pirates or criminals, but nooo, her attackers were people who'd known her. They hadn't been surprised to see her dressed like a hooker—because they thought she was.

It wouldn't matter if she wore the most respectable of designer clothing. They'd never let her forget her past. And she'd never escape them, not in Florida.

A little sick, she asked, "Can we leave now, Ben?"

Jake wrapped an arm around her. "You get Uzuri and Anne home, Ben. I'm taking Rainie."

* * * *

"Thanks for the ride," Rainie said as Jake parked his car.

Her voice sounded better, he thought, as if she'd finally recovered from whatever screwed-up shit had happened at the nightclub. "Not a problem."

"I can see myself in." She jumped out.

Jake joined her on the sidewalk and took her arm. "My mother would disown me if I didn't escort a lady to her door."

She gave a huff of exasperation, but then smiled. "Did you inherit that stubbornness from her?"

"Most assuredly." His spirits lightened. Not much kept this woman down. He admired that.

Didn't admire where she lived though. The damp night air brushed over his face as he walked her to a poorly lit, three-story apartment building. The closest streetlight was dark—shot out was his guess. The landscaping consisted of several dying bushes surrounded by weeds growing through sun-bleached bark mulch. How did Rainie stand it here?

Maybe it was the suit she'd worn, but he'd gotten the impression she had a good-paying job—so why live here? This wasn't a safe place for a woman.

As they approached the end unit, she rummaged in her bag for her keys.

Her wide shawl cover-up fell open, and he reluctantly pulled it back together for her while inhaling her light, sensual scent. "Better keep this closed."

"Excellent idea." Her eyes darkened, and the pain he'd seen during the confrontation reappeared. "I wouldn't want to give the place a bad name."

"Rainie." He touched her cheek, wanting to comfort.

"Sorry. Old history." She shook her head as if to dislodge the past. "I really appreciate the way you rescued me." Humor returned to her face. "You're a regular paragon of chivalry. I would have said a knight in shining armor, but you're closer to a gentleman pirate, like in old Errol Flynn movies or…or even Dread Pirate Roberts."

"Mmmhmm." Nice imagination. "Seems like a pirate should get a reward for saving a fancy lady. Doesn't the code of the seas state that after rescuing, then comes the ravishing?"

She had a gorgeous laugh, easy and open, sounding as if it came from inside her chest rather than a fake one from her throat. This was a woman he'd enjoy ravishing.

"I think those are more like guidelines than rules," she said seriously, although the glint in her eyes revealed laughter.

Moving closer, crowding her, he ran his finger down the sweet curve of her cheek. "You know, in a role-play, if booty isn't offered…it's taken."

Her color deepened, and the way her pupils dilated said she wouldn't be adverse to some rough sex and ravishing.

Then she blinked and shook her head. "No. No, I don't think so." She set her hand against his chest and stepped away.

"All right." He wouldn't push; she'd had enough stress for one night. He gave her hair a teasing tug, took the keys, and unlocked her door.

From the darkness inside, a whirlwind of a black-and-white dog assaulted her in a torrent of bouncing and barking.

She yelped and staggered back against Jake's body.

Fuck, she was soft. He steadied her and reluctantly released her.

"Oh my God, you scared me spitless, baby." Ignoring her dropped bag, she squatted to give hugs and scratches until the dog bounded away, turned two happy circles, and dove in for more.

"I'm afraid he might be a little crazy." She laughed as the pup ran out for another circle. Her gaze rose to Jake. "Is he supposed to act like that?"

"Totally normal." Jake grinned. "This your first small dog?"

"First pet ever," came the muffled response as she buried her face in the dog's fur. When she lifted her head, her pleasure was bright enough to melt icecaps. "I never knew how…how…*wonderful* a dog was."

She smiled at the pup. "Of course, you're absolutely the best dog ever, so other dogs might not measure up."

Never had a pet? Jake raked his hand through his hair. What kind of parents didn't give their kid…something? He and his sister had conned his folks into cats, dogs, rabbits, birds—even mice and hamsters and gerbils, until one too many escaped, and his mother had decreed a no rodent establishment. "How come no pets?"

"My mother didn't like animals. And later, when…Well. I never got a pet." She concentrated on picking up her spilled bag, and the light in her face dimmed.

As she rocked, trying to rise, he put a hand under her arm and helped her to her feet.

"Thanks." She gave him an uncertain look. "I appreciate you bringing me home. So—"

"While I'm here, I want to examine the dog. What's his name again? *Anger? Fury?*"

Her smile popped back out. "It's Rhage—with an 'RH'."

Right. Why the hell would she spell a name that way? Shaking his head, he lifted the pup and walked into the living room.

Pretty place. Rainie'd overcome the apartment's off-white walls and beige carpet by scattering bright floral pillows over her white-denim-covered couch and chair. Artwork of ocean vistas hung on the walls, and the coffee table and end tables were constructed of glass and driftwood. The entire room had a beach-at-sunrise ambiance.

Jake took a seat on the couch and stroked Rhage's soft fur. The dog was already filling out a bit. Eyes clear. Happy smile.

"Easy, boy. Let me check you over." He palpated the abdomen. Soft, non-distended. No tenderness.

Rainie sat down beside him, petting Rhage as she listened to her cell's voice messages. A junk call. A friend hoping to meet for lunch. The closure of a phone account for a Lily someone. Absently, she rubbed her forehead.

The alcohol was probably wearing off. Jake set the dog down and patted her thigh. "Where's your aspirin?"

"In the bathroom. Do you have a headache? I'll get you some."

"Stay put, baby. I'll find it." After tossing his suit coat over the back of a chair, he crossed the room, detouring to check out the shelves beneath the television stand.

She had a ton of books, mostly historical and contemporary romance novels. Even the suspense stories were—judging by the covers—still romance. The DVDs were predominantly chick flicks. The *Princess Bride* DVD had been played so often the cover was cracked. *Dread Pirate Roberts, hmm?*

Someone was a romantic.

In the bathroom, he rummaged for the aspirin and finally found it under the sink. With two tablets in his palm, he stepped out to an empty living room.

Loud voices drew him to the front of the apartment where Rainie stood at the door, talking with someone.

He stayed back, not wanting to intrude, although—wasn't it rather late for visitors?

An unhappy realization dawned. For all he knew, she had a boyfriend. Or two. Had a date planned.

But she didn't sound pleased with the guy. When her spine went steel-post rigid, Jake decided to step in.

On the front step, the man was focused on Rainie, not seeing Jake behind her in the shadowy hallway. The blond was good-looking enough, although his slick *GQ* impression was ruined by a fucked-up sneer reminiscent of Professor Snape in *Harry Potter.* The guy told Rainie, "I said this already. You make me happy; I'll make you happy."

Jake scowled. *What the fuck?*

Just in case his female audience missed the point, the guy patted his groin. Had a hard-on, Jake noted. *Jesus, what an asshole.* If Rainie wanted this guy, then, as a Shadowlands Master, Jake was going to go all Dom on her ass.

"And *I* told you *already*, Cory, I'm the office manager," Rainie said. "Not a whore."

"You look like a whore to me. Try behaving like one. You fucking go down on me"—Cory unbuckled his belt—"or the only money you'll make will be from hooking on the streets. Cuz you won't be working for me."

"Seriously?" Her voice went higher with her shock. "Cory, are you insane? You can't run that place without me."

"I can do anything I want to. And that includes fucking the staff."

She let out a growl of pure anger, but the asshole grabbed her wrists and yanked her out the door.

Jake shook his head in surprise. Alcohol must have impaired her reactions or she'd have emasculated the guy. *Oh well.* He stepped around Rainie and punched the asshole in the snout. Cartilage crunched satisfyingly.

"Fuck, fuck!" Hands clapped over his face, Cory staggered back. "Jesus!"

Gently but firmly, Jake pushed Rainie behind him, catching a glimpse of her wide eyes. "Easy, sweetling. Just let me finish this up."

He advanced on the asshole.

"What the fuck!" Cory'd regained his balance—and discovered his nose was busted. "I'm going to kill you, you—"

Right. A punch to the solar plexus doubled up the idiot. Jake quickly sidestepped to avoid any blood spatter—and hammered an elbow onto the guy's back over the kidney.

Cory hit the pavement with a pleasant thump. Crying and swearing, he curled into a ball.

Jake considered kicking the bastard's junk into his throat. *No, Sheffield, that would be overkill.* He turned to check on Rainie.

Hands pressed to her mouth, she stood in the doorway. Eyes wide and horrified.

Hell. She'd probably never seen a fight before. Might even like the asshole. Well, if she did, he was going to have a long, long talk with her.

Jake cleared his throat to get her attention. "Please tell me you two aren't friends."

She shook her head *no*, then called, "Hey, Cory."

The asshole had made it up to his knees. "You-you fucking—"

"I *quit*."

"And that answers my concern nicely." Jake guided her into her apartment—pushing a snarling Rhage back—and closed the door. With the pup trotting at his heels, he walked into the living room and settled Rainie on the couch.

Dropping down beside her, he pulled her close. "Your ex-boss is an asshole, sweetling."

"Yeah. He really is." When her lower lip trembled, she mashed her mouth into a flat line. "Looks like I'm unemployed."

"I'm sorry, baby. You know, you could take legal action."

She shook her head. "The company belongs to Cory's father. And Bart…he means a lot to me."

Compassion, again. He was beginning to realize how deep her caring spirit went. "Have you been working there long?"

She stared at the wall, looking little-girl lost. "A few years.

Long enough to feel the loss. *Hell.* "Do you have a plan in mind?"

Her face was still shell-shocked pale. "I—I guess I start job hunting."

"What exactly do you do? I know some people."

"No. But thank you." Her chin lifted. "I can find work, and I don't need much to survive. Not anymore." Her gaze turned toward the end table and a photo. A thin, white-haired woman posed cheek-to-cheek with a beaming Rainie, who looked about eighteen.

The grief in Rainie's face broke Jake's heart. Hell, she couldn't catch a break, could she? "Your grandmother?"

"Miss Lily. She…gave me a home when I was seventeen." Rainie's eyes gleamed with tears before she turned her head away. "She's gone now. So, aside from Rhage, I don't have anyone to spend money on."

With a whine, Rhage crawled into her lap, and she buried her face in his fur.

Jake stayed silent, hurting for her.

Yet the more he discovered about her, the more she pleased him. The woman was more than a fun-loving submissive with attitude. She possessed a deep well of character, one he wanted to explore.

Her first thought about losing Miss Lily was regret at not having the elderly woman to care for. And a self-centered woman wouldn't rescue an injured animal, ruin her suit, risk being bitten—or spend money on it afterward. Someone had a heart big enough to match her abundant body.

Jake glanced at the basket in the corner. Looked like the dog probably had more toys than Rainie—although Jake wouldn't mind checking her nightstand to see how many toys she did have. Putting that thought away for some time in the more distant future, he tugged on her hair, pulling her attention back to him. A change of subject would be wise, especially since he didn't plan to leave until he knew she'd be all right. "Your dog looks good, by the way, and I'd guess he's about two or three years old."

She turned her head. Paused. "Oh. Right. He's older than I thought." As she gently smoothed the dog's mustache, she asked, "What kind of dog is he? Can you tell?"

"Now, that's trickier." Jake studied the beast as he stroked the wavy soft—clean—fur. "Mostly poodle." Muzzle wasn't squished. Had a double coat that was fairly heavy. Fur fell over the eyes. Ears flopped. Interesting coloring with black ears and face, white on his whiskers, chest, and legs. "Might be part Tibetan Terrier. That's a good combination. Smart, friendly, not too hyper."

"That sounds like my baby. You're a hero, puppy." She kissed the top of Rhage's fuzzy head before smiling at Jake. "And so are you. Thank you for the rescue." Her grateful expression made him feel as if he could accomplish anything.

Jake managed a seated bow. "All part of the pirate-rescue service. Speaking of which…" He rose and retrieved the aspirin tablets along with a glass of water.

He squatted beside her and set the medicine in her hand. "Take the pills and drink all the water."

"For me?"

Did no one take care of her? "Yes. Drink up, sweetheart."

From the corner of his eye, he saw the dog wander over to a pile of soft blankets and settle in with a sigh.

Chapter Six

Why was Master Jake being so nice?

Holding the water and aspirin, Rainie regarded him. He was on his haunches, perfectly comfortable in that position. His rolled-up shirtsleeves showed corded forearms under a dusting of brown hair. Along his sharp jawline, his designer stubble was darker from the day's growth. His steady gaze was compelling. This Dom didn't flaunt his power, but kept it hidden like the strong current in a deceptively lazy river.

He'd saved her. After flattening Cory without even mussing his clothing, his only concern had been for her. He made her feel…special. Valued.

"Are you going to stay for a bit?" she blurted out and wanted to cringe. What was she thinking?

His eyes crinkled. "Do you want me to?"

This time, she took a moment to think, but oh, her desire hadn't changed. She'd craved him since she was sixteen. Sure, she was being unwise, yet, why not? As soon as she had the funds, she'd move from Florida and wouldn't see him ever again. She breathed out, accepting the pain in the same way she'd absorb the impact from a flogger. "Yes. Stay. But I don't want anything serious. A one-night stand is fine with me."

His eyes narrowed at her qualification. At the club, he'd picked up on the fact she wasn't searching for a permanent Dom. But still…it should be a relief to him now, right?

He didn't say anything…just looked at her.

Under his intent gaze, her entire body heated as if a desert wind swept across her skin. She could smell his cologne—a light scent that combined sex and male in one heady note. Her hand moved of its own accord, over his lean cheek, along the stern jawline.

His lips curved against her fingers. "You sure, sweetling?" he asked, his voice huskier.

Yet the glint of laughter in his gaze made her stiffen. "You're the Dom. Aren't you supposed to make all the decisions?"

He turned her wrist over and kissed it lightly. How could his firm lips feel like velvet? "Absolutely—after you say this is what you want. I need to hear the words." The resolve in his tone said he wasn't joking. "After that, since you're not a newbie, I stop only if you safeword with 'red.'"

God, it was as if he'd flipped open a hormone switch that sent all the blood in her body straight to her core. *Put up or shut up, Rainie.*

How rare for a man to be so straightforward. None of that "C'mon, baby, just let me…" And oh, she wanted him more than she could say. She leaned forward, her mouth almost on his. What would he taste like? "I'd like you to take me—in any way you desire."

He tilted his head in a formal acknowledgment she couldn't duplicate in a million years. "As you wish, buttercup."

Her insides instantly turned to melted jelly, but he didn't give her a chance to process how he'd sounded exactly like Westley from *The Princess Bride.*

He curved his callused hand around her nape and held her in place as his mouth grazed over hers, settled, and then took…slowly and so thoroughly she felt ravished without ever taking a stitch off.

"Mmm." He studied her face and smiled. "Let's have another."

When he halted the next time, she was dizzy, barely comprehending he was guiding her into the bedroom.

He stopped in the doorway, perhaps in surprise at changing from her cottage-style living room to an Italian Renaissance bedroom.

Although threadbare, the richly colored tapestries brightened the walls and faded Oriental rugs were layered over the beige carpeting. Her prize—an ornate Italianate frame bed—took up most of the room. Dark red, gauze draperies hung from a suspended metal frame to create an Old-World style canopy bed.

Smiling, Jake ran his finger down her cheek. "You really are a romantic at heart."

A shiver ran through her as he tilted his head back to study the well-anchored, rectangular frame that hung a foot below the ceiling. "Well." His low voice brushed like suede against her skin. "This has potential."

She bit her lip, belatedly realizing how many tie points the bed and frame provided. And this man was a Dom.

Perhaps she should have kept him in the living room.

"So…*wench.*" As his lips twisted into a cruel smile, he curled his fingers over the top of her bustier and yanked her forward. "I didn't save you from your sinking ship—and my crew—to receive a mere verbal thank you."

"Jake." Her eyes widened as he started unhooking the front of her garment.

"I'm ready to inspect what my sword has won me."

Oh God. Her heart pounded as the bustier fell to the floor, and air brushed her damp skin. He lifted her breast, teasing the nipple with a thumbnail. "I'm definitely going to play with these." The corner of his mouth tipped up. "Although you might not enjoy it as much as I will."

The sensuous threat sizzled straight to her pussy even as he unfastened her short skirt and shoved her thong down, leaving her in only a garter belt and mesh stockings.

"Those can stay on." Satisfaction filled in his gaze. "Very nice."

He pointed at the bed. "Up there, wench. Sit on the edge and await my pleasure."

She hesitated.

"Too slow." He curved his long fingers around the front of her neck and smacked her bottom hard enough to make her yelp.

A whine came from behind the closed door, and she realized he'd shut Rhage out.

Jake's gaze followed hers and filled with amusement. "No rescue for you, sweetling." He swatted her again, smiling at her squeak. "Tonight, you're mine for as long as I want to use you."

The hand around her throat was big enough to grip without shutting off her air…and yet, and yet…if he tightened his fingers, he could.

Knowing she was here alone with him sent little tremors up her spine. Not…quite…fear.

"Spread your legs for me now." The dark edge of threat sliced into her defenses like a razor through silk.

The burning from her spanked bottom and helplessness under his hands were affecting her, she knew. Nonetheless, her legs inched apart.

He ran his hand between her thighs. "I love a smooth, bare pussy. A pussy that gets wet from spankings is even better."

Doms discovered secrets. It's what they did. So why did each bit of knowledge he acquired make her as uneasy as though she'd surrendered part of her soul?

"Go." He pointed again to the bed.

She certainly didn't hesitate this time. As she planted her butt on the mattress, he rummaged her bedroom. He picked up several silky scarves from the golden brackets on the wall. Purse straps came from a shelf in her closet. Then he opened the drawer to her nightstand and made a gratified sound.

Embarrassed heat flooded her face. "No. You—"

"Eyes down, woman, or I'll blindfold you." He picked up a tube of…

God, that was the peppermint clit stimulant she'd recently bought and had been too chicken to use. She heard its wrapping tear and managed not to look up.

Hard hands pushed her knees apart, and he used the applicator to smear the stuff all over her throbbing clit, ignoring her squirming.

After tossing the tube onto the nightstand, he asked, "You don't own any nipple clamps?"

God, no. Her breasts were sensitive enough without pointed pokey clamps. She shook her head and dared a look at him.

His cheek creased as he looked at her. "That's all right, wench. I have other ways to torture female parts."

She considered grabbing a pillow and covering up the target area. But surely, he wouldn't push her past what she could take. She knew that. *Right?*

After examining the gauze canopy curtains for sturdiness, he repositioned the fabric along the metal rail. He tied two opposite sides together to form a kind of sling near the head of the bed.

Finding the candles in the wall shelves, he lit them. Then he checked her music selection on the iPod. When Kitaro's soft strains drifted from the small speakers, she knew he'd discovered her playlist labeled "Sex."

The man didn't miss a trick.

"Eyes down, Rainie," he warned her again.

She tried to obey, but had to—just had to—watch him.

He sat down in front of her and picked up the first of the scarves, rubbing it teasingly over her skin. Silky and cool. He wrapped it under and around her breasts in an intricate form of breast bondage and…just the sight of his strong fingers, the brushing of his hands as he worked, made her hotter than sex with anyone else.

Slowly, he tightened the knots, and her breasts were forced outward, the skin taut. "Very pretty," he murmured as he tied off the last knot. He took her mouth again in a long wet kiss, even as he caressed her now-tightly squeezed breasts.

"Lots of toys, but no nipple clamps," he said. "Must mean these babies are sensitive, doesn't it?"

And his damned bondage increased the sensation. Her "um-hmm" of agreement rose into a *mew* as his fingers circled her swelling nipples.

"Rainie." He brushed his knuckle back and forth over her jutting left nipple, sending a sizzle straight to her core. "When I told you to lower your eyes, you disobeyed me. Am I correct?"

She swallowed and nodded.

The controlled power in his gaze kept her trapped. "Since it matters so much to you, you may watch me. However—do you *want* to obey me, Rainie?"

His question was even. No judgment however she'd answer.

Did she want to obey him?

"Yes, Sir," she whispered. She really did.

"Then I'm going to punish you for the disobedience. Next time, if you don't agree with my order, you may question me. I might explain or relent. But you will obey. Clear?"

"Yes, Sir."

"Very good." His fingers closed on her right nipple, squeezing to the point of pain—and over.

Ow, ow, ow.

As his fingers continued the pressure, tears burned in her eyes.

"I'm sorry you have to suffer this," he murmured, stroking her hair with his free hand. "Breathe past it, sweetling."

Even as she inhaled through her nose, the sinking sensation of surrender closed like a wave over her head. He wouldn't allow disobedience and really would enforce his rules. The knowledge was…devastatingly erotic.

When his fingers released her, the blood surged into her breast with a sharp influx of relief and pain, and she moaned.

"Good girl." Jake licked her sore nipple. The moist heat increased the burn, then eased it. Her heart sped even faster as his tongue curled around the peak.

On her clit, the peppermint ointment warmed, increasing to a light burning. She squirmed at the influx of sensations.

He laughed and, with an easy movement, rolled her onto her back in the center of the bed.

"Jake. Sir!"

"Shhh." Smiling, he pushed her legs apart and knelt between them. As if he had all the time in the world, he teased her breasts, kissed her stomach, and took a long study of her pussy.

She closed her eyes. *What a place to look at.*

"The tube said peppermint." He had a brigand's grin. "I'll let you know if they got the flavor right."

Oh God, it was her most carnal of fantasies coming true—Jake Sheffield going down on her. A tremor went through Rainie as he lowered his head.

His breath laved her sensitive tissues, making the peppermint ointment turn both cold and exquisitely hot. "Mmm, pussy and peppermint—great combination."

The deliberate brush of his unshaven jaw on her inner thigh made her squeak and jerk. Made him laugh.

Even as his tongue teased circles around her clit, he slowly pressed a finger into her pussy. Her hips rose, and his free hand held her down.

She whined an objection.

"Don't move, little captive." He added another finger. "This is my body to enjoy—or to punish." The threat pushed her to try to obey, even as his fingers explored deeper inside her, wakening every nerve.

"God," she moaned.

"I usually suggest *Sir* or *Master*, but I suppose *God* is adequately respectful." Her snort made him chuckle. And then he sucked on her clit so forcefully her hips bucked at the thundering pleasure, and every thought drained right out of her mind.

When he lifted his head, she wanted to yank him back to the position. He licked his lips. "The ointment isn't as strong as breath strips, but it's got a good flavor."

"Oh well, that's a relief," she muttered. Her face felt like it was sunburned, so who was her sarcasm kidding? Knowing she tasted good *was* a relief.

"I wouldn't mind seeing some more squirming from the heat though," he said thoughtfully. "Next time, if I don't plan to do oral, I'll use something harsher—when my mouth won't be at risk."

Harsher? On her pink bits? Her head shook in an involuntary *no*, and he laughed, then his teeth closed on her clit, ever so gently.

As his tongue flickered over her trapped nub, an unstoppable tide of pleasure flowed through her. She wiggled, losing her hold on reality, and he pinned her hips and continued using his tongue as a weapon. Pressure built inside her, swirling low in her pelvis.

The ointment had made her so, so sensitive, and the teasing flicks on her clit kept her moaning as he thrust his fingers in, pulled out, again and again, relentlessly transporting her to a peak from both inside and outside.

She thought at one point that she was taking too long and tried to move. "Your turn." When she tried to pull him up to fuck her, he snorted and captured her wrists, holding them against her stomach to pin her down.

He didn't even need to speak—his actions showed he'd do—and take—what he wanted. Her head fell back onto the bed.

And he didn't lose a beat. His tongue tapped lightly on her increasingly sensitive clit, even as his fingers kept up a steady in and out.

God, God, God. She was there. Right there. Her muscle strained to the point of pain.

"Let go, buttercup," he murmured. "It's okay." He traced his tongue over her engorged clit and along the edge of the hood before rubbing ruthlessly.

Every nerve in her lower half went off as if someone threw a match into a fireworks booth. The zinging and exploding and sparkling spread upward until her whole body shook with the climax.

"Fuck, I love the way you come."

Dazedly, she opened her eyes.

Fingers still deep within her, he watched her intently. A slight smile curved his lips.

"Sir," she whispered. His turn. She should—

"I think you have one more in you." He lowered his head. His mouth closed around her clit, and he sucked…and rotated his fingers inside her.

"Aaah." Another wave of explosions ripped through her.

When she finally floated down from the vicinity of the ceiling, heat radiated from her skin as if her body'd been in a bonfire. Her heart still thudded enough to jostle her rib cage. "Am I dead?" she whispered.

"Not yet, wench. However, the ship won't dock for several hours, and I intend to have my way with you over and over again." Propped on one elbow, he lazily ran his gaze over her with obvious pleasure. "You might not survive."

His lips were tipped up at the corners. Teasing her. Oh God. She heard a sound escape her, the one a prizefighter would make when punched right in the stomach.

Because…because sex with Master Jake was better than dancing. What had she done? She didn't need to—want to—know this.

His regard intensified.

No. No, no, no. This evening was to be *fun*. Temporary. A one-night stand. Checking something off her bucket list—not creating an impossible-to-ever-meet memory.

"Sweetling, what's going on in that head of yours?"

Role-play, Rainie. Pirate talk. She hauled in a breath and put her head into the game. "Listen, you scabby-arsed, scurvy-brained…"

He blinked. "Damn, girl—"

"...thumb-sucking, syphilitic, slimy scalawag." She scowled at him. "I'll never, ever cooperate, no matter what you do to me."

"Oh aye, there's a challenge I'll take." He glided his powerful hand up her thigh and his squeeze made clear how strong he was. And just his touch made her core clench in response. "You'll cooperate...because I won't give you a choice, wench."

Damn, she knew how to make an evening fun, Jake thought as he stripped off his shirt and pants and sheathed himself, enjoying the way she watched him. Her open appreciation was a delight.

"On your knees now."

"Make me, you bilious, butt-scratching, baboon."

"Oh, I will, me buxom beauty." He rolled her to uncover her ass cheeks and smacked her hard enough to provide adequate incentive.

By the third swat, she was up on her knees, facing the head of the bed.

"Now you're in a nicer position, don't you think?" With his hand in the soft mass of her hair, he tilted her head back and kissed the pout from her lips. "Say, 'Yes, me wonderful Captain.'"

Her eyes lit with laughter and surrender, infinitely pleasing. "Yes, me wonderful Captain."

Holding the improvised drapery sling out, he said, "Arms against your sides. Put your head and shoulders through here.

That got him a worried glower, but she did as he ordered.

Before she had second thoughts, he slid the sling down her torso to below her breasts. Her lower ribs rested on the fabric. Most of her weight remained on her knees, but the sling supported her upper body. "It'll hold you, baby."

"Sure, it will," she muttered.

But when he shoved her legs farther apart, she was forced to trust more of her weight to the drapery swing.

After a second or two, she realized she couldn't straighten up...and that the sling had pinned her arms against her sides. She was trapped. "You...you *bastard*."

"My mother insists not." He rolled to his back and maneuvered himself between her legs until she straddled him with a knee on each side of his hips. *Perfect.* He liked having a woman on top, but in Rainie's case, if she were over him on her hands and knees, her breasts would hang too low for him to enjoy. And wouldn't that be a shame?

This way, the sling not only gave her some support, but also angled her just right to let him play. A hard-working pirate deserved some fun, after all...and he loved bondage in all its forms.

He ran the head of his cock over her wet pussy and pushed just inside. The sensation of moist heat shook his control. "Don't move, me beauty."

In open defiance—half for role-playing and half reality—she fought the restraints, trying to get her arms loose, trying to kneel up. She failed. Panting, she glared at him. "You..."

"You're stuck, sweetheart," he said quietly. He smiled into her vulnerable eyes, assessing her. Not afraid, but anxious, definitely. He'd stolen away her ability to control the sex—and they both knew he intended to give her a good fucking.

"Jake," she whispered in a plea to be released, but beneath it, loud and clear, was the desire to be taken. Was there anything more enthralling to a Dom than a submissive's need to be both cherished and ravaged? Than her need to feel safe—and scared.

"Shhh, you'll be fine, baby." He ran his thumb over her soft lips, slowly. Back and forth.

Her breathing slowed.

Then he made his voice cruel. Edged. "'Tis a shame, beauty, but I can do whatever I want to you. And I will." Even as her eyes widened, he curled his fingers around her hips, gripped…and yanked her down onto his cock.

Her neck arched, her mouth opened in a soundless cry. Fuck, she was slick and hot, and her cunt clenched around him, welcoming him to the heart of her. He held there, letting her adjust to his size.

Her back had arched, pushing her chest toward him in a pretty invitation. The scarves had made her breasts swollen and taut, so he cupped them and rubbed his thumbs over the nipples.

She made little whimpering moans, pain and excitement, as he continued stroking the softest of velvety skin. So fucking responsive.

As her core relaxed slightly, he gripped her hips and moved her up and down on his cock a few times, watching arousal overwhelm her anxiety. Beautiful. Then he pushed her up until the head of his shaft barely remained inside her. Time to add in another element—a submissive's joy in serving, in making her Dom happy. "Can you show me, baby, how still you can hold? For me?"

Blinking, she focused on him. She had the prettiest gold-flecked hazel eyes. So vulnerable. Like her body—open to him completely. She swallowed. "Yes, Sir." After a second, her leg muscles hardened, and she held the position.

"That's a girl. Look at me, baby."

As he rubbed his palms over her jutting nipples, everything she felt showed.

She had sensitive breasts—his favorite kind. He spread his fingers over the beautiful mounds and squeezed lightly. Her nipples contracted to adorable nubs as he teased them.

Her pupils widened until more black than hazel showed. Each inhalation brought him the scent of her musk and her unique spicy fragrance

As he studied her, he carefully increased the pressure to the edge of pain, learning what it took to pull her to that place where the world faded and to keep her there, piling sensation after sensation onto her pleasure.

Far before he was ready, her cunt clenched around him like a hot fist, and the insides of her thighs quivered uncontrollably against him.

"Damn, you're a delight, sweetheart." How long had he wanted to see her like this? Be inside her like this? With one hand, he cupped her face, caressing her damp cheek with his thumb. "Fuck, you're beautiful."

Even though her gaze had gone unfocused, her lips curved.

"Now, I'm going to take you hard, sweetling," he said. He gripped her breasts in the most intimate of restraints, hearing the soft whoosh of her inhalation. With one swift move, he shoved his hips up—burying himself to the root.

Her body shook from the impact, and her hair brushed with feather strokes against his chest. "Oh, *God*." Her clear voice had turned to a smoky hoarseness.

He made his tone stern. "This time, buttercup, I want you to ask before you come."

With a tiny nod, she acknowledged his order, and her mouth set into an adorable line of determination.

Her top half was pinned in the sling, holding her trapped, while he gripped her hips and pistoned into her softness, fast, then slow. *Absolute heaven.* The burn in his balls grew. The air itself thickened. The slapping of moist flesh blended with the music.

As her pussy muscles contracted, her whimpering grew louder. "Please. Please." She tried to lift up, to wiggle. "I need to come."

"When I choose." He refilled his palms with her breasts, preventing her movement, forcing her to take what he gave. What they both wanted.

Muscle by muscle, her body grew rigid, and her vagina clamped around him. She was panting, quivering with the need to go faster, and so he paused, holding his shaft barely inside to torture them both. "Look at me, sweetling."

Her wide eyes glowed in her pink-flushed face. "Pleeeze." Her voice was almost inaudible.

He pinched her nipples in the same rhythm as his thrusts had achieved. Her moan made him smile. But enough teasing. She was in a beautiful place—right at the edge—and needed no more stimulation.

"Come now, baby." He squeezed the velvety areolas and rolled, even as he thrust in hard and fast.

She gasped, and her cunt clenched him in a mind-blowing vise of pleasure. And then she was coming, wiggling, spasming, crying—and driving him toward his own climax.

Like a volcano, the pressure built inside him, squeezing his balls from within, then burning through his shaft in a wrenching eruption of heat and pleasure.

Slowly, slowly, his heart rate returned to normal. In blessed contentment, he savored the tiny erratic spasms of her easing climax. Her nipples unbunched; her flush lightened.

Using his abdominal muscles, he sat up far enough to kiss her generous mouth and nip the plump lower lip.

Her lips curved under his.

"You make a superb captive," he said, just to hear her throaty laugh.

"Sure I am."

He shook his head. She really was, and if she thought this was a one-night stand, she was in for a surprise. Smiling slightly, he kissed her again, taking his time, enjoying the feel of her…everywhere.

You're not done with me yet, sweetling.

After he'd cleaned himself up, he released her. As she cleaned up, he put the room back to rights, then tucked her into her bed. Obviously exhausted, sassy mouth silenced, she merely blinked at him.

Jake opened the bedroom door and tossed Rhage up onto the bed. As the dog curled up near the footboard, Jake slid in under the covers.

Rainie gave him a surprised look. "You're staying?"

Her lips were generous when he took her mouth. "I am." She was on her back, and he slid his arm under her head and cupped her closest breast in his other hand. Oh yes, he was going to enjoy the rest of the night. "Pirates do that."

She snorted softly. "Of course they do." Idly, she stroked his upper arm and traced out the tattoo on his deltoid—a *V* covering a caduceus and winged staff. "That's a medical insignia, right?"

"Mmmhmm. Army Veterinary Corp."

Her brow wrinkled in perplexity. "The military has veterinarians?"

"Since World War I, yes."

"Well, sure, but back then, they used horses and mules. Now…?"

"Now the soldiers use dogs." For bomb sniffing, among other things, and his memories weren't good. He'd lost friends, both human and canine, in Afghanistan. The ache in his chest and gut made it difficult to inhale.

Rainie curled her fingers around his arm, the pressure a comfort.

Don't be a wimp, Sheffield. He forced his lips to curve up. "We also treated normal pets on bases, did public health work, disease control." It hadn't been all heartbreaking.

"You're only five years older than me—maybe thirty or thirty-one—so when did you fit in a long education? Doesn't getting a veterinary degree take time?"

Now, how did she know his age? She'd obviously asked about him. "I skipped a grade in elementary school and did my bachelor's in three years. Four years to get the DVM, four of active service. Saxon and I bought the clinic a couple of years ago."

She stared. "Saxon? Our Saxon from the Shadowlands, who likes puppy play?"

"That's the man."

"Sweet-suffering fudgesicles, I need to get better gossip."

Jake laughed and rolled to his back. "Members rarely talk about their vanilla lives."

"True enough." She snuggled next to him and put her head on his shoulder. Her silky hair spilled over his arm and chest, tickling him.

Nice. And wasn't this a good position? He adjusted her breasts so one lay on his chest to fondle.

When she gave him an exasperated scowl, he gave her a warning look as his fingers traced over the lingering dents in her flesh. "I like sex toys as much as you do, sweetling. The difference is that I consider *you* one of my toys, and I intend to play with you off and on all night." He remembered the well-handled movie cover and added, "As the Dread Pirate Roberts, I have a rep to maintain."

Even as she gave a choked laugh, her body softened against his in a submissive's instinctual surrender. "As you wish."

* * * *

The next morning, Rainie yawned and tried to force herself to wake, but her muscles had the consistency of overcooked spaghetti. Aching spaghetti. Her arms were sore, as were her thigh muscles. The skin on her breasts burned. When she moved, she realized her pussy was tender. Because…

Because she'd had awesome sex last night. *Oh God.* With *Jake.* Her heart gave a painful thump as she held herself totally still, letting the thrill roll over her.

He'd let her sleep for a couple of hours. She'd woken when he pushed Rhage out of the bedroom again.

Ignoring her halfhearted objections, Jake had tied the thin bed curtains around her ankles to hold her legs up in a high *V* split. After teasing her orally…forever…he'd stopped right before she could come and taken her in his own version of missionary style.

With her thighs pulled out of the way, he went deeper than she was used to, and she was so primed, she'd started coming with his first thrust.

He'd laughed, settled in, and hammered her into another orgasm before getting off himself.

When he'd woken her again—before five a.m., damn him—she'd hit him. Her lips curved. Not a good move with a Dom.

He'd hauled her out of bed and onto her knees before she'd had a chance to finish swearing at him—let alone apologize.

Needless to say, he'd made sure she gave him a hell of a blowjob with a ruthlessness that'd make Dread Pirate Roberts proud.

But she'd enjoyed it. The man was wonderfully endowed, thick and long, with potently heavy testicles. And he had a sexy sense of humor. When she'd commented on his neatly trimmed manscaping, he'd grinned and answered, "If I prefer pussies to be bare, seemed only fair to partly return the favor."

After he'd come, she'd thought to go back to sleep. But nooo. The blowjob had been for refusing him. She'd gotten a damned *spanking* for hitting him. Then he'd used his hands and fingers and more toys until she was begging to be allowed to come. When he'd finally let her climax…well, her neighbors probably thought someone had been murdered.

No wonder she was sore and positively, completely satiated.

A noise made her jump, and she rolled over to see Jake beside the bed.

"You getting up now? On a Sunday?" she asked.

"A couple of dogs in the clinic didn't make it home on Friday." He'd already pulled on his pants. His shirt hung open, displaying his tanned pecs and where his curly brown chest hair narrowed to a line down his flat abdomen.

Still wet from the shower, his hair was shoved carelessly back. Why did he seem even sexier when not all neat and tidy?

"An attendant is there, but I need to check on them too," he finished.

She wiggled upright in the bed. He didn't sound upset that he had to get up early. Just matter-of-fact about his responsibilities. How long had she been around boys pretending to be men?

But even a decade ago, he'd already been a man. He was also a Shadowlands Master—the best of the best—and the first requirement of a good Dom was to accept responsibility for himself and his actions. "Got it. Do you have time for breakfast?"

His hands stopped in the process of buckling his belt, and he said in unconcealed hope, "You'd cook me breakfast?"

God, she'd bet he'd been an adorable child. "Sure. I like to cook."

Even knowing he had impeccable manners, she almost expected to hear a crack about her weight. But he said with open pleasure, "Works for me. I like to eat."

She slid out of bed and reached for her robe.

He slid it out of her reach. "Nope. You'll wear this." He pulled off his dress shirt and helped her into it.

He was tall enough that the hem hung below her butt cheeks, but…her full breasts pushed the front open. "I'll never get it buttoned."

"I don't want it buttoned." He took advantage by circling his finger around her nipples "I prefer these be accessible."

God, no matter how many times he'd taken her, he could waken her lust anew with just the dark desire in his green eyes.

An hour later, Jake sat back from the table with a supremely satisfied groan. "You can sure cook. That was damn good."

She flushed but managed to respond with a calm, "Thank you." She'd made him a customized spinach, cheddar, and sausage omelet—and added hash browns to balance out the healthy green stuff. The meal would keep a hard-working veterinarian going for quite a while.

Thinking of veterinarians, wasn't it funny that Saxon, the veterinarian, loved furry play? Of course, she wouldn't gossip about him or his career, but…during the next puppy and kitty role-play, she'd talk the submissives into coming down with a wealth of injuries. They'd be limping, with broken tails and crumpled ears, and whining at the big blond Dom until he "healed" them.

Poor veterinarian. Would he be at the Shadowlands next weekend? "I didn't notice Saxon at the club on Friday or even the week before. Is he all right?"

"Oh, he's fine." Jake's low growl was alarming. "He's been on vacation. But—"

"Has he done something wrong? Aren't you friends?"

"Don't look so concerned. I didn't murder him—although it was close," Jake grumbled. "You saw our receptionist, right?"

The blonde bimbo. "I did."

"Sax caved in to family pressure and gave her a job. She was—bar none—the most incompetent receptionist I've ever seen. Unfortunately, before we caught on, she did a number on everything in the computer, including the schedule. I fired her Friday."

"Oh." Rainie felt a twinge of sympathy for the poor receptionist. Deserved or not, losing a job really hurt. She cleared her throat. "So, did Saxon yell at you for dismissing her?"

"I beat him to it. I called and yelled at him yesterday and told him to haul his ass back by tomorrow. It'll take us both to clean up her mess." Tension tightened his mouth. "We'll have to assign a tech to answer the phone until we hire someone—but we don't have time to interview because of the disaster."

"Catch-22, huh?" Rainie hesitated. She needed to start making calls and get her butt into a new job, but…how could she not pitch in? A receptionist position wouldn't improve her resume, but certainly she could help the guys out for a little while. Until they found someone. "I don't know anything about animals but I'm superb at answering phones. If you want, I can fill in until mid-February."

"Seriously?"

"Hey, Rhage needs his vet in good shape."

"Done." He extended his hand across the table.

She started to take it and then pulled back. Now she had a problem. Work versus sex. She didn't combine the two. Ever.

Her inner self cringed at the thought of speaking her mind. But…this was the Dom who'd spanked her at the Shadowlands for not being honest. "Jake."

His eyes narrowed before he took her hand in his callused one. "Tell me, sweetling."

Even with his encouragement, the words wouldn't come.

"I need a refill—how about you?" She picked up their cups and rose.

In the kitchen, she poured the coffee, seeing the blackness swirl in the bottom of the cup. Why couldn't she refuse Jake—or other Doms? Her problem was due to more than being submissive.

With Miss Lily's help and the counseling she'd required, Rainie had learned that the uncertainties in her childhood—because of her mother and foster parents—trained her to be a *pleaser*. By knowing the cause, she'd managed to overcome the behavior.

But she'd never discussed the ugly habits acquired during her year on the streets. There, if a girl didn't give a man what he wanted, she starved or got hurt. Confrontations led to slaps, punches, kicks…or worse. Rainie had suffered it all before Shiz had taken her in. And even with him…she'd never said no. Giving in had been safer.

Well. Now that she recognized the reasons for her wimpy behavior, she'd work through it. And she'd not keep being a wimp either. She set Jake's coffee in front of him and met his patient gaze. "I… I don't mess around with my bosses."

"You got it out. Good for you." His smile was filled with approval.

And she deserved it. A glow of self-satisfaction filled her.

"*Mess around,*" he repeated. As the meaning registered, his smile turned rueful. "Hell. Well, hell." He ran his hand through his hair, messing it up even further. "Unfortunately, I agree. I don't screw my staff."

Relieved, Rainie sighed.

After a second, Jake rose. "You do realize though, I've never worked with an employee I'd previously fucked." Looking down at her, he ran his thumb over her kiss-swollen lips. "It's going to be difficult, sweetling…since I already want to take you again."

Chapter Seven

On Monday morning, Jake headed into the feline room.

"Jake." His buddy and co-owner of the clinic grabbed his arm and spun him around. Saxon's blue eyes and shoulder-length pale hair almost glowed against the dark tan he'd picked up on the Caribbean beaches. "That's Rainie."

"What?"

"That's *Rainie* out there answering our phones." Saxon hadn't looked so shocked since a subbie doing puppy play had actually bit him. "Bro, you might be a Shadowlands Master, but you can't just draft the submissives no matter how much we need a receptionist."

Jake laughed. "Jesus, Sax. If I tried conscripting the subs, Z would hand me, balls up, to Mistress Anne."

"So, you didn't…?"

"Rainie's between jobs and heard I fired Lynette. She volunteered to man the desk until the middle of February."

Saxon let out a sigh of relief. "Thank you, Deity of All Veterinarians."

"We can hope it works out. I didn't check for references. Hell, I don't even know what kind of job she had before." At Saxon's skeptical stare, Jake shrugged. "She's an honest woman. If she says she can do something, I figure she can."

"Pretty trusting for you, bro."

True enough. However…Jake shot him a pointed look to remind him of who'd hired Lynette.

"Right. Shutting up here."

* * * *

Not long before noon, a retriever pup was brought in, having tried to eat something sharp. After handing the case to Saxon, who loved surgery, Jake, who preferred his patients awake, took over the exams. Hairballs, cancer, ear abscesses, removing stitches. Helping and healing. He loved his job.

If only running a vet clinic didn't involve running a business, he'd be a happy man.

When he finally emerged from the exam rooms, Rainie sat behind the reception counter, looking as calm and collected as when she'd first walked in. Although she'd removed the jacket to her dark red suit, she was still too classy for the clinic.

He eyed her, trying to decipher what appeared different. *Ah.* Her tattoos were completely covered by her three-quarter-length sleeves. With her hair pulled back in a French braid, she was a poster child for professionalism.

"Doctor Sheffield," she said, making him smile with her formality. "When you're free, I have a list of calls for you to return." She gave him a notepad with several—completely readable—messages. "Nothing is urgent, and they're all willing to wait until you take a break."

"That's—"

"Your tech Ceecee said the kennel attendant schedule hadn't been done, so I took a stab at creating one. Kris gave me the pile of vacation requests from your desk and the usual hours each person works." She handed him a neatly labeled folder. "I printed out a tentative schedule and put it in here with the requests. I think I satisfied them all, but you should check it over and okay it."

"I could use you at my office. What are you doing working as a receptionist?" a new client holding a cat carrier asked from the waiting area.

Rainie smiled. "Just helping Dr. Sheffield out temporarily."

With her terrier perched politely beside her on the bench, Mrs. Pritchert peered over her reading glasses. "You lucked out with this one, Doc. That snippy receptionist last week wasn't worth the ink on her paycheck."

He found no discreet answer available, so he nodded his response, then studied the papers in his hand. "Excellent work, Rainie."

At his pleased smile, pink bloomed in her cheeks. *Submissive.* And delightful.

Obviously flustered, she rose to greet Mrs. Flanders, who'd brought in her grumpy Doberman. Even the techs were careful when dealing with the ancient canine.

But when the old woman dropped her checkbook, Rainie hurried around the counter to pick it up. She remained crouched and held out her hand. "Good grief, you're a big guy. You'd probably eat my little dog for breakfast and still want more."

Prince Albert's ears pricked forward. After sniffing her palm, he gave a butt-wiggle of approval. *Know how you feel, old man.* Rainie was soft, caring, and a real heart-tugger.

"Where is Rhage, by the way?" Jake asked, hoping she hadn't left the animal at home. A bored pup could rip an apartment to pieces.

"Under my desk. Kris was a sweetheart and took him outside when she walked the other dogs." Rainie grinned. "She wore him out so thoroughly he's been sleeping since."

Jake glanced over and saw the dog sprawled in a hand-fashioned bed. "Good enough."

"Are you taking your lunch now?" Rainie asked.

He snorted. "Hardly. Lynette never bothered to schedule breaks or lunches."

"Seriously?" She scowled. "That surly, sway-backed strumpet."

"Excuse me?"

She waved an airy hand. "I'm practicing pirate curses."

At the thought of her sumptuous curves beneath him while she cursed him like a fishwife, Jake laughed. And his body hardened.

She didn't notice, but with her beautiful mouth set into a determined line, she stared at her monitor. "I'll make sure you get time for lunch tomorrow."

He barely managed to refrain from stroking her hair. Instead, he took the folder she'd given him and headed into his office.

Saxon would be praying to his Deity of All Veterinarians to keep this woman.

Jake might set up an altar himself.

* * * *

The sun was rising when Rainie unlocked the clinic by herself two days later. Good thing Jake had given her a key since a client had arranged to arrive early to drop off her puppies to be vaccinated. Ginger hadn't wanted to be late to work.

Having experienced the joy that was Cory, Rainie understood all too well.

"Hey, come on in," Rainie said. With Rhage tucked under her arm, she held the door open for Ginger to edge past with her big box.

Rhage's ears pricked up at the squeaking noises.

"You can put them behind the counter," Rainie said. "As soon as one of the kennel staff is free, she'll get them settled in the back."

"I really appreciate you taking them early." Ginger set the box down and lifted up one of the puppies. "Y'all be good for Rainie, you hear?"

"Oh, they're *adorable*." When Rainie made an involuntary movement, Ginger put the tiny squirming ball of fur in her hand.

Plush and soft. Rainie held the baby up to her face, and a teeny tongue touched her chin.

Ginger grinned. "It's difficult to imagine they'll grow to seventy pounds or so." She rubbed the little perked-up triangular ears. "Shepherds make such cute puppies."

Rainie sighed. "I don't know much about animals, but so far, I haven't met an ugly puppy." And she'd managed to hold most of them. It was a weakness.

Rhage planted his paws on her knees, stretching up for a sniff.

"Don't worry, my hero dog," she told him, tucking the puppy back into the box. "You own my heart." Although the puppies had stolen a piece or two.

Ginger glanced at her watch. "I'm gone. I'll see you at lunch to get my batch of fuzzy-butts."

"They'll be ready for you."

In the wonderfully quiet office, Rainie worked steadily for an hour until the staff showed up, followed by the first appointments. As time passed, the waiting room filled.

Jake and Saxon were keeping up fairly well. It helped that the technicians handled the shots and initial exams. The clinic hadn't yet achieved the super-smooth functioning that was Rainie's goal, but the work was totally fun.

And then it wasn't.

A man entered with a slender black dog. "Rainie, what are you doing here?"

Her heart leaped at the familiar tenor—and crashed. She wiped away her expression. "Geoffrey, it's good to see you."

Her ex-fiancé looked…good. His lightly tanned face showed off his clear blue eyes and a new trim mustache.

"Are you working here?" he asked. His white shirt was stiff and bright, his silk tie perfect for the silver-gray pinstripe suit. Beautifully tailored, as always.

Not her. She grew keenly aware of the bloody splotch on her sleeve, and the stain from where Rhage had put his paws on her skirt. At least her legs were under the counter; a fleeing kitten had climbed her like a tree and snagged her hose.

"I'm working here temporarily." Submerging herself in the safety of business, she opened the schedule. "Ah, I see there's a miniature Doberman scheduled for a routine physical and shots. He belongs to Kailie Hollingsworth."

He smiled sheepishly. "She's my wife."

Married. Her mind went blank.

"Geoff, good to see you." Jake walked out of his office. The two men shook hands with the brotherly buffet on the shoulder that meant an extra dollop of friendship.

"Doing great. I don't know if you heard. Kailie is pregnant." Geoffrey's chest pumped up as if he'd invented procreation all by himself.

The first kick in the teeth hadn't even dissipated before the pain of the second hit Rainie. *Pregnant?* What happened to not wanting children for years, maybe not at all?

"Congratulations." Jake grinned. "That would be why you're stuck dealing with Kailie's demon Doberman?"

"That would be why. Kailie can't manage more in the mornings than looking green. At least, she has a ton of international clients and later in the day works well for contacting them." Geoffrey handed Jake the leash and nodded to Rainie. "It was good to run into you again."

"And you," Rainie managed past the blockage in her throat.

Jake turned a speculative gaze on her and Geoffrey. "You two know each other?"

Geoffrey smiled. "I think you were in Afghanistan when we were engaged." He lifted a hand and strode out.

She stared after him and then remembered Jake.

Eyes narrowed, he was studying her.

Her defensiveness flared. Swiveling her chair around, she faced the computer monitor. "The dog is on your schedule. I'll check him in."

He walked behind the counter and planted a hip on the desktop. Did the man have no concept of personal space?

"Engaged? So…how long did you and Geoff date?" His voice remained quiet enough that the clients in the waiting room wouldn't hear.

She gave an indifferent shrug. "I don't know"—*six months and twelve days*—"half a year, maybe."

"Quite a while. What happened to break you up?"

The surge of hurt made her eyes prickle. "That's not your business." She raised her chin. "You're my boss, not my Dom."

His intent gaze held the warmth of the sun. "I'm both. Seems like Geoff's into inertia, so I'd say if he stayed with you that long, something else derailed him. What happened, Rainie?"

The determined set of his mouth said he'd sit on her desk until she answered him—she'd seen the same determination when he'd pulled a massive St. Bernard out of a room. The dog's tail had whipped up under its belly as it had given in to the superior force that was Master Jake.

She gave in, too. "His family happened."

"Ah." Jake's smile flickered ruefully. "Status conscious. Appearance conscious. Shallow as a Disney cartoon."

"Mmm." His assessment was dead on. He didn't sound impressed with Geoffrey's family, as if they weren't worthy of his regard. She cleared her throat. With his family, Geoffrey'd been ashamed of knowing Rainie, acting like a cat trying to cover his waste. "Our relationship ended the day I met them."

She stared at her keyboard and willed Jake to leave.

His callused hand settled on her wrist, the warmth calming. "I see your hurt, baby. Still…knowing you both, I'd say you can find a better fit."

Right. Too bad for her that she wanted a gentleman Dom. The chances were slim that she'd find a gentleman who wouldn't mind that his woman was raised in the slums, in foster homes, and on the streets. Bitterness tasted foul on her tongue.

She shut her thoughts down and brought up the next bill on her computer. "I'm busy, Dr. Sheffield."

"Of course." Jake's light touch on her hair felt like a caress. "We'll discuss this some other time."

"I'll just pencil that little talk into the appointments." Not a problem. There should be an hour or two free on the day after the apocalypse. What year would that be?

* * * *

On Thursday, Rainie emerged from the dressing room in the bridal store, happily re-attired in jeans, sandals, and a peasant blouse. "No more bridesmaid dress fittings. Yay!" She danced across the floor to Gabi and Kim, who waited by the wall of mirrors.

Her two friends laughed.

"Gabi, thank you—and Sally—for picking a gown that's gorgeous on me." The clinging halter top and flowing skirt had totally made the most of her assets. "Made me feel like Cinderella at the ball."

Gabi beamed. "That's how I feel in my wedding dress. And we loved finding the perfect style for each of you. You should have seen the over-frilled frumpy rag I got stuck wearing in college." Gagging sounds ensued. "Thank God for the same-color, different-styles trend."

"I love my dress—and the deep blue color too." Kim patted Gabi's hand. Her bridesmaid gown would be a skin-tight sheath which displayed her perfect figure.

As Rainie took a chair near her friends, Kim asked Gabi, "By the way, did Master Z mandate a theme for this weekend?"

"I didn't check since"—Gabi scowled—"my *beloved* has said no Shadowlands this week. Marcus wants a little 'anticipation' for the honeymoon which means, starting Saturday, no sex either."

"Oh my God." Kim snickered. "He'll be so horny, he'll drag you out of the reception after one dance."

"He won't be the one dragging," Gabi said grumpily.

"What about you, Rainie? Do you know the theme?" Kim asked. "I'm in a dress-up mood."

"I didn't check either. I'm taking a hiatus from the club." When the other two stared at her, she moved her shoulders. "Jake and Saxon are my bosses at the clinic. Interacting with them at the Shadowlands would be…too much."

"Huh, I get how you might feel awkward." Gabi tilted her head. "But—"

"Here I come!" With the laughing announcement, Andrea popped out of a dressing room and strode toward the mirrors, the seamstress scurrying behind her like a mouse after a big cat. "Well? What do you think?" Her strapless gown exposed her beautiful muscular shoulders and golden tan.

"Wow." Kim clapped her hands. "You look fantastic. Like the Amazon Cullen is always calling you."

"Wonder Woman," Rainie said. "Girl, you've totally got to wear golden bracelets—you know, the bulletproof ones."

Gabi waggled her eyebrows. "Just be careful about wearing a Lasso of Truth. Cullen's liable to use it on you."

"He-he wouldn't bother." Andrea's golden-brown eyes filled with tears.

Gabi jumped to her feet and wrapped her arms around the taller woman. "What's wrong, girlfriend? Has he been mean to you?"

Cullen mean? Rainie knit her brow. Strict, maybe, but the giant Dom didn't have a cruel bone in his body.

Andrea shook her head. "No. It's…" Her breath hitched in a sob. The little seamstress bobbed in to hand her a handful of tissues, and Andrea wiped her face. "I'm being an idiot. It's just"—she peered at the wedding dress displays—"I want to get married. I'm ready."

"Well, finally," Kim said, smiling.

Rainie understood the lure of a wedding and having someone to spend a lifetime with, to trust and hold. "But, why the tears? Mast—um, Cullen has been proposing to you forever."

"He stopped." Andrea's eyes filled again. "He gave up on me. Or maybe he changed his mind."

"Fat chance," Kim said. "He adores you."

Gabi took a tissue and patted the tears from Andrea's cheeks. "He really does. He'll ask again." Her mouth set in a stern line. "You'd better say 'yes' next time, or I'll wallop you."

"Oooh, threat," Rainie cooed. "I'm getting all excited. Where's my flogger?"

The seamstress's mouth dropped open, and she backpedaled. "I think everything fits fine. Bring the dress upfront when you're done." Face a bright pink, she scurried toward the front of the room.

"Oops," Rainie whispered, sending the others into giggles.

When Andrea disappeared to change, Gabi dropped into a chair with a sigh and scrubbed her hands over her face.

Rainie exchanged glances with Kim and said, "Gabi, Andrea will be fine."

Kim added, "I'm not so sure about you. Is something wrong? Are your parents causing trouble?"

"No." Gabi grimaced. "Not really…aside from constantly adding more guests and demanding fancier food. But since they're not paying for the reception, they lack any leverage."

"So…?" Rainie prompted.

Gabi scowled. "They're unhappy about the 'double' wedding and about a ménage being included, so they're really cold to Sally. And worse, Galen's mom is just plain nasty and constantly criticizing Sally. "

Kim winced. "Sally's pretty vulnerable to parental disapproval."

"Yeah." Gabi slumped in the chair. "No one is openly rude. Sally—and I—could fight that—or the guys would. But Galen and Vance are out of town, and Sally won't rock Galen's relationship with his mother, so she hasn't told her guys anything. And, dammit, I figure it's her decision to make. Only I'm so frustrated."

"I don't agree since—" Rainie bit back the words. How would she react if someone interfered in her relationship with a lover? "No, I'm wrong. It's not your choice. But ugh, just imagine—Sally'll have to celebrate holidays with that woman." Galen's mother was the coldest person Rainie'd ever met. One glare from her and mice would flee a cozy heated building in the dead of winter.

Kim nodded glumly. "Guess we'll just have to shield Sally."

"As much as we can." Gabi scowled. "Just because Sally wasn't born to some rich East Coast family, Mrs. Kouros thinks she's not good enough for Galen."

Rainie's anger at the unfairness was slowly undermined by her dismay…and depression. Sally's handicap was merely from growing up on a small Iowa farm. What if Mrs. Kouros faced a slum-raised daughter-in-law like Rainie? The woman would go off the rails entirely.

Rainie thought of her wonderful night with Jake and how he seemed to enjoy having her in the clinic. He never treated her as something…less. Then again, he was a special sort of man. Maybe his years in the military had changed his perception of what was important.

However, if Jake's family thought their precious son might date a woman like Rainie, they'd undoubtedly react just as cruelly as Mrs. Kouros.

Rainie's chest constricted as her resolve deepened. Once her time at the clinic ended, she'd hunt for a job far away, maybe in the Northeast. When she eventually found someone to love, her manners and attire would be perfect—just as Miss Lily had advocated—and her past would be left far, far behind.

And she'd never return to Florida.

Chapter Eight

With Mrs. Morelli's miniature poodle cuddled in one arm, Rainie stood in front of Jake's pale yellow, two-story house and pressed the doorbell.

No one answered. As she breathed in the moist green scent of freshly cut grass, she listened.

No footsteps. The "horse country" was so quiet, she could hear the rumble of cars on a distant highway. The birds cheeping in the trees. And the thumping of Rhage's tail.

Hoping Jake would unload some of his grief, Rainie had tied Rhage on the shaded porch. He sat on his own special blanky, watching her closely. After being abandoned once, he wouldn't trust easily again.

She knew how he felt.

At the low whine of the dog she carried, she sighed. When Saxon had asked her to deliver Guido, he'd said Jake planned to spend his Saturday off at home. A truck sat in the driveway, so Jake was here.

But everyone at the clinic knew he didn't always carry his phone.

She turned in a circle. Tightly woven fencing enclosed the house's acreage. In the long expanses of green, colorful patches heralded the gardenias and azalea bushes beneath the oaks. But no Jake.

Maybe behind the house? Didn't he have a pool? Since no fence separated the front from the back, Rainie walked around the side of the house. Maybe she'd get lucky and find him sunbathing in the nude.

The poor excuse for a joke didn't lighten her mood. She was sad and even unhappier she'd have to break the bad news to Jake.

Behind the house, a screen-caged octagonal pool sparkled in the sunlight. Bright red-and-white striped deck chairs were scattered around the patio. Under the shade of the overhang, Jake slept on a lounge chair. He wasn't naked, unfortunately, although the bare chest was a good start.

Rainie opened the patio's screen door, deliberately making enough noise to waken him. Smart people didn't sneak up on war zone veterans.

He was on his feet before she had the door closed. "Rainie," he said slowly. Absently, he rubbed the sexy dark stubble on his jaw. His day off meant he hadn't trimmed his beard. He looked…rough. Dangerous.

Tempting.

"What are you doing here?" he asked.

"I—" Her momentary lust disappeared as she recalled her reason for the visit. God, how could she tell him? Her heart ached as she searched for words that wouldn't hurt him. There were none. *Mrs. Morelli passed on last night.*

Jake's brows drew together as he studied her face. His gaze dropped to the dog. When his jaw hardened enough to draw the skin taut, she knew he'd recognized Guido and why she'd come.

Grief filled his eyes for a moment before his expression smoothed out. He walked over and took the dog from her arms. "Thank you for bringing him."

"I'm sorry, Jake." She'd only met the tiny elderly woman once, but her sweetness had drawn Rainie in.

One of Jake and Saxon's first clients, Mrs. Morelli had requested they care for Guido if anything happened to her. Like Miss Lily, she'd viewed her mortality with equanimity.

"I appreciate you making the trip."

"Of course. I—"

"I'm sure you have things to do, and I should get Guido settled in." He walked away.

She stared at his back, surprised. Had she ever seen him so brusque? Only, he wasn't deliberately being rude. His normally smooth voice was almost harsh—as if forced through a tight throat. He made her want to cry for him…because he couldn't.

Jake stalked into his house, knowing he'd been discourteous, wanting to apologize, but not trusting his voice.

Goddammit.

He wasn't prepared for this. At the hospital last night, Violetta's doctor said she had a good chance of recovering. Apparently not.

"Take care of my Guido, Jake," she'd asked him. Her only concern had been for her dog. *God, Violetta.* His chest hurt—ached like a fresh stab wound.

At an unhappy whine, he cuddled the shivering dog closer. Yes, they both knew the world was a sadder place today.

Lonelier, as well. His footsteps echoed in the tile-floored room, emphasizing the emptiness. "Hadn't planned on having a dog, buddy," he muttered. "You'd better get along with cats, or we're going to have problems."

His two cats had hidden under his bed, but once they saw the intruder was a small canine—rather than a human—they'd be out and ready for war.

Speaking of problems… "I bet Rainie didn't give you a chance to piss, did she?" After detouring to the kitchen for a leash, he took the dog out the front door and stopped.

An ancient Civic sat in his driveway, and Rhage lay curled on a blanket on the porch. Rainie hadn't left? Jake stopped to pet Rhage, then walked Guido around the side of the house, retracing Rainie's path to the pool.

And there she sat with her back to him, in his lounge chair. She was watching the back door, probably hoping he'd settle before she knocked.

"Problems?" he asked.

She jumped a good foot—and had a fucking cute scream. Turning, she gave him a glare. "You sadist, you almost gave me a heart attack." She patted her chest, making her breasts jiggle in a way he had to appreciate.

For a full minute, he forgot his grief. "Sorry."

"I was worried about you," she said as he and Guido entered the screened area.

Once unleashed, Guido ran over to give her an enthusiastic greeting.

"You act like you haven't seen me for a month," she muttered, pulling the wiggling dog onto her lap.

"He's nervous," Jake said. "He knows something is wrong, and his person isn't here to fix it." *Would never be here.*

"Yeah." She snuggled Guido closer, murmuring, "It'll get better, honey."

Longing whispered through Jake. Lucky little pup to be the recipient of her affections and soothing caresses. "I notice you didn't leave."

"Observant that way, are you?" She set the dog down and held out her hand, expecting Jake to help her to her feet.

Manipulative little brat. He pulled her up and smiled at the logo on her pink button-up shirt: *Audit Me – Audit Me Now!* "What did you want to talk about?"

"Nothing, actually." She slid her arms around him. "I've never seen anyone so in need of a good hug, and I stayed to give you one."

He froze, almost hearing Gunny's snort of disgust, hearing him lecture: *"Pussy Doms need comforting. Real men don't."*

"You're here to care for the submissive. To take what you want. Not to lean on them."

"Stand on your own fucking feet."

But he wasn't leaning…exactly. With a sigh, Jake drew the sweet submissive closer and let her tenderness ease the chill in his heart. Something fuzzy settled onto his bare foot.

He pulled back far enough to see Guido lying beside Rainie with his muzzle on Jake's foot.

"I think that's a dog's version of a group hug. Or maybe he's hungry," Rainie said. She smiled up at him, innocence filling her face. "Me, too. Are you cooking me supper, then?"

He stared. She wasn't asking him if he wanted company, but just…pushing…herself into his evening. And fuck, he didn't want to be alone, especially not with a little dog who would constantly remind him of his loss. "Ah…how do you feel about grilled steak?"

"Warmly. I could feel quite warmly toward a good steak dinner." She bent to pat Guido. "Let me get Rhage, and I'll even help cook."

* * * *

Several hours later, Rainie watched as Jake rose to put the DVD away.

He'd tossed the back cushions of his toast-colored sectional onto the floor, leaving the wide bottom cushion for them to lie on side-by-side. It had been a comfortable way to enjoy television, but the evening had reached an end. She'd better head home.

With a sigh, she sat up and swung her legs to the floor.

Before she could stand, he rejoined her on the couch. "What did you think of the movie?"

"*Galaxy Quest* isn't bad," she said, judiciously. "Good choice."

He snorted. "Considering you had to have a funny movie with a romance and a happy ending, I'd say I did an excellent job."

"Hey, I gave you lots of alternatives."

"Sweetling, I have balls. I'm not allowed to watch movies with names like *Runaway Bride* or *27 Dresses*. At least, not in the first month of screwing around." His dark green eyes caught hers, held them, as he drew his finger across her lips. "We're not permitted a 'cute' romance at all…unless it's horror, sci-fi, or has really explicit sex."

"You don't get much X-rated sex in comedies."

"Now that's just sad." Still holding her gaze, he turned his hand over, trailing the backs of his fingers down her neck. When his hand closed, he had her hair in an unbreakable grip. He tugged, forcing her head to tilt back.

She couldn't move away as he took her mouth, penetrating with his tongue, exploring… Her mind spun under the onslaught as he moved closer.

She stiffened as he started to push her back—and he paused. Letting her decide. She shivered as she remembered sex at her apartment and how he'd made her verbalize her desire for him to stay. And how, after that point, she wasn't allowed to decide anything.

She wanted him tonight. So, so much.

No. She should leave.

"Jake, I didn't come here to mess around." Yet, what would it hurt? He was so sad; he needed her. And she wanted him. She'd lusted after him from the first moment, and the more she got to know him, the more she wanted him.

Tonight, she'd been afraid to find his home decorated in a snobbish-sophisticated style. Instead the landscaping was sweetly rural, the house older and decorated for comfort in creams and browns, with tall windows and ceiling fans in every room.

In the living room, a geometric design rug, thick enough to screw around on, covered the lime-washed oak flooring. A leather-topped coffee table practically begged for bare feet. The long sectional faced the usual hi-tech guy electronics, like the television that took up most of the wall. Another wall was all windows, framed by fan palms, and overlooking the rolling fields. The low bookcase against the third wall held military history and thrillers. She felt at home in his house.

And she could stay tonight. She *could.* She'd be leaving Florida soon. Having sex with the boss wouldn't affect her job; she'd be gone within a month.

As her resistance eroded, he knew; he pushed her back and followed her down. His lips were firm, knowing, yet soft enough to lure. His weight pushed her deeper into the cushions, and the anxious thrill of being overpowered increased when he set her arms above her head.

"Jake. What are you doing?"

"This." As he pinned her wrists with one powerful hand, she instinctively struggled and found herself helpless. The melting sensation in her depths said her body wanted that loss of control—no matter what her mind tried to tell her.

His hip rubbed hers as he sat up. For a moment, he studied her, and his lips curved upward. "Good," he murmured in his smoky smooth voice. "We agree. Tying you down is an excellent idea."

Her mouth dropped open. "We? I didn't say anything."

"Not verbally. But you have a very talkative body, sweetling." He reached past the arm of the couch and pulled something up—two Velcro cuffs attached to a thick rope. Swiftly, he slipped one cuff around her right wrist, yanked the Velcro tight, and did the same to the other. She had no chance to escape before he'd restrained her arms.

She glared at him, trying to ignore the internal flutter at how easily he'd immobilized her. "I didn't agree."

"Safeword's red, buttercup. Anything else is agreement." His eyes laughed at her as he adjusted the cuffs to a more comfortable snugness.

Sitting back, he considered her. "You're a bit overdressed." His voice came close to a purr. "Let me fix that for you."

She'd removed her sandals earlier. Now he yanked off her shorts, started to take off her thong, and paused at the picture of a four-leaf clover—directly over her clit—with green letters stating, *RUB FOR LUCK.*

"As you wish." Grinning, he pulled her legs apart and followed the instructions. His scraping strokes over the fabric grazed her clit, making it burn, making it swell. God, the man knew how to touch a woman.

He stopped long enough to yank off her thong, then ran his finger over her bare pussy. "I do like the way you keep yourself."

"Uh, thanks?" Yet his enjoyment made it worth the time doing Hazel's accounts in exchange for a waxing…and the Jesus-Help-Me agony of having the wax ripped off.

One by one, Jake undid her buttons, and the anticipation grew within her. When he opened her front-hooked bra, her breasts spilled out.

"Fuck, you're gorgeous," he murmured and the compliment put a happy beat in her heart. Cupping his hands on the sides, he pushed her breasts together so he could lick her nipples. His mouth was hot, his tongue wet, slick, yet slightly scratchy.

Her breathing changed to short little pants as he played, and she shivered when he rubbed his bristly chin over the damp areolas. Her back arched, pushing her breasts toward him. God, she wanted more. Wanted him. Wanted—

"Like being scratched, eh? Let's do more of that." Smiling slightly, he lifted the hinged top of his coffee table.

Her eyes widened at the wealth of BDSM equipment. "Oh my God."

"Why restrict myself to a one-room dungeon—I prefer to use the entire house." He opened a small, carved box and fitted stainless steel claws over the fingertips of his right hand. Like a cat's, each curved downward, narrowing to needle thinness.

A jolt of fear slid through her, and she tugged at the restraints. No give.

He lifted his hand.

"No!" The word burst from her. "I don't like needles."

With his unencumbered left hand, he captured her chin. "Look at me."

She couldn't pull her gaze from the sharp glittering claws. Her hands clenched.

"Look. At. Me." The subterranean note in his order tugged on something deep inside her.

Her eyes lifted. Met his. Read the control in his steady green gaze. *Jake—this is Jake.* The breath blockaded in her lungs sighed out.

"Better." Laughter tipped his lips. "However, be aware that I consider 'no' to be a delightful addition to an evening. A safeword will work. *No* turns me on."

Oh God. Why did his pleasure in screwing with her limits make her hotter? She made a frustrated—worried—sound.

A crease appeared in his cheek. Turning his needle-tipped hand over, he skimmed over her hard-peaked nipples with only his bare knuckles. Not the claws.

Her hands relaxed.

His grip tightened on her chin, holding her face for his perusal. And then he drew the claws lightly from her right shoulder all the way to her wrist.

No pain. Just a long tickling array of scratches. Her skin tingled afterward.

"Breathe, Rainie," he said softly.

She exhaled and sucked in air.

His laugh was sexily husky. His left hand stayed curved around her jaw, trapping her while he raked his clawed fingers along her stomach. He pressed sharply enough to not tickle, hard enough to remind her of the sharpness of the points.

Down they swept…toward her mound.

Every muscle in her body tensed. She started to draw her thighs together to protect the very, very exposed tissues.

"Don't move, subbie." His order held a growl that kept her legs in place.

The claws moved upward, then wandered to and fro over her torso. Below her breasts. Across her stomach. Above her mound. He made slow circles, small circles, wide circles.

The skin of her stomach grew more and more sensitive, then as if he'd turned a rheostat, her entire body became intensely aware of everything—the strength of his hand on her face, the scrape of his jeans against her hip, the cool air touching her damp pussy.

He ran the claws over the top of her breasts and paused, hovering over her left breast with the claws spread in a circle.

She squeaked in protest. *Not there. No.*

As he drew his fingers together, the needle tips scraped toward her nipple, panic-inducingly dangerous yet terrifyingly erotic. She was aroused, so, so aroused, panting for air and somehow frozen in place.

His gaze traveled from her face, her shoulders, her hands, and back to his claws. One tiny needle dragged over her nipple with enough sting to send a sizzle through her. To have her pussy throbbing with need.

Jake smiled as the slow application of sensual pain drew Rainie closer and closer to an orgasm.

He picked up his hand and started to set the claws on her other breast. But no. He wanted more. Wanted to see her climax with a need that was probably equal to her own. She came more beautifully than any woman he'd ever seen.

Turning sideways, he touched her mound with one bare finger. Her breathing went staccato for a moment. Unhurriedly, he fondled her pussy, enjoying the naked smoothness of her plump outer labia. Her darkly red inner folds were carnally slick. Ready for him. But he could wait…a while.

"I think you need a little more to occupy you," he said. "I wouldn't want you to get bored."

Her tiny snort held both laughter and exasperation…and a hint of worry.

With his free hand, he took a rabbit vibrator from the toy box, choosing a size slightly smaller than his own cock, so he could enjoy filling her when he took her.

Her eyes widened, but a warning look kept her from speaking.

He wet the vibrator in her juices and slid it up into her cunt. She was puffy enough the vibrator stretched her, and she inhaled sharply. *Perfect.* With the rabbit in deep, the small vibrating ears barely brushed her clit. With a few clicks of the controls, he set it to a wavelike rhythm, from slow to fast.

She made a gloriously helpless noise. Her hips lifted. Wiggled. The color in her face increased, her lips such an inviting red that he took himself another probing kiss.

His dick throbbed its own demand, but he wasn't through playing with her. He sat up and simply enjoyed the sight before him. What was there about having a submissive tied on his couch, open to his use? And when the submissive was Rainie? All soft and round, color high, quivering with arousal and anxiety. *Sheer fucking loveliness.*

So. She was filled with the dildo, clit teased by rabbit ears. Time to top off the array of sensations with something sharp.

Lowering his voice to a warning growl, he said, "Don't move, sweetling.

I don't want to hurt you…too much."

A shiver shook her brutally enough her breasts quivered.

Still sitting beside her, he laid his claw-tipped hand on her left breast, letting her feel the pinpricks of pain.

Her moan of protest made him harder than a rock.

Using a pulling motion, he dragged the claws down Rainie's breast until the points converged on her pointed, dusky nipple. Her poor areola tried to bunch tighter. To add to the fun, he rolled her other nipple between his unadorned thumb and fingers.

"Stop," she whispered. Against his hip, the muscles in her thigh grew rigid with her approaching climax.

"No," he whispered back and stroked her breast with the claws again. "Do stay nice and still when you come, baby, or these might draw blood." The skin on her breasts was delicate, her nipples even more so.

She gave a muted whine of protest and tugged at the restraints. Her hands clenched as she tried to exert control over her impending orgasm.

"Poor subbie," he murmured. Each breath brought him the scent of her arousal, and the insides of her thighs glistened. He reached down and reset the rabbit's rhythm to a quicker build-up with a pause before starting over again.

As she shuddered with the fresh onslaught of vibrations, he gave her two more strokes of the claws. Then he switched to her other breast, leisurely drawing the points to the pink tip. There he paused to dig in the sharp claws slightly.

Sweat broke out on her upper lip. Her thighs trembled as fear of being cut warred with her unstoppable orgasm. Her breathing held a delightful moan with every breath.

There was a sheer glory in driving her to this point—to where she was submerged in sensation alone, to where she was focused only on what he gave her, hearing only his voice… Keeping her nipple trapped in sharpness, he laid his free hand on her mound, scissoring his fingers on each side of her clit so he could lift it right against the rabbit ears' vibrations. "Come for me, sweetheart."

With a low wail, she climaxed, still struggling to hold still. The effort would internalize the spasms so her orgasm would last—at least to her—forever.

As her muscles went limp, her skin glowed with the light sweat covering her body.

Gorgeous.

He dropped the claws onto the end table so she could clean them later and fully appreciate their sharpness…before the next time when he'd use them on her pussy.

Rainie felt…satiated, as if every nerve in her body had imbibed chocolate cake. With thick frosting. And sprinkles. She was drowning in after-sex repletion.

Yet, when her eyes opened to Jake's heated, assessing gaze, she was ready to go again. And again. As long as he wanted her, she wanted him.

Even more, she needed him to get his own satisfaction—needed to give that to him. To make him happy.

Because he was Jake. Amazing, incredible, impossible. From his absolute control and ability to read her, his perfect technique, his harder than rock body, to his intoxicating scent of light pine and musk—the man totally turned her on.

But she could have controlled that. Unfortunately, there was more to him. The outgoing personality and easy sense of humor that disguised a consummate Master. His affection for people and animals. His sense of honor. And…his kindness. Yesterday she'd found a note. Jake had ordered that an impoverished senior wasn't to be billed for anything more than medications. The incredible knowledge of all that was Jake washed over her in a downpour of desire.

She looked up and realized he was considering her thoughtfully. A shiver ran up her spine. "Why are you looking at me like that?"

His lips curved. Jake's smile could never be cruel, but ruthless…definitely ruthless. "I'm deciding what position I want you in when I bury my cock in that soft pussy of yours."

Oh.

Her core clenched. Still…no need to let him have everything his own way. He'd put the claws down; her courage was returning. "Well, Sir, feel free to tell me if and when you ever decide."

He grinned and tapped the small logo on her shirt, *Audit Me – Audit me Now!*

"You gave me the idea, subbie—seems as if you must be due for an internal audit."

Imagining the…tool…he'd use to perform the audit, she shivered, then made a loud huff. "I'll have you know that my ledgers are well balanced."

He cupped her breasts and ran his thumbs over her exquisitely sensitive, abused nipples. "Oh, baby, I agree. You definitely have some fine assets."

"Sir, you can play with my assets any time."

With a grin, he whispered, "I intend to."

His kiss was gentle…at first…then his tongue plunged inside, and he simply…took. Possessed. Plundered.

When he stopped, he gave her a quick smile and opened the Velcro wrist cuffs. He removed the rabbit vibe, and her insides clenched around the emptiness.

"New position, babe."

Her head spun as he helped her sit up. The floor chilled her bare toes, and she looked around, feeling as if she'd traveled to an exotic land for the last hour.

He patted the wide bottom cushion. "Kneel here and hang on to the back of the couch."

As she turned and maneuvered herself into position, her knee slipped and she flopped down, half onto her side—far too much like a beached whale. *God.* She loved herself and her curves—she *did*—but her clumsiness summoned up memories of school gym classes, of being the fat girl, of being ridiculed.

As Jake pulled her upright, she felt…ugly. Her arm pressed over her rotund stomach as she longed to be skinny and graceful and…and everything she wasn't. Forcing away the maddening tears, she managed a weak laugh and said, "Let me try that again." She started to roll up onto her knees.

His grip on her shoulders stopped her. "One minute, baby. What happened?"

"N-nothing." Her voice quivered. God, she was such an idiot. "I'm fine." She shoved at his arms.

"Bullshit." Sliding his hands down to take hers, he squatted in front of her. "You looked as if I'd slapped you."

"You're such a…a stubborn…"

When his chin lifted slightly, her words dried right up. Calling a Dom stupid could lead to pain and not the good kind.

"Rainie?"

He wasn't going to let it go, was he? She huffed in exasperation, but at least her tears were gone. "Sir, I'm a big woman, and mostly I like that. But society is…can be…cruel." She scowled down at her wide hips, feeling immense.

He studied her for a long, long minute, then tucked a stray lock of hair behind her ear. "We all have those moments, baby. Bear in mind, though, I really enjoy your shape. You're a fantastic playground."

"Excuse me?" Her tone came out on the icy side.

With his hands curled over her knees, he kissed the inside of her thighs. "Now, some playgrounds only have swing sets. I suppose that's all right, but in my opinion, the more, the better. As it happens, I like ones with slides." He nuzzled her stomach.

"And jungle gyms." Cupping her breasts, he teased the nipples taut again, then rose to his feet. In a swift move, he lifted her, set her on her knees, and with unyielding hands, positioned her to face the back of the couch.

"And merry-go-rounds." He kneaded her full buttocks before whispering into her ear, "The playground that is your body could keep me entertained forever."

As he kissed the hollow between her neck and shoulder, his open hum of enjoyment erased her unhappy memories, replacing them with sizzling hunger.

"Don't move." He ran his fingers along the top of the couch to her right. A Velcro cuff popped out from a hidden pocket beneath the upholstery.

Another cuff? "How many of those do you have?"

"Lots, sweetling." He secured her wrist and pulled another cuff from the left side.

As he finished, her shoulders rested on the top of the couch, her arms restrained toward each end. Her breasts dangled. In the air, her bottom tilted up, stationed above her feet.

He stood behind her, bathing her in his heated gaze before lightly slapping the insides of her thighs. "Open for me, baby."

She wiggled her knees apart and jolted as he ran two fingers through her wet labia. When she tried to lift her torso, a heavy hand between her shoulder blades kept her in place. "Stay put, subbie, or I'll spank that gorgeous ass."

One merciless hand pinned her, and his other massaged her buttocks.

Restrained. Touched. Her body heated with a smoldering desire.

His playground. As he touched, he'd stop to slide a finger inside her pussy or stroke around her clit—as if he wanted to see her wiggle.

She couldn't help herself.

He was openly enjoying himself—using her in precisely the way he wanted.

His ruthless handling drove her into a floating surrender. *Take me; take everything.* Her whole body softened.

"That's right, sweetling," he murmured, leaning in to kiss her cheek.

She couldn't feel any embarrassment or worry with such open approval.

A second later, she heard a zipper and a condom wrapper. Her body trembled in anticipation, and then his cock pressed against her pussy. And stopped. The rabbit vibrator had left her slick…and very swollen. She hissed as he rocked his hips to work his shaft in. When the broad head breached her entrance, he stopped.

Her stretched core throbbed around the intrusion. All of her, every cell, felt alive and begging to be touched.

He ran his hands down her back, leaned forward, and kneaded her breasts. The claws had left the delicate skin abraded and so, so sensitive. When he rolled her abused nipples between his fingers, her insides clenched around him…and he laughed.

Jesus, how much control did the man have? Was he going to stand there with his dick only partly in her? She wanted…wanted to be taken. Hammered hard. She tried to push back onto him, but her arm restraints allowed no movement…and he noticed her attempt.

"Bad girl." Amusement underlay the stern tone. A stinging smack hit her right buttock, and the flare of pain made every nerve in her pussy sparkle and spasm. Three additional spanks followed, hard enough to leave her ass cheeks feeling scalded.

God, she needed him more than she could bear. "Please." Her breath escaped in sharp little pants. "I want…need…you to take me."

"When I'm ready, Rainie. When *I'm* ready." He leaned forward again and kissed the back of her shoulder, nuzzling her, driving her crazy. Sadistically taking his time, he pinched her nipples and teased her breasts until they swelled to a throbbing tightness.

Finally, he straightened, and his big hands curved over her full, full hips.

"Fuck, I love your ass. Next time, I'm taking you there."

Without waiting for her response, he rammed into her pussy, hard and fast and deep.

The surprise, the stretch of sensitive tissues, the exhilarating knowledge of being taken for a Master's pleasure blew through her. Her neck arched as the shock hit, and he was already pulling back and driving in again.

God, yes.

Hands gripping her securely, he hammered her. "Look at those ass cheeks quiver." He paused to fondle her buttocks, rotated his hips as if to be sure every inch of her pussy had been wakened, and resumed. Each deep penetration started a shockwave low in her pelvis to travel up her center.

And she loved it. Loved… No. With an enticing wiggle, she squeezed her internal muscles to please him.

His laugh rolled out. "There's the cunt I love." Leaning forward, he wrapped his long arms around her waist. His right palm pulled her stomach and mound upward, forcing her clit to poke out…for his left hand to find. His callused fingers brushed tantalizingly against the nub.

As the exquisite sensations engulfed her, she groaned and everything inside her bore down. A coil of pressure at her core tightened, growing, expanding, taking over her body, her control. The ache in her shoulder, the awkwardness of the position, the tightness of the cuffs—all disappeared, leaving only the stroke of his merciless, knowledgeable fingers and the ruthless impalement on his thick cock.

Her body tensed, thighs quivering, as he drove her to the peak. *Almost…almost…*

He stopped.

Her moan of protest was loud in the room. He pulled back slightly to edge her legs out wider, then gripped her ass cheeks, pulling them apart. This time his cock penetrated deeper than any ever had before, invading her body so thoroughly, so intimately, as Jake took her over completely.

The onrushing tidal wave of orgasm slammed into her, sending her over. And over. And over.

* * * *

Jake woke before dawn, lying on his back. Rainie's head rested on his right shoulder, and her thick, wavy hair covered his chest. Her softness against his side and the light fragrance of her shampoo had him hardening. But damned if he wanted to—or could—move.

She had him pinned down on one side. On the left, Rhage and Guido lay curled against his hip and thigh. Normally he'd insist the dogs sleep at the foot of the bed, but his two rescue cats had staked out that territory. Patton, the Manx, was draped over his right leg, MacArthur, the tiger-stripe, on his left.

Good thing he didn't get claustrophobic, he thought drowsily. On the contrary, even with his grief for Violetta still fresh, he couldn't recall feeling more content.

Sure, being surrounded by animals always made him happy, but this ease was deeper. As if the woman lying next to him had carved new channels in his soul and filled them with her ever-flowing joy.

He half snorted at the thought. Any minute now, he'd break into *The Sound of Music* or something. Gunny would have been horrified.

Guido stirred and raised his head. With a whine, the dog jumped off the bed to sit by the door.

Seriously?

Another whine.

Fuck. But he couldn't blame the beastie for the impact of a changed environment, different routine, and new food on his system. Carefully, Jake disentangled himself from the various bodies.

Rainie murmured inaudibly and rolled to her other side. He eyed the pale roundness of her ass with prurient thoughts, sighed again, and motioned the dog out of the room, taking Rhage as well.

A few minutes later, as he sat on the edge of the concrete slab, he heard the porch door. A glance over his shoulder gave him a treat.

In his T-shirt, Rainie was all curves and beautiful legs. Her multi-colored hair waved over her shoulders, her eyes were sleepy, her mouth swollen from his kisses.

Nice. Very, very nice.

She pulled a chair close to him and sat. "Dogs?" she asked, her voice beautifully husky as if she'd had all the high notes fucked away.

Made a man proud.

He pointed to the field and the two dogs stalking and pouncing on field mice with abysmal success.

"At this hour?" She snorted. "You know, when I drag home from work, Mr. Energizer Puppy's raring to play. All evening. It's a good thing I'm out of school or I'd flunk."

School? He leaned his shoulder against a post. "What were you going for?"

"Uh…an MBA."

His brows rose. Hell, he'd known she was smart, but… "That's great, Rainie. And you got it?"

"Finished in December." When she smiled down at him, the golden streaks in her hair glinted in the moonlight.

She smelled of his soap from the shower they'd taken. He liked her in his clothes and scent. "No wonder you're so good at everything in the office."

The compliment made her eyes light. "Thanks."

"And what did you plan to do with that fancy new degree?"

"Find a fancy new job…somewhere." She added lightly, "I need a position where I can wear all my suits."

"Well, you do look stunning in them." The thought of her leaving the clinic shredded tiny bits from his contentment.

In the moonlight, the dogs flushed a rabbit and chased it across the grass, barking madly.

"He may have too much energy, but I'm glad you made me keep him." As the dogs trotted back, panting happily, Rainie laughed.

A shame she hadn't had a dog growing up. "Your mom disliked pets?"

"Not exactly. It's just that owning a dog would have meant rental deposits. And…she didn't want to care for anything."

Ah. Rainie's tone was even, not bitter, but her face was easy to read. "Not even you?" he asked softly.

As if to avoid the question—and him—she leaned back in the chair.

He put his hand on her calf, keeping contact whether she wanted it or not. "Rainie?"

"Yes, even me. She took off with a guy when I was twelve and never came back."

"You ended up with your father?"

"No, he left when I was seven."

"*I was seven,*" she said. Didn't have to think to remember her age…which meant it had been nasty. Memorable.

"Did he die?"

"Walked out on us."

"Jesus." He stood, scooped her up, and took her place in the chair with her on his lap.

"Jake, no, I'm too heavy."

"Hardly." Even if she were—being smothered in soft, fragrant female flesh would be a fucking fine way to go. He pulled her closer, marveling how there wasn't a place on her that was bony.

When he nipped her jaw, she shivered…and his cock began to lengthen. No, she needed cuddling and conversation, not sex. The subject was childhood. And abandonment.

A shame irresponsible people couldn't be spayed—or neutered—as easily as dogs. "Who raised you, baby? Relatives?"

"Didn't have any. I got foster care."

Hmm. He knew guys who'd had decent, loving foster parents. Knew others who'd suffered. Rainie lived her life with joy and laughter, but…she had formidable emotional defenses. "So the foster home didn't allow pets?"

"Neither of mine did." Her grim tone told him even more.

"That sucks." In the clinic, affection flowed from her in a river, washing over animals and people. If, as a child, she'd had no one to spend that love on, it'd have been like damming up the Mississippi.

He'd try to make up for that lack.

He guided her to her feet and stood himself. A whistle brought the dogs, panting and quivering with happiness. "Back to bed, crew," he ordered, ushering her into the house.

"It's almost dawn."

"It's Sunday. We're going to sleep in." He tucked an arm around her as he led her to the bedroom, feeling the rightness of having her beside him.

"Been wondering, buttercup. What kind of a bribe will it take to get you to cook breakfast?"

The slight tilt of her lips told him exactly what inducement she was considering.

As he ran his hand over her luscious ass, he smiled. Wasn't it amazing how great minds thought alike?

* * * *

In her apartment, Rainie tossed another bra toward the overloaded suitcase on her bed. Three pieces of underwear fell off the pile onto the floor.

"Babe," Jake said, amusement in his tone. "Don't you have a bigger suitcase?"

He was laughing at her, damn him. She eyed her carry-on. It really was too small.

Each night since last weekend, Jake had coaxed her into staying at his place. And she'd loved that—but hated having to visit her apartment every morning to change outfits. If he didn't own two cats and now Guido, they might have alternated. But the felines were used to freedom.

Besides, Rhage loved Jake's fenced acreage. And she always gave her sweet puppy what he wanted. Really, she was doing all this for the dog: working with Jake. Having sex with Jake. Sleeping with Jake.

She opened another dresser drawer and considered the shirts. Jake wanted her to pack some clothes and keep them at his house. And she'd finally agreed.

Since finding Rhage, she'd spent more time with Jake than in half a year with Geoffrey. Every day, she fell more and more into…liking him. Caring for him.

"How did this happen?" she muttered.

Jake walked up behind her and pulled her back against his chest. Gripping her hair, he tilted her head sideways, giving him access to nibble on her neck. His beard stubble tickled, scraped, and the slight sting of his teeth was soothed by his gentle lips. Hard and soft, pain and pleasure, sweet and cruel. He never gave her a chance to get her bearings.

"It happened, Rainie." He nipped her earlobe. "And I'm damned pleased. Aren't you?"

Under his level, questioning eyes, all she could do was nod. "I… Yes. I am." Very pleased. Very happy.

And very scared. She felt as if she'd been floating in a meandering river and suddenly an undersurface current had grabbed her. Her emotions were being swept along with no chance of escape.

She reached up to touch his lean cheek. When had she come to care so much?

He smiled slowly. "Keep looking at me like that and you'll get fucked instead of packed."

A snort escaped her. She retreated, pointing at him with an accusing finger. "You are insatiable." And she loved it.

"Quite true, where you're concerned." Blatantly adjusting himself in his jeans, he turned to study the clothes scattered over the bed. "Bigger suitcase?"

"In the closet." She turned back to the dresser and selected another set of underwear. With more room, she could—

Behind her, the bed squeaked as Jake tossed the suitcase on the mattress. Latches clicked.

"Well, well, well. I am impressed." Jake's baritone had lowered, turning an edgy hot as if he'd descended into the fires of hell.

With a red thong in her hand, Rainie glanced over her shoulder. *Oh crap. Wrong suitcase.*

The oversize black suitcase lay open, showing how she'd customized the interior with Styrofoam and padding to hold dildoes, vibrators, gags, edible oils, and…everything. "I arrange sex-toy parties. Those are the samples. My stock. That's not the right case."

"Baby, this is the perfect suitcase." Jake picked up a pair of fluffy nipple clamps and gave her a Dom's assessing stare. One that made her entire body soften. "Remove your blouse. And bra."

"Jake." Her mouth had gone dry—and her pussy was dampening, preparing for him. "I-I don't… The toys are for parties."

"How come I never get invitations?" Laughter teased the edges of his eyes. "Don't worry, sweetling. I'll buy whatever I open."

She gulped. "But—"

"Rainie," he interrupted and picked up a gag. "Want me to use this?"

"No." Yes. *Oh yes.* "I'll keep—"

"I'll be damned. You do." His gaze turned more intense.

Oh shit. She backpedaled, heading for the door.

Hard hands closed on her arms, and he tossed her onto an empty place on the bed. A second later, he'd pushed the pretty red gag into her mouth and was strapping it on.

As she made irritated noises and struggled, he mercilessly stripped her clothes off—and picked up a set of nipple clamps from the case.

Not nipple clamps. "Mmmmh, mmmmh!" She tried to roll off the bed.

He swatted her ass, rolled her onto her back, and straddled her, holding her down as he applied the damn things.

Ow, ow, ow.

"Damn, those are pretty," he murmured. With a finger, he rang the little hanging bells.

She glared at him—and he laughed. But he hadn't made the clamps too tight, and as he fondled her breasts, the ache in her nipples turned wonderfully exciting.

"I think we'll have to make time to visit your apartment more often. This canopy setup has definite benefits." He knotted one of the hanging drapes around her right knee, then another on her left, forcing her thighs widely open. After an evaluating look, he shoved a pillow under her hips to open her more widely. Bare and exposed.

She should feel embarrassed, but the appreciation in his gaze and the heat simmering under her skin burned it away.

After a quick search, he placed one of Rhage's squeaky toys in her hand. "I might not be able to differentiate between your screaming and a safeword, so use that."

Screaming?

From the suitcase, he removed a tube of lube, and his hand hovered over the array of anal plugs. "According to your Shadowlands trainee files, you've done anal play."

Oh, the Gods of Cruelty have struck again. She nodded. She loved being taken anally. And hated it. It felt too…intimate, too…possessed. And yet nothing quite equaled the sensation.

"Good." He chose the smallest plug—*thank you, God*—lubed it, and pushed it in with no fanfare, ignoring her wiggling. The slight burn and the stretch and wakening nerves made her clit throb and need.

Her gaze took in the wonderful bulge beneath his jeans. She was so ready to have sex.

Instead, he turned and dropped additional anal plugs beside her.

She stared at him and made a sound. A bad sound.

He gave her a terrifying smile and picked up a vibrator. "After you come—each time—I'll reward you with a bigger plug."

The restraints held her open as he ran his finger around her clit. "Don't worry, sweetling. The biggest one will be…me."

Chapter Nine

With a depressed sigh, Rainie finished updating her resume at Jake's kitchen table. Now that the task was completed, she needed to send out applications. Get a job. Move.

Misery grew like a weed inside her.

For a while, she'd escaped thinking about the future. Between wedding chores and the clinic, she'd been busy. Then there was Rhage, as well. And—her new man took up even more time.

I have a man.

She could feel her lips curling up into an idiotic grin, but didn't care. She loved it all. Loved having her life filled with activities, loved having a dog, loved being involved with Jake Sheffield.

From outside came the sound of a mallet striking metal. She rose to peek out the window.

Across the green swath of grass, Jake was attaching what looked like a chain wastebasket to a tall pole. Jake had decided to set up a disc golf course.

Admittedly, the game was fun, although she'd never been able to hit the broad side of a barn with a Frisbee. Actually, she was lucky if the disc stayed in the same zip code. But ever since last Sunday when Jake had dragged her out for some "fun," she'd been improving.

And both Rhage and Guido loved Frisbee catch. They'd gone out with Jake today, obviously in hopes that he'd play with them again. But he was focused on getting the course done so he could start having weekend Frisbee golf and grill parties.

Only he'd used the word "we." *"We can have…"* The way that made her feel, with hope and sadness so intermingled she couldn't pull them apart.

As she watched, Jake peeled off his shirt and tossed it over the pole. His wide chest gleamed in the sunlight, and her thoughts scattered before a rising wind of lust. *Down, girl.* He wasn't stripping for a show but because the sun was too hot. *Shame on me.*

Feeling guilty, Rainie poured ice tea into a sports bottle and grabbed a couple of the cookies she'd made the day before. If nothing else, she could go succor her man.

She sure didn't do much for him—all she gave him was food and…well, and sex. Nothing emotional. Nothing real. Her lips turned down. She'd come to need him, but the reverse wasn't true at all.

When the screen door banged shut behind her, the dogs raced across the grass to bark and bounce around her.

"Look at you two. Were you helping your human?" They were so happy to see her, to be outside, to be together. As she dispensed scratches and ear tugs, her heart felt so full it was tender.

Jake said they'd probably been raised in one-dog families, and now they'd found themselves a "pack." She knew the feeling.

Jake was on his cell as she approached. He'd shoved his hair back off his forehead, and the sun glinted in the thick brown strands. When he saw her, he winked and kept talking. "Yes, I'll tell the housekeeper to have the fridge stocked. No, Mom, I won't check on Jennifer's kitchen. If she left stuff in there, she can clean it out herself."

His family was due to return from Europe next week, Rainie remembered. She handed him the bottle of ice tea.

His pleased smile was enough to melt every ice cube in the bottle and her bones as well. Tilting his head back, he drank, and his Adam's apple moved in his hard, corded neck as he swallowed.

As she watched—and perved—her mouth grew dry and the air heated.

The work of pounding in the iron poles had pumped up his muscles until his tanned skin stretched taut over his rock-hard biceps, delts, and pecs. He gleamed with sweat, and his light scattering of chest hair had matted down, allowing flat brown nipples to show. On the back of his forearms, his veins stood out, daring her to trace them with her tongue. His jeans hung low on his hips, giving her a mouth-watering view of the ridges of his abdominal muscles. The bulge of his package in those jeans was growing.

She jerked her gaze up.

Lowering his phone, he said in an intensely masculine growl, "If you keep those hungry eyes on me, I'll show you all about sex in the sun."

"Oh my God, you're talking to your mother—you can't..." She sputtered, knowing her face had gone beet red. How could he have said such a thing with his mother listening? At a loss, Rainie held out a cookie. "Eat this, and stop whatever you're thinking!"

His deep laugh reverberated through her, filling her heart with happiness. Then he glanced at his phone and...turned the mike back on. "Still here. Just had to deal with something for a moment. Yes, tomorrow is Marcus and Gabi's wedding. It's a shame you won't return in time."

Before Rainie could escape, he nabbed her with a long arm around her waist. Holding her against his front, he rocked his hips, teasing her with his thick erection. One big hand kneaded her ass.

He said into the phone, "Nadia's actually working? With William Renard? Well, maybe I'll run into her tomorrow."

Another long flow of indecipherable words came through the phone before he responded, "I love you, too, Mom. Put him on."

I love you, too. Trapped within the curve of Jake's arm, unable to flee, Rainie stared up at him as his sentiment resonated down into her center. The very same words—*I love you*—lived inside her heart just waiting to be released.

No. No. Absolutely not. No, she didn't love him. Couldn't love him. *Ever. Wrong.*

She tried to take a step back, and he drew her closer. Even as he answered his father about a business matter, he pressed a kiss to the top of her head.

The affectionate gesture hit her resolve with the weight of a sledgehammer. And as the broken pieces of her future fell around her, she was wondering…what would it be like to stay?

But what about her past? Her jaw firmed. The cruel people from her past—as well as the memories—would find her, over and over. She'd never escape.

Yet, she'd had experience in dealing with the jerks who judged her, and she'd survived so far.

She leaned into Jake and breathed in his scent. If the assholes' verbal abuse was the cost of staying with Jake—and God, she wanted to be with him—she could handle what they dished out.

She could.

* * * *

The gods had smiled on Gabi and Sally, Rainie thought, gifting them with a flawless wedding day. The gauzy clouds overhead grew denser near the horizon, softened the sun, and kept the temperature perfect. The light sea-scented breeze blew any bugs away and ruffled the vivid blue-and-white blooms of the annuals and vines.

Rainie dodged a caterer, stepped around a woman carrying a tissue-wrapped gift, and hurried toward the bridal suite.

Behind her at the entrance to the ceremonial garden, Jessica and Linda were going over last minute details with the wedding planner. Although both women were gowned in the rich blue of the bridal party, they'd managed to sidestep the walking-down-the-aisle portion.

It hadn't been easy. Linda had tactfully refused, then refused again, and finally told the brides that Master Sam would handle the next refusal. Neither Gabi nor Sally were about to annoy the Shadowlands' notorious sadist.

Faced with the same pressure, pregnant Jessica had informed the brides that if they persisted, she'd either go into labor or—even worse—inform Master Z of every trick the two brats had pulled in the club.

Awesome threat.

Grinning, Rainie walked through the main entrance of the bridal suite. Decorated in quiet colors of cream and khaki, the suite held a small kitchen, bathroom, and dressing room. In the main space, which combined a living room and a beauty parlor, counters, sinks, and mirrors lined one entire wall.

Right now, chaos ruled. At the counters, three hairdressers were finishing Kim, Beth, and Andrea. A makeup artist was putting the last touches on Gabi's face.

Doing a mental count, Rainie nodded. Gabi and bridesmaids were accounted for.

In the center of the room, Uzuri and Kari lounged in the beige suede chairs. They, along with Rainie, were Sally's bridesmaids. Rainie cleared her throat. "Where's the second bride?"

"In the kitchen," Gabi called.

"No, she came out and went into the dressing room." Kari jerked her head toward the back. "She's been there a while."

"She looked a little upset," Uzuri said. "I wasn't sure whether to check on her or not. Maybe she's got an attack of nerves?"

Over getting married? That didn't seem like Sally. "I'll take her in a Sprite and see if she wants to talk."

But when Rainie reached the kitchen door, waves of animosity seemed to pour forth.

The two voices were unfortunately familiar. Gabi's mother. Galen's mother—Mrs. Kouros. The Queen of Petrified Nastiness was conversating with the Empress of Icy Bitchiness.

How had either warmed up enough to procreate? Rainie grinned, imagining some poor guy trying to fuck one of them. With one thrust, his cock would ice over…and shatter.

Her smile faded at what Galen's mother was saying. "I don't know where Galen found her, but he could do so much better. She is quite coarse. Common."

"It's a shame she didn't stay on the farm where she belongs," Gabi's mother agreed. "Her graceless presence lowers the entire tone of the wedding—as do her gauche relatives."

Rainie's teeth ground together. They meant Sally, and Sally's charming brother, wife, and their adorable children.

"It is a shame, but Galen is quite determined to proceed." Mrs. Kouros gave a chilled sigh. "I fear I will have to endure her when—"

"I daresay that is exactly what Sally is saying to herself right now." Rainie didn't bother to lower her voice. Miss Lily would have been horrified at the incivility.

Stepping into the room, Rainie faced the obsessively thin, older version of Cruella de Vil.

Mrs. Kouros stared down her nose at the intruder. "Excuse me?"

"I doubt there is an excuse for you," Rainie said. "Your son managed to find a beautiful woman who makes him so happy he laughs now—and I'd say that's a rarity for him, although understandable, considering who he has for a mother."

Mrs. Kouros drew back as if she'd been slapped, and Gabi's mother's expression turned cold. Colder.

"But, having been raised by you," Rainie continued, "Galen knows exactly what he does and doesn't want in a wife. He searched for a warm, spirited woman, one courageous enough to save his life. Or did you forget you wouldn't have a son at all without Sally?"

When no answer was forthcoming, Rainie tsked-tsked. "You did forget. Oh well, mental deterioration is common at your age."

Gabi's mother stepped forward. "Listen, you—"

"No, you two pay attention now. This is a happy time, and you are destroying the mood. I want you both to leave this suite right now."

Mrs. Kouros had recovered. "You don't have any say here."

Rainie gave them a threatening smile. "I'm commonly known as a brat. And I can assure you that if you don't stay away from the entire bridal party, including the brides, I will make you the center of a scene the likes of which you've never known. Screaming, hair-pulling, ripped clothing, scratched faces."

She paused for breath. Fury edged her voice. "Just *try* me."

They backed away, clear to the other side of the kitchen. Mrs. Kouros opened the kitchen door and…

Dear God of little cats and dogs. Dressed in a black tuxedo, Jake stood right outside. From his stunned expression, he'd heard *every single word.* He stepped aside to let the two Bitches of the Year flee and turned to watch them scurry down the sidewalk on their high heels. He pointed his gaze at Rainie and cocked a brow.

Wasn't it just fate that her voice chose that moment to dry up?

His lips quirked. "Z sent a heads-up. Guests will start arriving in a few minutes."

Rainie choked out. "I'll tell everyone."

With a polite tilt to his head, he closed the door. Through the open window, she watched him stride away.

He'd heard. She stood in the empty kitchen and shook. Her face felt hot. Cold. Hot. The man she…admired…had listened to her ream out two distinguished women. Like poor white trash. Or a crude, rude, graceless girl from the slums.

Like her own mother.

She'd ruined the entire wedding with her stupid mouth. *Please don't let anyone else have heard her.*

She straightened her shoulders and walked into a mob. All the bridesmaids and brides were gathered around the door.

No, no, no. God, what had she done? "I thought I'd kept my voice down."

"Actually, you weren't that loud," Uzuri said. "But we heard the squeaks from the road kill and, um, moved closer."

When Gabi met her gaze, Rainie wanted to cry. *I attacked my best friend's mother.* She bit her lip. "I'm sorry, Gabi. I was—"

"Entirely honest and direct." Gowned in white satin, Gabi hugged her. "I just wish I had it on tape, dammit. Now I have to remember it all for Marcus."

"You don't hate me?" Rainie choked out, and then, worse, so, so much worse, she saw Sally. Who was crying.

God, she'd ruined her entire—

"I've never had friends like you," Sally whispered. "Ones that would stand up against pressure like that." Sally wrapped her arms around Rainie and hung on tight.

Oh. Breathe. She pulled in a shuddering inhalation, blinked hard, and hugged Sally back. After the water cleared from her eyes, she managed to look around. She saw the same approving expression from everyone in the room—as well as more tears.

"Stop it, all of you." The makeup lady scowled at the bridal party. "I used waterproof, but there's only so much it can do. No crying until after the ceremony."

As the room exploded with laughter, there was a sound like a gunshot.

Unfazed by the screams, Jessica stood at the counter pouring frothing champagne into tall flutes. She lifted one. "Here's to the Battle of the Bitches where the best maid won."

Next to her, Linda laughed, winked at Rainie, and handed out glasses.

* * * *

Jesus Christ. Still stunned—and laughing—Jake reached the groomsmen's quarters.

Fucking amazing job. Rainie had taken on those two witches and flattened them. How many people would have the courage? Those two women were the human female equivalent of huge, aggressive Brazilian Mastiffs. In comparison, by fighting weight and disposition, Rainie would be closer to a sweet fluffy collie. But she'd taken them on, defended her friend, and conquered.

He'd have to figure a way to reward her tonight. Damn, he was proud of her.

He stepped inside the room set up for the groomsmen. The masculine décor of dark wood and leather was lightened by a floor-to-ceiling view of the shore. One mirrored wall had a long counter where Marcus, Dan, and Nolan were finishing the last touches to bow ties, pocket silks, and cuff links. Drinks in hand, Vance and Galen relaxed in the leather chairs in the room's center. Saxon, Raoul, and Cullen stood by the chest-high bar, conversing. Near a window, Sam sat at a table, reading a newspaper.

Jake cleared his throat loudly. When he'd gained everyone's attention, he announced, "Z requests the groomsmen be at the wedding garden in about five to ten minutes to seat people."

Cullen nodded. "We'll be there."

"You've got time for this, then." Saxon poured and handed Jake a shot of Ketel One.

Jake checked over his friend. "Nice mixture of tux and Viking barbarian." To do justice to his tux, Saxon had pulled his long hair into a neat queue. His jacket was open, showing off the silver waistcoat. "You look good, bro."

"I do," Saxon said smugly. He'd been asked to step in as a groomsman when Holt had been unexpectedly called out of town. Although the brides and grooms possessed family and friends who could participate, they'd kept the wedding party to Shadowlands members.

Surrounded by the relaxed group of friends, Jake had to appreciate the decision.

When Saxon returned to his discussion with Cullen, Jake took an empty chair next to Galen and asked, "The photographer and her helper passed me as I left the brides' suite. Wasn't the assistant supposed to be here?"

Vance grinned. "Yeah. She fled when Cullen started stripping."

Cullen glanced around at the sound of his name.

Jake eyed him. "I thought you finished dressing an hour ago."

"I did." One elbow on the bar, Cullen swirled his drink. "Next time, she'll ask permission before busting into the men's quarters."

Every guy in the room laughed, even Nolan. Galen lifted his glass, toasting Cullen.

Galen. Hell.

Jake took a hefty swallow of the vodka, let it burn its way down, before facing a man he considered a friend. Jake judged himself diplomatic, but this was out of his depth. Yet, if positions were reversed, he'd want to know—and sooner rather than later. "Listen," he started.

Galen straightened at the grim tone. "That doesn't sound good."

"No. When I went to the bridal suite…"

As the retelling of the battle continued, Galen's expression turned dark.

"Galen," Vance said. "We knew this might happen. Your mother is…who she is."

"Ayuh. And she had her chance," Galen said quietly. "I'll ensure she excuses herself once the wedding is over. She won't attend the reception."

"Agreed." Vance gave Jake a chin-lift. "We appreciate the info, and we'll thank Rainie when we get a chance."

Jake nodded. Their Sally was a delightful submissive, younger than Rainie in some ways, but with the same exuberance of spirit. Perhaps, that's why it had taken two FBI Doms to tame the girl.

As for Rainie… Jake smiled slightly. He considered himself just the subbie-tamer needed for her.

Not men to postpone an unpleasant task, Vance and Galen set their drinks down and left.

As Raoul joined Sam by the window, Cullen settled into a leather chair across from Jake.

"Hey, bro." Saxon took the other seat. "We've been so busy I didn't ask how your new pet worked out."

Jake raised an eyebrow, thinking Sax meant Rainie, then realized he referred to Violetta's dog. "Guido is fine, although the little bastard dug up three of my pepper plants." He grinned. "He's decided he's a cat now, so MacArthur and Patton drafted him into the feline army."

"That's pitiful. Ruination of a fine dog."

"Nah, they keep him busy enough he hasn't had a chance to mope."

"Was the delivery girl useful?" Saxon's light brows quirked upward.

Now, he meant Rainie. Jake scowled. "I appreciate it…but you shouldn't have sent her. I was damned rude to her."

"I bet she understood." Drink in hand, Saxon extended his legs, totally at ease. "When she's not playing prankster, she's a comforting woman. I figured she might help."

"I shouldn't need help," Jake growled. "I can deal with things myself." *Jesus, did he think Jake would dump his troubles on—*

"Andrea thought that, too," Cullen said quietly.

"And she is right," Jake said. "A Dom stands on his own feet. Shouldn't need—"

Cullen shook his head. "No, buddy, that's what she thought about herself. Her father played hell with her perception of independence. Took a while before she realized we're just human, and it's all right to lean on someone else."

Jake imagined Gunny's growl of outrage, but he said mildly, "How can a Dom be strong for the submissive if he needs her help?"

"No one gets through life without needing some support," Cullen answered. "A Dom has to be honest with himself and his submissive. And—"

"Time to go, gentlemen," Nolan interrupted. "We've got guests arriving."

As he followed the others out the door, Jake set aside the argument. Dammit, he respected Cullen. Fine man; fine Dom.

But he was wrong.

For half an hour, Jake escorted guests down the curving path through crimson roses, under the jasmine arbor, and then across the manicured grass to the white chairs decorated with silver and blue ribbons. In the front, blue flowers cascaded from the arch of the white gazebo, and beyond that, the sandy beach rolled down to the blue-gray waters of the Gulf.

The day was peaceful with the quiet conversations of the guests and waves sighing on the shore. The palms dotting the edge of the grass rustled in the light wind.

As the sun dropped behind the bank of clouds, the grooms and groomsmen took their places, half on each side of the gazebo. Z stood at the apex, and his black on black attire lent his justice-of-the-peace appearance a dangerous edge.

Jake turned as the bridal party appeared. The chairs had been arranged to provide twin diagonal corridors, and on the left one, Kim headed the line of Gabi's bridesmaids. Kari led Sally's posse. Upon reaching the front, Kari took a place beside her husband Dan, and Kim beside Raoul.

When Uzuri and Beth were halfway down the aisles, Rainie and Andrea followed, glancing across the center seats at each other to keep in step.

Jake smiled. Hell, most men seeing Rainie would have to smile. In contrast with Andrea, Rainie was shorter. Rounder. And so happy that the light seemed to increase when it struck her.

He'd never met a woman like her. From the way she was transforming their clinic, to her pleasure in Rhage, to the way she'd defended her friend, to the way the animals—and owners—instinctively trusted her.

She was...amazing. What they had was amazing.

He intended to hang onto her.

The music changed, and the audience rose.

Much to their fiancés' bemusement, the two brides had decided on a traditional entrance.

So Gabi's father escorted her.

Sally's father, who apparently was a total asshole, hadn't been invited. However, in Jake's opinion, Sally had found someone better. She'd asked Sam to act as her father and walk her down the aisle.

And the sadist—who terrified every submissive in the Shadowlands—had choked up with tears in his eyes.

As they came down the aisle, Gabi's father moved like a robot, far more concerned with his dignity than with his daughter. Upon arriving at the front, he handed his daughter off to Marcus and strode away.

In contrast, Sam kept his gaze on Sally, openly pleased with the girl's sparkling joy. He brought her to a halt at the gazebo and offered Galen her left hand, Vance her right. After kissing her cheek, he shot her men an easily interpretable stare—*treat her right or answer to me.*

When Sally made an undoubtedly impertinent comment, he barked a laugh.

He paused to give Marcus the exact same warning look. Touching Gabi's cheek gently, he said something too low to hear.

And, Gabi, having easily dismissed her own father, smiled at Sam and blinked back tears.

As Sam took his seat, Z cleared his throat and began, officiating the ceremony with the dignity and polish everyone expected from him. With an occasional revision to accommodate Sally's ménage, he blended together a psychologist's hard-won knowledge with a Master's even harder-won wisdom.

Vows were exchanged. Rings were exchanged. Most of the women in the audience were dabbing at their eyes.

Amused, Jake shook his head, then caught the look Marcus offered his woman. Openly loving and proud and possessive.

Next to him, Galen held Sally, resting his cheek on top of her hair, as if he'd acquired something so precious he feared to squeeze too hard. After exchanging a long pleased look with Vance, he passed her to his partner.

And Jake found himself blinking back tears.

Weddings, truly a treacherous battlefield. His gaze rested on Rainie. Hazardous or not, he planned to win the skirmish and take her home tonight.

Chapter Ten

Both exhausted and fizzing with happiness, Rainie stood at the floor-to-ceiling windows overlooking the Gulf shore. From the dark waters of the Gulf, white frothy waves rolled up onto the beach. In the rising wind, the tall palms shook and bowed.

Behind her, dinner over, the reception was going gangbusters. Filling the center dance floor, an older crowd gyrated crazily to the old tune, *The Twist.*

Most of the over-fifty crowd were business associates invited by Galen's mother and Gabi's parents. In the interests of harmony, Gabi and Sally had caved in…and for a while, Rainie'd wondered if any relatives were worth the bother.

But in the past couple of days, Vance and Marcus's loving, supportive families had demonstrated what a family could be—and made her wish she had one.

A flicker caught Rainie's eye as the light of the moon gleamed off the sails of a boat gliding toward the marina. What a gorgeous location. To her delight, despite a fair amount of parental pressure early on, the brides had held out for their beachside wedding location. Gabi and Marcus had romantic memories of playing together in the waves, and Midwest-born Sally had loved the idea of a true tropical wedding.

Rainie smiled. If Sally wanted something, Galen and Vance would work their asses off to see she got it. Although "legally" people in a ménage couldn't "marry," the men had wanted their Sally to have a beautiful, traditional wedding ceremony, so despite any objections, that's what she'd gotten. Even Gabi's mother quailed when faced with Galen's implacable stare.

Rainie had practiced that expression in the mirror and added it to her personal arsenal. In her future corporate position, she'd need all the firepower she could wield.

However, the reception wasn't the ground on which to employ such weaponry.

Here, people fought their battles with beautiful attire and graciousness. Turning away from the windows, she smoothed her gown and looked around for possible dance partners. She saw Shadowlands members scattered throughout the room.

Near the head table, Kim, Andrea, and Kari chatted with their husbands.

In the center of the room, Beth was dancing with Nolan. Who knew the rough Master could actually dance? Dancing with the couple who'd chosen him as their submissive, Tanner looked blissfully happy.

Like a good pregnant woman, Jessica sat beside Linda, both their Masters nearby. By the punch bowl, Uzuri'd nabbed a sizzling hot man.

Anne was dancing with a young man who was obviously star struck and hardly a challenge to the Mistress. Rainie frowned. Anne better be careful or she'd be on the receiving end of one of Master Z's infamous *talks*.

In the center of the dance floor, Gabi and Sally were showing off steps from the bachelorette party, and somehow their virginal wedding dresses transformed the exotic dancing moves to breathtakingly sexy.

Off to one side, the Shadowlands' security guard Ben stood with Galen and Vance. As they talked, the two grooms watched their bride with wide smiles. Ben's gaze kept drifting to Mistress Anne.

As the song came to an end, Rainie moved out. She should check in with the brides in case they needed something. After that—

Around the side of the room, Jake was heading toward her.

Her heart skipped a beat. Not knowing how late her bridesmaid's duties would keep her, she'd told him he was on his own, and she'd go home to her apartment after the reception was over. Now she regretted her decision; she wanted to sleep in his arms.

But, either way, at least she'd get to dance with him.

Unfortunately, even as she watched, Gabi's parents intercepted him. Rainie considered a rescue, but from the way Mr. Renard clapped a hand on Jake's shoulder and shook his hand, they were well acquainted.

Despite his annoyance at the delay in reaching Rainie, Jake shook hands with William Renard and answered the man's question. "My parents are enjoying their trip. Thank you for asking." He smiled. "They made a stop in Paris before heading home."

"I can't believe you didn't join them," Mrs. Renard said. "Certainly you'd have more fun in Europe than running that clinic of yours."

Jake shrugged. "I get bored on vacations." Although a holiday with Rainie might defeat boredom nicely. He glanced over his shoulder, but she'd been pulled out to the floor by Uzuri, Saxon, and Holt.

She really could dance…

He'd noticed her talent at the Shadowlands and the bachelorette party. Here she was simply having fun and looked incredibly sexy in that floaty-skirted gown. "Damn," he said under his breath.

A body blocked his view. Irritated, he sidestepped.

Two soft hands clasped his. "Jake, don't you recognize me?"

Startled, he glanced down to see a slender woman. Dark copper hair in an up-swirl style, gold designer dress, sultry blue eyes. "Nadia." His distant cousin looked beautiful, as always. "It's good to see you. Mom mentioned you might come. Is your husband here as well?"

"Oh, we've been divorced for ages. That's why I took a job with

William's law firm." A pout crossed her expression as if she were miffed Jake hadn't kept track of her.

He had, at one time. As an undergrad, he'd chased her until his tongue dragged on the ground, but she'd scraped him off in favor of richer prey.

"I'm sorry about the divorce," he said politely. "However, I'm sure William is pleased to have your expertise. I imagine he keeps you busy."

She drew closer. "He does. But I can always find time for you."

"We'll have to have a drink one of these days." Over her shoulder, he noticed Rainie heading for the drink table. "Excuse me, please."

"Of course." Nadia rose up on tiptoes to kiss his cheek. "Later, honey."

* * * *

Rainie managed only a gulp of punch before Jake steered her away. Typical Dom—he hadn't even asked if she wanted to dance.

Then again, slow dancing with Jake was *almost* as good as having sex with him. She snuggled closer. "*Truly Madly Deeply*. I love this song."

"You're welcome."

"*You* got them to play it? Is that why they played two slow tunes in a row?"

He rubbed his cheek against hers. Although his hands were positioned properly, he kept her plastered against him…and the half-erection he boasted. "Did I mention that in high school, my friends and I had a garage band? I know from experience that a good bribe works wonders on a playlist."

She breathed in his cologne, spice and pine, and melted even closer.

"This one was worth every penny since I've been wanting to dance with you," he murmured. "I'd like to find a closet and do more, but the staff's monitoring the private areas. Maybe the beach though…"

Thinking he was joking, she laughed. "You are…" The heat in his gaze made her swallow hard. Maybe he wasn't joking. "Um. I'm not dressed for sex in the sand."

"Mmm." He nuzzled her temple and set her heart to pounding. "I wouldn't put you in the sand, buttercup. I'd bend you over a table, hike up your gorgeous gown, and take you from behind."

He rubbed his chest sideways to tease her breasts. "Because that way I can reach around and play with your nipples…using my right hand."

What about his left hand? "Behave, Sir."

"Now the left"—his voice lowered—"my left hand would tease your pussy."

The flames sizzling over her skin might well ignite her clothes. As she dampened, she tried to step back. His arms flexed into iron bars holding her captive.

"I like your little whimpers when I'm balls deep," he whispered. "I like how your cunt squeezes my cock as you come."

He was liable to make her climax right there in the middle of a crowd. As her legs wobbled, he laughed.

"Jake." Linda walked through the dancing couples. "Sam says you're in charge of summoning the two limos for the newlyweds. It's time."

"I'm on it." With his usual impeccable manners, Jake escorted Rainie to the edge of the dance floor and kissed her fingers. "Enjoy yourself, sweetling. I'll be back in a bit."

"Right," she said under her breath, watching him stride away. Jacob Sheffield in a tuxedo had to be one of the wonders of the world.

He made her feel so special when he danced with her. Talked with her. Laughed at her jokes and teased her. His gaze said he thought she was beautiful.

But... She winced. *Mr. Politeness-Itself* Sheffield had witnessed her tirade at the evil mothers, Mrs. Kouros and Mrs. Renard. Why hadn't he mentioned her behavior?

A knot formed in her stomach as she remembered his ease with Gabi's parents—and they with him. The totally snobbish Renards wouldn't converse with someone they considered beneath them. But he was at their level.

Her shoulders tightened. She hadn't missed how Jake attracted female attention—like the redhead who'd made a play for him, kissing his cheek and rubbing her breasts against his arm.

But he left her to dance with me.

"You must be Rainie." Like a witch materializing out of black smoke—obviously summoned by Rainie's unhappy thoughts—the redhead approached. Wine glass in hand, she gave Rainie an insolent scrutiny, making her aware of each hair out of place, of every bulge of her hips and stomach, of how her chin was round, not pointed.

"I've heard quite a bit about you tonight." The woman's snide tone established she wasn't applying to be one of Rainie's BFFs.

"How odd," Rainie said evenly. "I haven't heard a thing about you." A feeble comeback, but better than none.

"I can see how Jake would enjoy a woman like you for a quick fling," the redhead said. "There's a certain appeal to fat and coarse, at least for a brief change in diet." Her flawlessly curved eyebrows lifted to complement a delicate sneer.

Rainie stiffened. *What in the world?*

"However, since I know the Sheffields, I suggest you don't get comfortable. Men rarely marry beneath their class, and you, my dear, are so far below you're barely out of the gutter."

Before Rainie could find a response to the unexpected vitriol, the bitch spun on her high heel and stalked away...back to the Renards, who were staring at Rainie as if she'd crawled out of some lagoon for monsters.

After a second, Rainie got it. Gabi's mother had unleashed the woman as her own personal attack dog.

Turning her back, she fought the sickness trying to crawl out of her stomach. Yes, she'd been rude to Mrs. Renard and Galen's mother, but only in defense of her friend—and with good cause.

Being attacked for a background she hadn't chosen, that wasn't...wasn't *fair.*

Then again, was it fair in college when boyfriends like Geoffrey took her home, then dumped her after their parents disapproved? Was it fair when teens like Mandy had ridiculed her in the classrooms?

Or, worse, at the Sheffield's house? Tears pricked the backs of her eyes and burned in her throat. The redhead was right about the Sheffields. They were elegant. Refined. Cultured.

Rainie closed her eyes, remembering. As a foster child, she hadn't visited anyone's home, not until popular, charming Jennifer Sheffield invited Rainie to her birthday party. Rainie'd worn her coolest, prettiest clothes and spent hours getting her hair and makeup just right. She'd walked into the Sheffield's home, with her ugly backpack slung over her shoulder. In wonder, she'd stared at the parquet floors, the antique furniture worn to a smooth patina, and the paintings with vivid colors and textures. Everything merged to create breathtaking beauty in a way she'd never seen before.

And there had been another kind of beauty as well. Jake had been there.

Staring blindly at the dance floor, Rainie heard the song change to *Nobody Knows it But Me.* Could a tune get any sadder? *Crying inside* was right. She realized she was backing away from the music, from the guests.

At the Sheffield's, she'd learned an ugly lesson—that clothes and manners only took a person so far. When mean people discovered a vulnerability, like a distasteful background, they'd tear away at it until the victim bled to death.

She'd been wrong to think she could stay. To love Jake. All her work to improve herself would be useless if everyone knew her past. And she'd be Jake's vulnerability. Being with her could hurt him. She must—*must*—move away. But escape meant leaving Jake.

Don't cry, don't cry. Breathing through her nose, she forced the tears back.

"Hey, are you okay?" Beth appeared and took her hand.

Nolan was a step behind. The clean lines of his black tux emphasized his facial scars and the deadliness of his dark gaze. This Master was scarier than Master Sam. "What happened?"

"N-nothing." Her voice broke. Nolan's eyes narrowed, and she added hastily, "I'm fine."

He put a finger under her chin, tipped it up. His eyes turned blacker. "Who upset you?"

Damn him for noticing. For caring. Tears blurred her vision. "No one. I-I'm just...hey, it's a wedding. Females are supposed to cry." She took the tissue Beth handed her and wiped her cheeks.

"Females are supposed to be honest," he growled, and, to her horror, looked past her.

The redhead had disappeared—*thank you, God.* But Mrs. Renard stood with two of her stuffy women friends. Watching. Gloating.

"I'm thinking Gabi's nasty mother was rude or did something, probably because Rainie gave her a few home truths." Beth leaned on Nolan and stroked his huge biceps through his jacket. "Oh, my most wonderful, majestic King of Kings, could you drag that woman out onto the dance floor and make her uncomfortable."

His expression didn't change in the slightest, yet amusement lit his cruel eyes. He studied Rainie, the tissue in her hand, and returned his gaze to his submissive. "I can, little rabbit." Without another word, he strolled toward the women.

"Beth," Rainie whispered. "No."

Beth squeezed her hand. "Shhh, I want to enjoy this."

He escorted Gabi's mother to the dance floor, and his big hand completely wrapped around her upper arm.

The woman gabbled protests and was ignored. When her voice rose, he gave her a Master's stare. One the Shadowlands really should patent.

Mrs. Renard shriveled on the spot, mouth shut completely.

"Go, Sir." Beth was giggling worse than Sally on her silliest day.

"Beth, he shouldn't—"

"He should. Gabi gave the guys orders. If her mother caused trouble, a Master was to drag her out to the dance floor and go all Dom on her ass."

Rainie tried to laugh. "That's mean."

"Gabi's mom is mean." Beth squeezed her hand. "What did she say to you?"

"Nothing, really. A friend of hers simply rubbed my nose in an indisputable fact." One she'd tried to forget. "Jake is rich."

"His family is." Beth considered. "I guess that makes him wealthy as well. But he doesn't care about money."

Sure, he didn't.

Beth's mouth twisted. "You don't believe me."

"I've had some experience with these matters," Rainie said. "Jake might not be concerned now. After all, he's a guy. Guys think with their dicks. And a dick has a fairly short-sighted range of ambitions."

Beth choked on a laugh.

"But parents don't have the dick handicap. So if their beloved heir brings home a woman like me? One ugly scene ensues." As Geoffrey's family had demonstrated.

"Jake's not the kind of man to give in to pressure."

"I know." That was part of what made him special. "But, seriously, causing a family blowup isn't a good thing to do to someone who"—*you love*—"is so nice. Jake needs his family."

He doesn't need me.

"Rainie…" Beth protested.

Rainie hugged Beth and whispered, "Thank Master Nolan for me, okay?"

As Rainie stepped back, her escape path was blocked. The woman was a grandmotherly age, but this *grandmother* would turn heads no matter how old she got. It wasn't just the flawlessly made-up face and hair, and the exquisite ice-blue gown which set off her dark hair and gray eyes, but her sheer composure. Nothing would upset this woman.

When I grow up, I want to be her.

The lady had undoubtedly heard Rainie being a total crybaby. *Wonderful.* Rainie straightened her shoulders. "Ma'am, may I help you?"

"Why, yes, you may." The smile was charming with a hint of reserve. "I'm Madeline Grayson. I believe you know my son, Zachary?"

Master Z's legendary mother? *God, help me.*

Rainie drew her shoulders back and pulled on her shawl of perfect manners. *Etiquette, I got this.* "It's delightful to meet you, Mrs. Grayson. I'm Rainie Kuras, and this is my friend, Beth King."

"Lovely to see you again, Beth. I thought the landscaping you did for the Leighton's beach house to be very fine."

"Thank you." Beth turned as the music changed. "If you'll excuse me, I need to reward—uh, rejoin—Nolan."

"Of course." Mrs. Grayson tilted her head in a mannerism reminiscent of her son's. Only when Master Z did it, submissives tended to kneel.

Mrs. Grayson's attention turned to Rainie. "Zachary informed me you achieved your master's in business administration with a specialty in organizational management?"

Master Z had talked about her? To his mother? *There were no words.* "He's correct."

"He speaks extremely highly of you, as do your professors."

My professors? Why would she have—

"And you're working in a veterinary clinic now?

"Yes. For Dr. Sheffield."

"Helping out, yes." Her smile was gracious. "I did hear about Jake and Saxon's…problem…with office staff."

Rainie smothered her smile…and yet, she couldn't help defending the guys. "Jake and Saxon are superb veterinarians. Their failing was to not thoroughly check out a family recommendation."

"Yes, I spoke to Saxon about the lapse," Mrs. Grayson said mildly. "Now…" Her chin lifted slightly. "Although Zachary recommended you, he doubted you'd be willing to relocate. However, I overheard some of your conversation."

Rainie felt her face heat. "I see."

Mrs. Grayson handed her a card. "I recently bought an advertising company in New York and am taking it in a different direction. Thus, several management positions will soon be open. Would you be interested?"

New York? So far away from… Yet, she'd always planned on moving, at least until she'd started daydreaming. But daydreams were nothing on which to build a life. She had no future here. Not with Jake Sheffield.

And she refused to cry in front of this indomitable woman.

Rainie swallowed. "I'm very interested. However, I've committed to the clinic until mid-February. I can't—it wouldn't be fair to leave them in the lurch."

"Good for you." Mrs. Grayson gave an approving nod. "I'll be interviewing for another couple of weeks, so you have time to decide. Since my son has infallible instincts, I think I can assure you of a position. Please do give me a call."

With a brisk nod, she glided away.

"Oh my God." Rainie glanced down to see if the floor had disintegrated beneath her feet. She wanted to scream, do a victory dance, shoot off fireworks…and burst into tears.

How could she leave?

"Sweetling, are you all right?" Jake's firm hand closed around her arm. He turned her to face him and ran his hands up and down her arms. "I saw Mrs. Grayson with you. She can be a bit intimidating."

Rainie forced her numb lips to form the words. "She was…nice."

"Good." He pushed her hair back, his fingertips leaving a wake of sensation, ripples that spread through her body. "Linda is herding the guests to the entrance to wave Gabi, Sally, and the men off. Afterward, the place closes, and we're free to go."

"Oh." She had duties. What was she thinking? Too obsessed with her own problems to do her job. "I need to check in with Sally."

"She's over there." He guided her toward the head table. "Spend the night with me. We can pick up Rhage on the way."

Her whole life had changed in the last hour, from the redhead to Mrs. Grayson…and Jake didn't know. He still thought… Her heart felt squeezed between two abrasive surfaces, sending flares of pain outward with every beat. "Jake."

He spotted Sally. "There she is."

How could she do this to him?

'Men rarely marry beneath their class, and you, my dear, are so far below that you're barely out of the gutter."

How could she stay? If she remained here, it would be because of her own selfish need to be loved. And she'd wind up harming Jake. She couldn't hurt him. She would *never* hurt him.

Her life was drained out onto the floor, leaving a stiffening corpse behind. And she wanted the chill, needed the ice, or she'd never get the words out. "Jake. She offered me a job. In New York."

He halted so suddenly she tripped. "Mrs. Grayson? New York?"

She nodded. "Management. Like I've always wanted." *And you'll be free of the low-class woman who'd ruin your life.* Even if—someday—she grew enough to be equal to him, he'd never move out of this state. Veterinarians didn't relocate. "I'm going to accept."

"You're leaving? Just like that?" His hand dropped from behind her waist, and he stepped back. "Decision made. No discussion?"

The disbelief in his eyes stabbed through her ribs and right into her heart.

Jake took another step back. He'd been thinking marriage; she'd been thinking career. Last year, he'd been butted by a ram. The massive animal hit, sent him flying, and knocked the air out of him so completely he hadn't managed to inhale for a good minute.

This was worse.

He stared down into Rainie's wide eyes, a compelling mix of green and brown that normally sparkled like a sunlit cypress forest. Fucking beautiful. Tonight her eyes were dimmed. Worried.

She should be. *Jesus.* She was leaving. Going to New York. Hell, Z's mama had probably offered a bonus for moving—a few extra bucks to treat their relationship like an annoyance to be discarded.

Just like that.

Fuck, maybe he was the only one using the word *relationship*.

"Jake?" She put her hand on his arm.

"Congratulations." The word tasted bitter. "Guess I need to start interviewing new staff right away."

"I—yes. I told her I'd stay until the middle of February, like I promised you."

"Aren't you an honorable...person?" he said, and despite his care, sarcasm invaded his tone.

She flinched. "It's best for both of us."

"Uh-huh. Glad you had the brains to realize I needed someone to make my decisions for me." He removed her cold fingers from his arm. "I believe that answers the question of whether you're coming over tonight."

His jaw clamped over further foolish words, and he strode away, leaving his plans, his life, and his heart behind him in a pile of ash.

Chapter Eleven

She might not survive two more weeks in the vet clinic, Rainie decided. At the reception room counter, she hit the backspace and retyped in the correct amount. Perhaps she wasn't screwing up the files as badly as the old receptionist, but only because she rechecked every entry three times.

With a sigh, she stroked the ancient, stick-thin cat snoozing in her lap, grateful for its jagged purr. Grateful for any comfort.

When Jake had walked away from the wedding reception two nights ago, she knew it was for the best. Because really, what did they have between them? He'd been happy with her, sure, but he didn't truly need her. Any woman could give him food, sex, and someone with whom to talk.

She'd been right to sever their relationship. She'd found that out quickly enough.

At the reception, after waving off the brides and grooms, she'd joined the exodus. In the parking lot, the nasty redhead had been talking to Jake. Laughing and flirting, she'd gotten into his car.

Jake had driven away, redhead beside him, not looking back once.

She'd hated him then, as pain had driven deep, deep into her heart. And yet…she couldn't blame him.

Rainie hit *SAVE* on the document and pulled up another bill. Considering the cruel way she'd broken off their relationship, he wouldn't pine over her. Only…couldn't he have? At least for an hour or two? The hurt of seeing him with the redhead had been horrible. Even worse was the hurt of not being with him now…

The melody of her days continued, but the low notes of pain were only getting louder.

Poor Rhage didn't know what was wrong with her. He'd lick the tears from her face, sit in her lap, and try to coax her into playing with him. But holding the little dog was bittersweet, because Rhage had been the one to bring her to Jake.

Why, oh why, had she said she would work in the clinic these last two weeks? Every time she saw Jake or heard his voice, her heart shredded even further.

But she couldn't leave until they hired someone else. Even if she hated Jake—and God, she never could—she had to be fair to Saxon.

Okay. Okay. Get over yourself. Like the survivor she was, she straightened her spine and printed the last bill and put it into a folder, ready for Mrs.

Atkinson to pay when she picked up her pretty, newly spayed cocker spaniel.

Rainie wrinkled her nose at the other folder, which contained her ideas for the clinic: Expanding into an emergency hospital. Stocking and selling specialized foods and medicines. Offering boarding. Streamlining the scheduling with new software. Improving the invoicing system and...*enough.*

She opened a drawer and tossed the folder inside. As with the suggestions for Bart's tow truck company, her notions for the clinic would simply die away, not wanted, not used.

Around her, the place hummed with quiet noises—a complaining cat in the feline room, low voices from the treatment area, cupboards slamming in the pharmacy. The waiting room had emptied as the staff took lunch. Despite emergencies, Rainie usually managed to give everyone a chance to sit down and eat. Since she'd come, the stressed expressions and general unhappiness had disappeared.

The clinic needed her. And she was happy here. Involved in everything. The animals added an incredible dimension of reward she'd never known before. *I don't want to leave.*

The emaciated cat in her lap rubbed her fingers, marking her with his scent as if to emphasize she belonged...here.

Way to realize that too late, Rainie.

But, even if she'd known, she'd still need to leave. To get away from her past.

No, she had no choice, especially since Mrs. Grayson had offered this big chance. In New York, she'd make herself into someone better. Respectable. Classy. And she'd never have to run into old classmates or be called a whore again.

At the thought, she smoothed down her jacket. She'd worn her most conservative suit for its ability to deflect Jake's cold stares. If her clothing could only deflect the way her heart leaped at the sound of his voice—and even his damned footsteps. When had she learned what his boots sounded like?

Swallowing the ache in her throat, she looked up as Jake strode out of the pharmacy room.

"Rainie."

"May I help you, Doctor?"

A muscle in his jaw tensed. "Can you schedule an exploratory abdominal surgery, please?"

"For?"

"Old Buckingham, Jed Parker's basset hound. Probably has cancer."

"Oh no." *Oh God.* The elderly man was crippled with arthritis and lived in the country. "He will be all alone without Buck. His son lives in Miami and doesn't get over here often. And—"

Jake cupped her cheek; his thumb brushed away the tear she shed. And then he simply stood there, staring at her.

She put her hand on his wrist. Pushed. "Don't, Jake."

He didn't move. His piercing green eyes shot steely anger through her ribs, straight to her aching heart. "How can you leave, Rainie? You love it here. People share their personal lives with you." His gaze took in the Siamese curled in her lap. "You cry over puppies and carry cats around. What the hell will you find to like in some frigid advertising company?"

Her mouth opened, but the words didn't come out. She, who never had trouble expressing herself, was mute. "I..."

He waited and then let her go with a disgusted noise. "Not the first time I was mistaken about a woman," he muttered, picked up a chart, and headed to Exam Room Two.

Yes, you're wrong about me. He had no idea who she'd been. How having her in his life would impact his own future, his relations with his family. She closed her eyes, feeling her emotions boil up out of control.

Why did he have to act as if he cared about her? He didn't. When he'd learned she planned to move? *Snap*—he'd found himself another woman before even leaving the wedding grounds. He was rich and important. His world didn't admit her.

But...God, she hated making him unhappy.

"Mrow-ow-ow." The cat's complaint sounded like a feline buzz saw.

With her back still to the waiting room, Rainie checked her lap, but the Siamese lay sleeping. She stiffened. Had someone come in while she was talking to Jake? How had she not noticed?

Because Jake took up her entire world.

She plastered on a smile, spun her chair around, and saw Master Z.

He wore a white shirt and a dark gray tie that matched his eyes. She'd helped Jessica pick the tie out a couple of months before. "You're in white," she said like a total dumbass.

"Indeed." His eyes crinkled. "I work with children, pet. A psychologist in all black is frightening."

"Um. Right." She straightened, realizing he held a cat carrier. "Can I help you?"

"Jessica and I realized Galahad is due for his shots. Can you fit him in?"

As he spoke, she brought up the records on the computer. "He's not due for another couple of weeks."

"However, I'm here now." He set the carrier on the counter.

Such a scruffy cat for a sophisticated person like Master Z. The huge feline had scars, ragged ears...and narrowed eyes. That was one pissed-off kitty.

"We've missed you at the Shadowlands," Master Z said.

God, she'd missed everyone too. She struggled to get her dejected expression under control. "It's mutual."

When Rainie extended her fingers for the annoyed cat to sniff, Master Z watched. "My mother reports you plan to relocate to New York. Do you think you'll enjoy it there?" His voice was relaxed. Just making conversation—as if the Shadowlands owner had ever made casual conversation in his life.

"Probably. Hey, if the city were that bad, your mother wouldn't live there."

He gave her an easy smile. "She wouldn't reside in New York if her existence depended on it. Although she buys companies around the world, her home is Sarasota."

"Oh." Rainie felt despair slide through her again. Soon she'd leave all her friends behind. "I'm sure I'll adapt quickly enough."

"You make friends easily, yes. But, Rainie, you and Jake seem good together, and you love Florida. Why did you accept my mother's offer?"

He'd heard her talking with Jake. The…the *snoop*. Her mouth turned down, and yet, under his compelling silence, words slid right out of her. "I have to live in a place where people don't know my past. And to become more…*more*. Besides, Jake found a better woman. Someone of…of his class." Of Z's class, as well.

He regarded her thoughtfully. "I think you're mistaken, pet. I doubt Jake is interested in anyone but you."

Joy zinged through her and then dissolved in the light of reality. "No. I saw them—I mean, I'm right."

He considered her as those silver-gray eyes held her in place. Then his grin flashed, taking her by surprise. "I'll make you a wager, Rainie. If I lose, I'll pay for Jessica and Gabi and Uzuri to fly to New York and help you get settled in."

Her fingers closed on the edge of the counter. Have friends with her in her new place? She *wanted* that. The only thing better would be Ja— *Stop.* "What's the bet? And what if I lose?"

"If Jake proves he's not interested in…the other women…before Friday, you'll return to the Shadowlands. And there you will spend the evening serving him with total trust and total submission."

"No," she gasped.

He lifted an eyebrow.

Jessica and Gabi and Uzuri. In New York. They'd help her settle in, ease the strain of the move, relieve the loneliness.

But, what if she lost? Could her heart withstand another night with Jake? "He won't do it. He's interested in…her, and even if not, he doesn't want me any longer."

"We'll leave the decision to him." Z poked his fingers through the carrier's wire door to stroke his battered cat. "I won't tell him about the wager unless you lose. If you do, you'll call me, and I'll explain the rules to him that evening."

Friends in New York. *One more night with Jake.* "Okay, you're on."

"Good." Z's silvery-gray eyes met hers, trapped hers, and his voice deepened. "Rainie, you're wrong about who suits him. And who you are. And what is important in life. You think long and hard before you make a mistake."

* * * *

His family had returned to St. Petersburg on Monday. On Wednesday, Jake took Saxon to supper at their house. The cook had outdone herself with preparing an it's-nice-to-be-home meal, then gone home to her husband. So the casual dining room held only his parents, his younger sister, and his best friend.

As the talk of their European vacations swirled around him, Jake contributed absent-mindedly while fuming inwardly. Rainie hadn't smiled all week. Even the clients noticed. Mrs. Flanders had scolded him and ordered him to fix whatever was bothering her.

Difficult to do. Damn him for being an idiot and getting involved.

"...Jake?" Jennifer lifted her eyebrows.

Everyone waited for his answer.

"I missed that," he said. "What did you ask?"

"I ran into Nadia, and she said you two were dating. When did that happen?"

"Who's Nadia?" Saxon scowled. "Is this why Rainie hasn't laughed for three days? You might have mentioned you broke up."

Fuck was the only word that came to mind. He ignored Sax to frown at his sister. "Since when does having a post-party drink mean I'm dating someone?"

"Who is Rainie?" his mother asked.

No, fuck wasn't enough. Clusterfuck was more like it.

His mother didn't rule her children's lives, but she was an advocate of staying informed. "Jake?"

No help for it. "Remember Lynette, the receptionist Sax's uncle recommended? She screwed up the office so badly I fired her. Rainie has been helping out." He gave Saxon a flat stare. "However, Z's mother, Madeline Grayson, offered Rainie a position in New York, and she's moving soon. I'll call in an ad to fill the receptionist spot tomorrow." He should have acted sooner but hadn't been able to face the task.

"Well, that sucks." Saxon scowled. "I wanted her to stay." He glanced at Jake's father. "She had Lynette's mess straightened out within a day, took on the staff schedules and the payroll, as well. She's been researching more efficient software. And she keeps notes on what's required to expand into an emergency hospital."

"And you call her a *receptionist*?" Jake's father laid his napkin beside his plate and leaned back.

"She just completed her MBA," Jake said. "Her last job was managing a towing company. Since the owner hated business, she kept on taking on new projects. She's enthusiastic that way." Not so enthusiastic about relationships.

But he couldn't escape the memories... Rainie surrounded by puppies. Coaxing a homesick cat out of the sulks. Dancing with heart and soul. Kneeling before him. Laughing with him.

His chest squeezed painfully. He'd miss the joy she brought to everything she did.

Now get over it.

"Someone who thrives on multitasking is the perfect office manager for your clinic. If she likes that, she'll probably find a large company a tad stifling," Jake's father said.

Quite true. She didn't seem to care though.

As his mother poured decaffeinated coffee, his sister served the dessert.

"Interesting name." Jennifer set a piece of key lime pie on Jake's plate and said, "I knew a Rainie once. A girl in my class who dropped out. She ran away from her foster home, which made me unhappy because I wanted to get to know her."

Jake stiffened. Rainie'd been in foster care. "Sounds like our"—*my*—"Rainie. Why'd she run away?" And why hadn't she mentioned the running away part?

"I'm not sure. I heard some nasty rumors about the foster home she lived in. The man—" Jennifer grimaced. "Well, there are always rumors. Like after that, Mandy said Rainie was staying with a drug dealer."

Mouth tight, Jake's dad tapped his fingers on the table. "How old were you at the time?"

"Um. I was studying for my driver's license," Jennifer said.

Jake pushed his pie away, appetite gone. Then Rainie'd been sixteen…and living with a dealer? His softhearted woman who cried over old dogs and their owners?

"So, big brother," Jennifer said, trying to lighten the table conversation. "Were you *dating* this paragon of efficiency?"

"Obviously not seriously or she wouldn't be moving to New York." He winced at the bitterness in his voice. With a forced smile, he added, "Which is as well. Her priorities differ from mine."

"Oh." Jennifer's gaze flickered over his face, and then she bit her lip and turned her attention to her pie.

"Well…" His mother's expression held sympathy. She'd always been able to read him like a book. "How is Nadia doing with her job?"

"Fine," Jake said. "She's an excellent choice for Renard. One good snob deserves another." At his mother's choked-off laugh, he smiled slightly, remembering when he'd thought Nadia exemplified the ultimate in womanly perfection. But young men grow up and learn to cherish the beauty hidden beneath the surface.

Rainie was beautiful inside and out.

Ignoring the conversation around him, he toyed with his pie and thought about Heather, his prior girlfriend. They'd been good together, and she'd been an easy person to love. He'd missed her cheerful company, but…but not with this profound ache, as if he'd accidentally sliced a hole in his chest.

When he heard Rainie's voice in the clinic, his body warmed, not with lust, but just…happiness. Seeing her with puppies, he felt like gifting her with a half dozen simply to keep that smile on her face. Always, he wanted to sit next to her and share in her joy.

But her glow had been missing since the wedding. He'd done that—or she had.

She was unhappy; he was unhappy. Couldn't she figure this out? Why wouldn't she talk with him, dammit?

The plate and pie he was playing with disappeared, and he looked up with a scowl.

Sax gave him a smile. He forked up a big bite of the half-smashed pie and popped it in his mouth. "Sorry, bro, but if you're not going to enjoy something tasty, you're going to lose it."

Chapter Twelve

Late the next night in a restaurant's private dining room, Jake sat back in his chair and listened to the other Masters and Mistresses talking. The various conversations were drawing to a close. The monthly Shadowlands M&M dinner was almost over.

As the waitress set a beer in front of him, Jake smiled at her. "Thank you."

She gave him a timid nod. Poor woman. While taking their orders, she'd actually been shaking. But Z had eased her fears, Cullen had teased her, Marcus had paid her one of his silver-tongued compliments. Even Nolan had found a smile for her.

She'd relaxed slightly…probably as much as possible when faced with all the firepower of the Shadowlands, let alone the conversational material. The argument they'd had about blood-play would disturb anyone but a sadist.

"Any more concerns?" Z asked from the head of the table.

"A small one." Anne turned to Jake. "I heard Rainie is moving?"

He nodded.

"So we're down to two trainees?"

"Less," Jake said. "Tanner told me he's joining the Colton household. Only Uzuri is left."

"That's a shame about Rainie." Marcus frowned. His face was deeply tanned from his honeymoon. As he gestured, the wide gold band on his hand flashed in the dimly lit room. Gabi had told Jake she'd picked a ring so "ginormous," every woman in Florida would see he was taken. "I'm going to miss the girl, and so will Gabi."

And so will I. The Shadowlands wouldn't be the same. Rainie had added a special flash of brightness and color to the club. And to his life.

He caught Z's gaze on him and stiffened. Much as he respected the owner of the Shadowlands, Jake didn't need his counseling.

"In that case, meeting adjourned." Z got to his feet.

Jake rose with the others and after the general round of farewells, he took his beer to the bar to finish. Wasn't as if anyone waited at home for him—except for a small dog and two cats. *Pitiful, Sheffield.* After all, his "black book"—the cell phone's contact list—was filled with numbers to call if he wanted female companionship.

He didn't.

"Hey, buddy, you're still here?" Cullen's voice boomed over the noise of the television and nearby conversations. He slid onto a barstool beside Jake. Probably a month or so past due for a haircut, he had to brush his brown hair out of his eyes.

His dark red, button-up shirt fit him well—except for some rather suspicious bulkiness under the left sleeve. Gauze bandages, perhaps? Cullen was an arson investigator—not the safest of career choices.

Jake nodded at Cullen's arm. "What got you?"

"Falling beam. Got a bit scorched before I knocked it aside." Cullen caught the bartender's attention and pointed to the Guinness on tap. "Beer's a hell of a lot easier—and tastier—to swallow than pain pills."

Jake studied him. Cullen was probably well over two hundred pounds, but that wasn't his first beer. "How about I drive you home when you're done self-medicating?"

Cullen drank past the foam to the dark brown liquid and heaved a pleased sigh. "No need. Andrea's out with friends. When I told her I wanted to overindulge, she volunteered to pick me up."

"Good enough." Jake turned his attention back to his beer.

Cullen grinned. "Does this make me less of a man then? To ask my submissive for help?"

Hell. Gunny would have said yes—that a Dom should manage his own problems. Jake rolled his beer bottle between his palms. He wasn't sure he agreed; Cullen was one of the strongest Doms he knew.

Cullen's mouth tipped up when Jake didn't answer. "Who told you a Dom couldn't show weakness?"

"Professor in grad school. A Marine Gunnery Sergeant who served in about every war zone since Moses and had so many medals he could've used them for weight lifting." Jake frowned, remembering his first sight of the battle-hardened vet. Jake had been maybe twenty-one? Young enough to hang on the Dom's every word. "He introduced me to the lifestyle. Mentored me."

Gunny'd missed the camaraderie of the Marines. Missed having younger men to supervise. Upon discovering Jake's interest in BDSM… Jake grinned and shook his head. In hindsight, he realized Gunny'd been delighted to find someone like Jake to train.

"Got it." Cullen drank half his beer, and then leaned an arm on the bar top. "Not a surprising stance considering the Marine mentality. However, I disagree. Much as we Dominants hate to admit it, we're human. You can pull off that infallible, invulnerable shit if the submissive only scenes with you occasionally, but the façade will fall apart in a relationship."

Jake stiffened. "You're saying being strong is a pretense?"

"Sometimes. We *are* strong. We also get hurt and need help." Cullen glanced at his burned arm. "Last I looked, even Doms lose loved ones or jobs or pets. We need to mourn. We get depressed." He smiled. "Some of the best sex of my life was the night Andrea bratted me out of a black hole. I needed her, and she knew it."

Jake scowled. "I don't—"

"Giving is a two-way street, buddy. Don't deny your submissive the pleasure of being able to help you. Of knowing she's needed."

The pleasure of helping. His mentor had denied anyone that satisfaction, hadn't he? *"I'm fine, Sheffield. Don't need help."* Gunny's color had been gray, his age finally showing after his most recent heart attack. He'd been crippled up. Jake had wanted so fucking badly to assist—and been refused.

Was it strength that'd kept the old Marine from accepting any support…or a kind of weakness?

"There he is. And Jake too." Andrea's slightly accented voice drifted across the bar.

Jake glanced over his shoulder, relieved at the rescue. *Fuck.* Seemed like his life since meeting Rainie had been a mess of confusion.

"Jake, it's good to see you." Andrea smiled at him, then her Dom. "Sir."

Cullen pulled her between his long legs. "Jake just reminded me you're the best thing in my life."

"Jake is right." Andrea's smile softened into pure beauty. "I love you, *mi Señor.*"

"I love you, too. Marry me, little tiger. We—" Cullen swore under his breath and released her. "Sorry. I've had too much to drink."

"*Sí.* I will." Andrea's answer was swift and sharp. "Marry you."

Cullen's hands clamped onto her arms so hard she squeaked. "Sorry, love, but…you'll marry me?"

Her eyes gleamed with tears, but her smile would rival sunlight. *"Sí."*

"Fuck," Cullen muttered. "You said yes—you really did." His craggy face split in a huge grin as he pointed at Jake. "You're my witness."

"Got it covered."

"No escape for you now, love." Cullen pulled his captive closer.

Grinning and trying to give the two some privacy, Jake spun on the barstool—and came face-to-face with Heather. "Hey." She'd cut her hair, he realized, and the brown strands curled around her face. "I didn't realize you were in town."

"It's good to see you, Jake." She took the hand he held out and kissed his cheek. Her scent was still lightly floral, her lips soft. "I was at a convention in Orlando and popped over to visit friends here."

Of course, the Shadowlands submissives would be part of her gang of buddies.

"We arranged for me to drop Andrea off so she can chauffeur Cullen home in his truck." Her smile brightened. "And probably celebrate their engagement."

"Probably," he agreed, hearing the sounds of someone being thoroughly kissed behind him.

When a person at the bar muttered sourly, "Get a room," Cullen laughed. With Andrea tucked against his side, he kissed Heather's cheek, slapped Jake's shoulder, and was out of the restaurant in seconds.

"Well." Heather stared after them. "I didn't even say congratulations."

"I don't think they noticed." Jake took a drink of his beer. He was happy for Cullen, no question about that, but felt pretty damned sorry for himself. How pitiful was that?

But the woman he wanted had dumped him in favor of her career. And here was Heather, who'd done the same. Fuck, he needed to reevaluate his handling of relationships.

He motioned to the bartender. "What can I get you, Heather?"

She hesitated before sliding onto the barstool Cullen had vacated. "Just a diet soda," she told the bartender before asking Jake, "How is the clinic doing?"

"Busy." If they could have kept Rainie, they'd have expanded. "How's your job?"

"Wonderful." Her smile was still sweet. "I've been promoted."

"Good for you. I'm sure you earned it." She would have. As a submissive, she'd always given a hundred percent. He couldn't imagine she offered less to her career. "You look happy. Apparently, you made the right decision."

Her gaze dropped, and her weight shifted on the barstool. "I did. Although, I almost changed my mind and stayed, you know."

Jake watched her as he took a slow sip of beer. "No, I didn't know."

"I was torn." Her hands opened and closed in her lap. "If you'd said you needed me…if you'd given the slightest hint that losing me would upset your life, I'd never have been able to leave."

Jake straightened, winded as if she'd kicked him in the gut. "What fucking *hint*? I love"—when had the word turned past tense?—"loved you. I don't understand."

"I know." Gaze on her drink, she traced a finger through the condensation on the glass. "You know, we all love our family, friends, even pets. But, a person doesn't *need* a dog. They're not essential to happiness. It's not a give-and-take relationship."

"I never treated you like a pet." *Jesus.*

"No." She huffed in exasperation. "But people who start a life together, they rely on each other. Lean on each other. Know each other's weaknesses and worries so they can assist."

"Right. Go on."

"You supported me. But…I never did that for you. I didn't make any difference in your life. You didn't need me."

"Heather—"

"I gave you nothing you couldn't get from a couple of friends and an occasional sex buddy."

Jake straightened. "That's not true."

"I know," she whispered. "I know now. But at the time, that's what I thought." She laid her hand over his on the bar. "Because you never let yourself show you're not invulnerable."

He scowled. What the fuck was it with people wanting him to be weak?

"Doms are supposed to be strong. Submissives want someone to lean on."

"I do. I found a Dom," she said. "And he showed me what bothered me about you and me, Jake. It's that I never felt as if I gave you anything important. A relationship—even a D/s one—is two people growing stronger together than they would apart. Not one tree standing alone with another leaning on it."

Her smile wavered a little. "You know, submissives need to give just as much as Doms need to protect."

Shades of Cullen. Jake's brows drew together. Sipping his beer, he considered. Gunny had shown him how to dominate, how to flog and whip and all the various scene techniques. But…maybe, just maybe, his mentor hadn't demonstrated how to maintain a long-lasting D/s relationship—because Gunny hadn't known how. He'd had three divorces under his belt. Jake had figured the women couldn't take the stress of loving a professional soldier, but perhaps something more fundamental had been lacking.

Fuck. Jake met Heather's gaze. "I did need you."

"I eventually reached that conclusion." Relief and sorrow showed in her eyes as she rose. "We've both moved on, but…friends?"

He kissed her lightly. "Friends."

As she walked from the bar, Jake watched her, seeing her appeal and sweetness. In all reality, their relationship might have worked if he'd been different. But…the bond he had with Rainie contained even more potential. Was more fulfilling.

When Rainie left, her loss would gut him in a way he'd never experienced before.

"Submissives need to give just as much as Doms need to protect." Did Rainie find it easy to leave because she didn't believe he needed her? He closed his eyes.

She was a woman who loved fulfilling the desires of everyone and everything around her—pets, friends, Doms. And her lover hadn't let her do anything for him. *Fuck, I'm an idiot.*

There was more to her moving away though—a compulsion he didn't understand.

But in order to get through to her, he'd have to show her he needed her…and that he'd fight to keep her with him.

* * * *

On Tuesday, a cold snap had blown off the Gulf, giving a bite to the moist air. A light breeze rustled the leaves of the maples as Rainie left her car and joined Jake in front of a popular Irish bar. She glanced up at him, relieved the strain on his face had faded.

The last few hours had been bad. Actually, they'd had an easy day until late afternoon when a cop arrived carrying a bloody mess. Saxon and Jake had done their best to save the animal. According to Ceecee, they'd tried long after most vets would have given up, but the dog had been too badly injured.

When Jake had come out of surgery, face set with misery, Rainie's eyes had filled with tears. He'd started to turn away, then hesitated and said, "I know after-hours isn't in your job description, but I'm... Would you come with me for a drink? For company? I...need you."

He needed her. She could do something to help. Despite her sadness, her heart had been lightened.

When they reached the bar, Jake pulled open the door and smiled down at her. "Thanks for taking the time to join me."

She fought back her first response, *"I'd go with you anywhere,"* and offered instead, "You're welcome."

The crowded bar smelled of beer and frying food, with hints of cologne and perfume. From the corner dedicated to darts came a light *thunk*, then high-pitched cheers and groans.

Hand on Rainie's arm, Jake checked for a table.

She waited silently, cherishing even the smallest impersonal touch of his hand, storing memories for a future without him.

Jake ran his knuckles over her cheek. "You know, you're excellent company, even when quieter than normal." The sun lines at the corners of his eyes creased. "Maybe *because* you're quieter than normal."

Jostled out of her melancholy, she stared at him. "You're-you're *insulting* me? I was kind enough to join you and—"

A roar went up from the crowd watching basketball on the bar television. Rainie glanced over, noted the scoreboard—Miami Heat in the lead—and added her own, "Woot! Woot! Woot!" She was totally going to win her five-dollar bet with Saxon.

"There's a table." Taking her hand, Jake tugged her after him. His grip was strong. Warm. Familiar. And she wanted to hold on forever.

As he threaded their way through the rough-hewn tables, she smiled at various acquaintances. To her dismay, Mandy and Jefferson from her high school sat at one table. Her stomach clenched. Did they have to turn up everywhere?

It was as if they were walking, talking reasons of why she had to leave the Tampa/St. Pete area.

Then Jake stopped at an empty booth far too close to them. *Dammit.* She should have told Jake to pick a different bar. This one was far too popular with the locals.

Since flinging her arms out and screaming at the heavens, *"Just shoot me now,"* wouldn't help—no matter how satisfying—she simply took a seat across from him. At least her back was to the rest of the room.

"What can I get you folks?" A waitress in jeans and a skimpy top appeared.

"Rainie?" Jake prompted.

"A Frozen Mudslide." To Jake's raised eyebrows, she explained, "It's like getting chocolate, dessert, and alcohol all at once. Good for the end of a crap day."

When his eyes darkened, she regretted her words. Why had she been stupid enough to remind him of the dog's death?

But his smile reappeared. "Women and their chocolate." He nodded at the barmaid. "Make that two."

"Won't work for you, dude," Rainie said. "You see, the soothing effect of chocolate is diminished by too much testosterone—and I think you're at toxic levels."

Jake snorted.

As the giggling barmaid left, Rainie realized something. "You let me order. Without interfering or taking over."

"Ah." He leaned back comfortably, his long legs stretched under the table, catching Rainie's ankles between them. She tried to move, but his legs trapped her. And her hormones burst out of the gate like racehorses when the bell sounded.

"I like being in control for sex, sweetling," he said easily. "However, I don't need to be in charge all the time."

"Unless I try to put mushrooms in your eggs?" Her last morning at his house, he'd delivered a stinging swat to her ass as well as a lecture on why fungi were not to be confused with food.

His grin flashed in the dim bar lights. "'Tis most distressing when a subbie tries to poison her Dom."

Her Dom. He never would be again. "Mushrooms or not, making breakfast is not sexual."

"Sure is. Whenever a female is in a man's house, it's all about sex. Showering is sexual. Meals are sexual." He grinned ruefully. "It's a guy thing."

"Like I said, toxic amounts of testosterone." No joke. Every moment in his house had been infused with anticipation of being ravaged on the couch or fucked on a counter…and she'd loved it.

To Rainie's relief, the barmaid interrupted the conversation to drop off their drinks.

Jake eyed his suspiciously. After a drink, he swirled the glass and drank again. "Good stuff."

Rainie smiled. "Thanks." She took a sip, closed her eyes, and moaned appreciation for the sublime combination of chocolate ice cream, Baileys, and Kahlua.

When she opened her eyes, his gaze met hers—hot with lust.

Her expressions of enjoyment stopped abruptly.

But, after clearing his throat, he returned to their conversation. "Seems like your Shadowlands notes said you wanted a part-time Dom. Not a full-time one."

No, this would not be a topic they'd discuss. Not when the subject increased her sense of loss. "Nothing I'm going to worry about now, since it'll be a while before I get settled in and find a new club."

The muscles in his jaw grew taut, and his eyes turned an ice green.

He still wanted her to stay. The realization tightened her throat. *Don't cry.*

Don't cry. Don't cry. She forced her lips to tilt up. "So, what do you think of Miami Heat's chances against Orlando?"

"I think you are changing the subject," he said softly. "We're going to—"

A man crowded their table. "Rainie."

Rainie looked up. "Bart? Aren't you supposed to be in Europe?"

"Yes." He almost spit the word. His stocky frame was rigid with a fury she hadn't seen since one of their truckers committed a hit and run. "I had to cancel our plans…to come back and save my business."

Cory must have made a mess of things. No surprise there. "I'm sorry Cory—"

He slapped the table so violently the glasses rattled. "I hired you when you had no references. Gave you a good salary. Responsibilities. *Trusted* you."

*Wait…*he wasn't mad at Cory, but at *her*. Her breath clogged in her chest. "Yes, you did. And I worked my butt off for you."

He leaned in, glaring into her face. "*Sure* you did."

"That's enough." Jake rose.

Bart ignored him. "You walked out the door the minute I needed you. No notice. Left my boy in the lurch."

When Jake stepped between them, Bart made a disgusted sound. "You aren't worth yelling at."

He stomped across the room, pushing people out of his way.

Rainie stared after him. *But, but, but…*

"Rainie." Jake sat next to her and tucked her into his side. "Easy, sweetling."

Bart disappeared somewhere in the room. She couldn't pull her gaze away. The music and conversations were drowned out by the clamor of pain in her head. In her heart. He thought she'd walked out on him. He'd *yelled* at her. She put her hands over her mouth to hold back the sobs.

"Shit." With gentle fingers against her cheek, Jake forced her to look at him. "Baby, I've seen you remove the hide from two old dragons. This was just one man, and he was wrong. Why didn't you lay the truth on him?"

"He is"—her voice broke—"he was a friend. Gave me a job. Trusted me. Just like he said." Self-loathing poured blackness through her veins. "I should have tried harder to work with Cory."

"Rainie, his son attacked you. You didn't walk out."

"Oooo, is the whore crying?" The whisper came from the nearby table of classmates.

Rainie stiffened as the comments grew louder. "Look, Sheffield's got it bad. Is he pussy-whipped or what?"

She tried to pull away. Jake shouldn't hold her. Shouldn't—

His head tilted, and he scowled. His arm was an unmovable iron bar around her.

"Let me go," she whispered.

"The rude assholes really do bother you, don't they?" He tipped her face up again, but she closed her eyes to avoid the disgust that must be in his.

"Babe, they're fucking insecure, needing to drag someone else down to feel adequate. Ignore them."

What? Her gaze met his. He didn't appear angry with her. Or disgusted.

His lips quirked. "What did you think I was going to do? Toss you out of the booth in case your unpopularity with a few losers might be contagious?"

She barely kept from nodding.

He stared. "Seriously?"

He honestly didn't care what her classmates said? He'd called them losers. Her fingers were icy. Little tremors shook her body.

But Mandy and Jefferson *were* losers. She closed her eyes as the truth sank into her bones. She had friends, teachers, mentors who considered her valuable. Strong. Why did words coming from *losers* upset her so badly? Maybe her judgment scale was skewed if nasty comments from those she didn't respect weighed more than opinions from people she valued. Somehow, someday, she needed to think about that.

"Rainie." Jake squeezed her shoulder. "That old guy, Bart. He needs to hear the truth."

Misery was a heavy anchor, dragging on her heart. "He thinks his son is a good person."

"Mmmhmm. He might hope, but I doubt he believes it. He's hurting because he thinks you let him down. *You*, he trusted."

Even knowing she should shift away, she couldn't leave the comfort of Jake's arms. She leaned her forehead against his chest as she tried to work out what to do. How did a person choose a path when each ended in pain?

But Jake was right. Bart thought she'd betrayed him. Even worse, if he didn't comprehend the dangers of leaving Cory in charge, Bart could lose his company.

But…oh…facing Bart would be much more difficult than merely walking away.

This time when she retreated from Jake's embrace, he let her. She firmed her trembling lips. "You go on home. Thank you for the advice."

"What are you planning?"

"I'll talk to him." God help her.

"You're not facing him alone, sweetling." He rose and helped her out of the booth. "I won't butt in, but I've got your back."

Her eyes blurred with tears. "Don't be nice, damn you." She slapped his arm, knowing she was one small second from bursting into noisy sobs.

"Right." The lines fanning from his eyes creased, although he didn't smile. His knuckles brushed a tear from her cheek gently enough to make her heart ache. "I'll work on being mean."

"Th-thank you."

She'd broken up with him. So how could her love continue to grow and expand until her heart felt filled to bursting? How could that be?

As they wove through the tables, she spotted their destination in a booth under a bank of night-black windows. Bart and his wife, Tilly, on one side.

Cory sat on the other side. Clean-shaven, groomed, suited up and looking like a Boy Scout—except for his swollen nose still bearing yellowing bruises.

When Bart spotted her, he rose. Watching his face darken with anger was like taking a knife in the chest. When had she come to love the gruff old man? Why hadn't she ever told him?

Her regrets were like an echo in a rock-lined valley. *Too late, too late, too late.*

Cory saw her and stiffened. "What the fuck is she doing here? Beat it, bitch."

"Cory," his mother gasped. *"Language."*

Rainie pulled a shield around her heart. If she didn't speak now, she'd never find the courage again. "Give me one minute, Bart, and I'll leave you alone." Chin up, she held the old man's gaze.

"Spit it out, Rainie." Bart's jaw was tight.

Behind her, Jake stepped closer, giving her the warmth of his body. Of his support.

Cory glared, malice coating his expression.

She swallowed and forced the words out. "You never knew this, Bart, but I first met Cory when I was sixteen and living with a drug dealer."

"A drug dealer? Sixteen?" Tilly gasped. Her face changed, worry filling it—and Rainie realized it was for her, a teenager in a bad situation. Bart's wife had a heart as big as his.

Bart merely nodded. "I knew. Lily told me." His bushy brows drew down. "Why would Cory have been there?"

"He came to buy drugs." This was like wading through a swamp of ugliness with the muck of her past dragging at her feet. "Then he wanted to buy me for s-sex. Had a fight with Shi—with the dealer and Cory ended up thrown into a dumpster."

She saw Bart and Tilly's expressions. Complete disbelief. It hurt, and her momentum faltered.

Jake squeezed her waist. "Go on, babe," he murmured.

God, she loved him.

She forced her gaze back to Bart. "When I got a job with you and realized Cory was your son… Well, it was an unpleasant surprise for both of us."

"You are full of bullshit," Cory burst out. "Bitch, I never met you before and—"

"Be quiet." The dominance that had made Jacob Sheffield a Master in the Shadowlands filled the air.

Cory turned pale, and with a jerky movement, slid as far away in the booth as he could get.

Well. The wonder of having her own hero at her back loosened her throat, letting her continue. "The day before I quit, Cory took over the scheduling. You know Larry tends the baby when his wife works, and he needs those afternoons off. Cory ignored the *requested-time-off* slips and scheduled him anyway. Larry had a fit, and Cory fired him."

"Fired Larry?" Bart looked as if someone had punched him. "He's one of the most reliable ones there. Cory, you—"

Rainie continued, "After I wrote out Larry's paycheck, Cory ripped it up and said he wouldn't pay Larry, even though he'd worked all month. We argued."

"That's bullshit," Cory snarled. "You—"

Rainie never looked away from Bart. "Cory kicked me out of the office. That was on a Friday. The next night, he showed up at my apartment, and he was high on drugs. Probably coke. He told me…"

Her gaze met Tilly's, and her voice closed down.

God, she couldn't do this. Not to that sweet woman. Rainie tried to take a step back and bumped into Jake.

He put an arm around her waist, anchoring her against his side as he spoke to Tilly. "Ma'am, I'm sorry to tell you this. Cory told Rainie that if she didn't give him a blowjob, he'd fire her. He told her he could do anything he wanted, including fuck the staff."

"No. No," Bart whispered. His eyes turned to Rainie. Appalled. Filled with pain.

"I… Yes." This was like kicking a helpless puppy. "Cory grabbed me, and Jake punched him."

"You fucking bitch! I never touched you!" Cory jumped to his feet. "And I've never met your asshole boyfriend."

"Want me to break your nose again?" Jake stepped around Rainie. "Sit. Down."

Rainie's knees almost buckled. Cory dropped back onto the bench.

Bart stared at his son's bruises. "You said you'd fallen down." The color drained from his face, leaving his lined skin gray. He sagged.

As his wife took his hand, she was choking back sobs.

Oh God, what had she done? "I'm sorry, Bart," Rainie managed to whisper. "I'm so sorry." She hesitated and then fled, pushing her way to the front door.

"Rainie." Jake followed her out.

In the distance, thunder rumbled, and the palms lining the parking lot bent under the advancing storm.

Rainie turned to face Jake. Another person she'd let down. He'd lost a dog at the clinic, and he'd needed her—and she'd used him. Ruined his evening with her own problems. She hadn't helped him at all—because, once again, her past had returned. Hurting her. Hurting others.

"I'll take you home," Jake said.

"No." She took a step back, distancing herself. "Thank you. Thank you for…for being here. But, I'm not good for you."

"That's not true, Rainie."

"I want to be alone."

His jaw tightened. "I don't—"

She shook her head. "My choice."

As she walked away, she could feel the tie between them stretch and thin and disappear. The wind whipped at the tears streaming down her face, leaving only coldness behind.

* * * *

Jake watched Rainie as she sat at her desk in the clinic. She looked like hell. Her color was so pale he could see the blue veins at her temples, the shadows under her eyes. She moved as if even her muscles hurt.

She'd undoubtedly spent the night suffering for Bart and his wife. Yes, she was the type to take on that guilt.

Fuck, he wanted to hold her.

Instead, he opened the fridge, grabbed a couple of energy drinks, and handed her a can. "You need that. Drink it."

She blinked at him and half smiled. "Your presentation lacks finesse, but thank you."

"You doing all right?"

Her lips drew up into a wry smile. "The fact you fetched me an energy drink means I'm not going to win Miss America today, huh?"

He smiled back. "Pretty bright, aren't you?"

"That's me." She pushed her hair out of her face. "Jake?"

She hadn't braided or coiled her hair today. Not that he'd complain. The way her hair fluffed over her shoulders made him remember burying his fingers in it. "Mmm-hmm?"

Looking down, she opened the can. Turned it around in her hands. Finally said, "Last night, you heard what my old classmates were saying, and I was surprised at your reaction."

"Because I didn't beat them up for you?"

From her startled expression, she hadn't even considered he might have defended her that way.

Now he rather wished he'd mopped the floor with them. "I don't try to defend against whispering. Open rudeness, yes. Behind the back is—"

"No, God, no, I didn't want you to… Sheesh." Her hands closed on the can, denting it. "No, I simply noticed you weren't embarrassed or—"

"About what assholes are farting about?"

At her appalled stare, he grinned. "Sorry for the crudeness."

"Well. Right." Her fingers loosened. "It's just… When people don't like you and you'll never change their opinion, it must be nice to not really care."

Jake's eyes narrowed. Once again, he was realizing just how much she did care what others thought. "Rainie—"

She straightened. "So, can you fit in a walk-in?"

Totally changing the subject. He glanced at the waiting area, nodded to the three clients who waited with their pets, and answered, "I finished the buckshot extraction on the Doberman. So, yes, I should be able to take another."

The reception door opened and closed. "Jake," a woman called across the room.

Jake let out a sigh. The day lacked only this. "Nadia, what are you doing here?"

"Why, I told you last night." She glanced at Rainie, and her lips twisted into a smirk. "Remember? I said I'd drop by to take you to lunch."

As the bitch's claws ripped through Rainie's skin and ribs and heart, she forced her face blank. What Jake did with *Nadia* was his own business. After all, he liked the woman. Had left with her after the wedding. Rainie should wish them well.

Not going to happen.

She checked her blouse in case blood was leaking from the far-too-accurate heart shot. When Jake didn't say anything, she looked up.

Eyes narrowed, he regarded Rainie…reading with a Dom's uncanny perception every single emotion she was feeling. Dammit.

"Jake, honey, are you ready to leave?" Nadia asked, her voice thicker than cold molasses.

Ignoring her, Jake touched Rainie's cheek with a gentle finger, holding her gaze trapped for…forever.

Finally, he straightened. "Nadia, last night when you *called*"—his glance at Rainie undoubtedly caught the surprise and relief on her face—"I said I didn't have time for lunch. Or anything else you offered."

"Oh, Jake." Nadia's pout took full advantage of her well-collagened lips. She gave Rainie a look of disdain. "I certainly hope someone like *her* hasn't come between us."

Jake gave a short laugh. "Nadia, there is no *us*. I dated you years ago, before you married. I have no interest in seeing you now. At all."

The whispers from the waiting room clients grew audible.

Jake turned his back on Nadia, leaned a hip on the desk, and said to Rainie, "The lab work on Brennan's rabbit came back, and I need to change the antibiotics. Can you get the owner on the line?"

"I—of course. Right away, Sir."

His lips quirked at her submissive slip, but he simply opened a folder and flipped through the contents.

The outer door made its distinctive hiss, and Rainie gave a quick glance up.

Color almost purple, head held high, Nadia stalked out.

The elderly man in the waiting room had his hand over his mouth, but his shoulders were shaking. The woman with the cat carrier winked at Rainie. The one with the poodle gave her a surreptitious thumbs-up.

Rainie's body hummed with amazement. *Jake didn't want the redhead.* Eventually, her fingers managed to bring up Mr. Brennan's file—without any mental input, thank goodness, since her brain had taken an extended leave.

Annoyed with herself, she huffed out a breath.

And Jake turned his attention back to her. The power in his gaze made her hands turn clammy. "Problem, Rainie?"

"N-no, Sir." Realizing she'd called him "Sir" again, she flushed.

The sun lines beside his eyes crinkled, and he bent to whisper in her ear. "Did you know that each time you call me 'Sir,' you lighten my day?"

The resonance in his voice shivered through her, and then he disappeared into the treatment area, leaving her staring after him. God, she wanted him so badly. Thank goodness, she'd be gone before he sucked her into—

Oh no. What had she done?

The blood drained right out of her head with an almost sucking sound. She must have moaned, since Rhage came out from under her desk to press against her legs. As her fingers teased his soft ears, she tried to swallow past a dry throat.

You stupid, senseless, slow-witted squid.

Master Z had got her. Got her good. She watched her hand reach for the phone. Punch up the contact. Wait. *Don't answer. Don't answer.*

"Shadowlands." Master Z's voice couldn't be mistaken for anyone else's. His power sizzled through all the miles between them, probably making the telephone wires shake as violently as she was.

"This is Rainie," she said almost in a whisper. *Pull it together.* She forced her spine straight…and watched her fingers tremble. "You…won, Sir. The bet."

"Indeed."

He let her hang for only an eternity or two before he said gently, "You will come to the Shadowlands on Friday at nine. Tell Ben to notify me when you arrive."

Total trust. Total submission. With Master Jake. Her gaze instinctively lowered as she whispered, "Yes, Sir."

Chapter Thirteen

When Jake arrived at the Shadowlands, he swung by the bar where Raoul sat talking to Cullen. "Men," Jake greeted.

He received chin lifts.

"I thought you said you needed time off," Raoul said. "Did you change your mind?"

He hadn't. The Shadowlands held too many memories of Rainie. "Not exactly. Z asked me to stop in and talk to him." And had refused to discuss *the problem*, whatever it was, on the phone.

"He's in the back." Raoul nodded toward the rear of the club. "Near the cages."

"Thanks." Jake slapped Raoul on the shoulder and headed through the room, walking past the various scenes, inhaling the scents of leather, light perfume, sweat, and fear.

With Jessica curled in his lap, Z sat in a black leather chair, watching a newer Domme practice with a flogger. He noticed Jake's approach and squeezed his submissive's shoulder. "Can you give us a few minutes, kitten? I don't want to put you in the position of keeping secrets from a friend."

Jessica frowned at him. "What evil thing are you up to now?" When her Dom didn't answer, she gave a cute grunt of exasperation, then rubbed her cheek against Z's in a pretty surrender.

As the little blonde walked away with one hand on her rounded belly, Jake took a seat. "What's up?"

"Thank you for coming in." Z picked up his drink. "Did Rainie mention our wager?"

Rainie and Z? "No." Jake shut his mouth on the questions and waited.

"She thought you wanted to be with another woman—one more suited to your *class*. I bet her that you would demonstrate her error."

What the hell? "My class?"

"Indeed."

Jake scowled. Rainie must have seen Nadia at the wedding. Nadia was beautiful; it was true. But Rainie seemed more comfortable in her own body than most women Jake had met, small or large. "What's this 'class' bullshit?"

Z steepled his fingers in consideration. "Has she spoken of her goals in life?"

"I know she's studied for a career in business. She wants a management position—a high status one."

"And why did she choose high status as a goal?"

"Isn't that what every businessperson wants?"

"Not any more than all vets want to handle horses." Z smiled slightly. "Her friends say she loves your clinic—the animals, the challenges, the people. My question—which she wouldn't answer—is why she'd give up a job she loves to do something else. And why she said she had to '*be more*.'"

Jake's eyes narrowed. "Be more what? She's already..." *perfect.* "I don't understand."

"Nor do I. Which is why I made the bet."

Jesus, if Z made a bet with a submissive, the consequences could get ugly. Jake straightened. If Rainie were uncomfortable with the penalty, Z would damn well back off. "What are you going to make her do?"

Laughter lit Z's gray eyes. "She agreed to come here tonight to serve you in total trust and total submission."

"Me?"

Z rose. "She's in the dungeon waiting for you, Jacob. This might be a good time to get some answers."

As Z walked away, Jake stood...and sat back down.

She had to serve him. To trust him—although she obviously didn't or he'd know her background. She'd been reluctant to tell Bart about living with a drug dealer. Jennifer had mentioned the streets. Foster care. Running away.

Most people were happy to confide their pasts, ugly or not. If Rainie was so reticent, was she...ashamed? He needed to know.

And goals. The assholes the other night had really bothered her. And she wanted to be *more*.

Jake stared at the wall. Z's bet gave him one night—and there would be a lot to accomplish in only a few hours.

Planning came first.

And then he'd get some answers.

* * * *

Her knees hurt. Head down, Rainie shifted her weight from side to side. Behind her, someone used a paddle on their submissive, and the slapping of flesh was loud in the rock-walled dungeon room.

How long had she been in here, anyway? Had Master Z forgotten her?

No, he never forgot anything...except maybe a grocery-list item. Jessica's report that the Master could be occasionally absent-minded had been a surprise.

Because he was never inattentive in the Shadowlands.

Maybe Jake didn't want to see Rainie. At the dismal thought, she blinked back tears. Determinedly she turned her attention to the sounds around her—the moaning from the other side of the dungeon, the clip of a Domme's heels. A sigh. A laugh.

Boots appeared in her field of vision. Black, scuffed at the toes. Black jeans.

Her heart lifted and actually bounced like a beach ball as her gaze rose. A heavy leather belt around trim hips. Broad shoulders under a black collared shirt—one of the slim-fit kind that showed off hard pectoral muscles and his narrow waist. *Jake. My Jake.*

Only he isn't. Why did she have to keep reminding herself of the fact? Why did each repetition hurt more?

His top shirt buttons were open to show the tanned skin of his chest. His shadowed jaw was tight; he looked angry. Did he even want to be here?

She dropped her eyes before meeting his gaze. Unhappiness was a solid lump under her sternum. *Don't cry.* She dug her fingers into her thighs so the pain would drive her tears back.

The bare skin dented under her nails. Bare legs, bare ass, bare everything. When Master Z had led her into the dungeon, he'd pointed to the corner and ordered, "Strip completely, kneel, and wait for Master Jake's directions."

And now Master Jake was here.

"So, you're to serve me tonight with total trust and total submission," Jake said. She got nothing from his voice—not sarcasm, not surprise, not enthusiasm.

He didn't sound like her Jake at all…because she'd hurt him more than she'd realized. More than she'd thought possible. The last thing she'd ever wanted to do was cause him harm. She bit her lip, wanting to beg him to understand that she wasn't the right person for him.

But he'd sent the perfect Nadia away. And come back and touched Rainie.

She swallowed. "Yes, Sir."

"Good enough." He offered his hand to help her rise. "I'm in the mood to work you over hard, so this is fine timing."

A quiver of anxiety and longing lodged low in her belly. How pitiful that she'd let him do…*anything*…just to have him touch her.

She followed him to the back corner. The wax play area was set up with a disposable covering on the bondage table. The heavy stone table next to it held a lit candle.

Wax could feel wonderful—or hurt like hell if the Dom was in a sadistic mood. How angry was Jake? But he'd never take out his anger on a submissive. He'd call off a scene first…wouldn't he?

"Rainie."

She dragged her gaze from the flame to look up into intent eyes. "Yes, Sir?"

"Total trust?"

She winced and let go of her doubts. "I'm sorry, Sir. I do trust you."

"You trust me with your body." He helped her onto the table and positioned her on her back with firm, impersonal hands. "But not with your emotions. Or your past. Or your future." His baritone had chilled to be as emotionless as his expression.

I don't like him this way.

Yet his quiet accusation hit the bull's-eye. The realization she'd deliberately hidden herself from him—from her Dom—was a blow severe enough to make her tremble.

With deliberate movements, he pushed a wedge under her ass to tilt her hips up and wrapped cuffs around each thigh before clipping them to the side table hooks. As he tightened the straps, her knees were forced up and out to the sides—giving him an open pussy playground, especially after he positioned her butt on the table's edge.

Another band across her low abdomen ensured she couldn't wiggle away from whatever he had planned.

When he applied a forehead strap, she barely kept from whining. Not being able to move her head made everything seem far too restrictive. More straps went over her arms, crossing both above and below her breasts.

He walked around the table, tightening or loosening the fastenings to an even snugness. "Your safeword is red. For cramping, numbness, tingling, or discomfort you can't handle, use yellow. Understood?"

"Yes, Sir." Her heart grieved for the affection missing from his voice.

"Excellent." He stood close, filling her vision and blocking out the room. "You're a beautiful, intelligent, loving woman, Rainie. Why do you think you're not good enough for me?"

The question dropped out of nowhere, a tornado ripping up her internal landscape and stealing her breath.

She had no answer for him.

He gave her time to respond and then shook his head, letting his disappointment in her silence show.

Tears prickled her eyes.

"If you don't want to talk to me, I might as well use this." After placing a squeaky toy in her fist, he gagged her with a black silicone pacifier. It wasn't as gag inducing as the huge penis ones, but the soft roundness filled her mouth completely.

Inhaling through her nose, she could smell Master Jake's evergreen-forest cologne. It was like a hint of freshness in the rock and leather scent of the dungeon.

"Bite down on the gag, if you need to," he said calmly. "Use the squeaky toy to safeword—or when you're ready to speak."

When. Not if.

His palm was warm against her cheek as he bent. "You're going to talk to me, sweetling. The only question is how much you'll subject yourself to before that point."

At the terrifying determination in his voice, she involuntarily pulled at her straps, but she was completely restrained.

He leaned his forearm on the table, his face inches from hers. The stern set of his jaw reminded her of the steely core beneath his usual charm. "I don't know what's happening in that head of yours, Rainie. But before this evening is over, we're going to explore it, even if we journey back to your birth."

She bit down on the gag. No way would she talk about her horrendous childhood.

"Total trust. Total submission. You're one of the most honest people I know, Rainie. You wouldn't renege on the bet."

Her mind went blank as she realized the depth of Master Z's trap.

When he paused, giving her a chance to respond, she told her fingers to squeak the toy, to talk to him. And everything in her stayed immobile.

He waited another second before brushing his lips against hers. "Don't worry, Rainie. You're going to tell me everything." His face was expressionless as he put a pair of sunglasses on her.

The room turned dark. Even worse, the lenses curved like magnifying glasses, distorting the surroundings like funhouse mirrors, enlarging objects and people.

"I'm going to fuck you eventually," he said softly, "but first I'll ensure the sensation is increased for both of us."

What did he mean? Was he planning to do chemical play?

He positioned a rubbery-feeling circle above her clit, extending almost to her anus. He held it in place with one hand. With his other hand…

The circle dug into her skin even as something seemed to pull on her clit and labia. There was another surge. The drawing sensation increased. And increased. And increased.

Unsure if the device hurt her—or just scared her—she whimpered.

"All right, I'll leave it at this pressure for a while and see how you do."

Pressure. Her eyes widened. He had a pussy pump on her—a suction device. Now she recognized the feeling. It didn't really quite hurt, but was extremely disconcerting, as if a giant mouth kept sucking on her entire pussy.

She looked up at his looming presence in her shadowy world and couldn't make out the features of his face.

His hands were warm as he massaged a light oil into her stomach and breasts. "You have the softest skin," he murmured. "Like silk." His callused fingers scraped lightly as he rolled her nipple, making it peak.

A sultry hunger flowed to her core, adding to the sensations. Having his hands on her again was the most bittersweet of pleasures.

Jake idly caressed Rainie's full breasts as he contemplated her response. Her color had heightened. Her nipples beaded tightly.

Knowing he needed to unsettle her quickly tonight, he'd removed her ability to move, to speak, to see. Her pussy belonged to him, and the constant pressure from the suction device would enforce that awareness. But she was still too much in her head.

Time to up the game with the next step. He put wet towels on the stone table. A bowl of water with ice. A table knife. The candle had a stand to prevent accidents. His toy bag held aloe cream.

Lifting the candle, he visually noted the height before letting a drop fall on his inner arm. The pleasant splat was followed by a spreading warmth. Not too hot, at least for him.

He looked down at Rainie. The glasses hid her eyes, but with the curved lenses, the flame probably appeared huge to her. With consideration for her more delicate skin, he raised the candle an extra foot of height to ensure the wax had more time to cool. A drop fell on her shoulder.

She jumped. Gasped in surprise—but he didn't hear any sound of pain.

Using his fingertips, he pried up the hardening blob. Beneath, her skin was slightly pinkened. Just right.

And so he began.

Wax play was as engrossingly fun as finger painting in kindergarten. Even more than the artistic enjoyment in creating interesting patterns, he had the delight of using a woman's silky skin and curves as his canvas. Add to that his Dom's pleasure in taking a submissive up and up. He increased the heat, the amount, the timing, until Rainie was straining upward and yet flinching away from each drop.

Her face turned pinker. Her lips reddened with her arousal.

Speaking of which… He set the candle on the table and assessed his artwork. White lines of wax crossed her torso, circled her breasts, and thickened on her lower abdomen. *Gorgeous.*

The quick-release on the suction device ended the pressure. He removed the cup and surveyed the results.

Her clit and pussy lips had puffed up to three times their normal size. "Very pretty."

When he ran his finger over her beautifully swollen flesh, she sucked in a breath. Yes, she was much more sensitive. And her labia already glistened with her arousal.

Damn, he wanted her—but he wanted all of her, not merely her body. Answers came first. At the head of the table, he pulled the gag from her mouth. The mini-dildo pacifier had cute bite marks in it. After wiping her lips, he pushed the glasses up onto her forehead.

"You're looking a little dazed there, sweetheart," he said. "What's your name?"

She swallowed and whispered, "Rainie."

Even before talking to Z, Jake had wondered about the gaps in his knowledge of her. Her father, then mother had abandoned her. She'd been in foster care. But…she'd run away and possibly been with a drug dealer at sixteen. And Miss Lily had given her a home at seventeen. *Wherever you are, Miss Lily, thank you for your care.*

"Pretty Rainie. You're being such a good girl." Murmuring in a low voice, Jake stroked *his* submissive—because, dammit, she *was.* He ever so slowly traced the skin not covered by wax to ease her into a calm state. "The wax looks gorgeous on you, baby."

She relaxed under his hands, her gaze losing focus.

In the same quiet voice, he asked, "Why'd you run away from foster care?"

Rainie's mind had taken up residence somewhere else. But with the question, a darkness slid into her, like a rain cloud over the sun. Foster care. "Mr. Evans tried to…" Her lips had trouble forming the words. "Ripped my dress." Her borrowed clothes had made her look almost as nice as the popular high school girls. "My pretty clothes for Jennifer's party."

"Jennifer? For Jennifer's Sweet Sixteen party?" a husky voice said.

"Invited *me*." To be invited to Jennifer's home was…beyond cool. And the house was sparkling clean, lushly beautiful. It even smelled different, like flowers and pastries. She'd been late. Heard the sounds of people having fun when she came in. *"Go through the living room to the back patio, miss."* Only halfway there, she'd glanced in the door of a game room and seen...

Her feet had simply stopped. *"Look at him..."* Surrounded by his friends, the boy—no, the man—moved with a lean power. Hair a shaggy brown, eyes a mesmerizing green. She'd never seen a man so beautiful. So decent and strong.

"Look at who, baby?"

"Jake…brother." Then the laughter started, right behind her. Horrid. Cruel. She flinched at the sound. *"Hey, Fat Girl, who you looking at." "Jesus, she's staring at Jake." "Like you'd ever get him."* She flinched.

"Tell me, baby. What's wrong?"

"I'm ugly. Trash."

The voice held an angry edge. "Who said that?"

"Jenn…friends." Her legs shifted, but straps held her down. "Run." Tears filled her eyes, a harsh sob escaped. *Run, run home.*

"Jesus, that's it." A calming hand settled on her legs. "You ran home"—the voice growled—"from *my* place, and the bastard attacked you."

She tried to nod. "He said I deserved it. Asked for it."

"He lied."

At the snap in the Dom's voice, her head started clearing. What had she told him? *Trash.* She'd called herself trash. *Oh God.* Her eyes blurred with tears, and she shut them tight. *Let the world go away. Please, God.*

Instead of more questions, he kissed her. "I love your lips, sweetling." He kissed her again, tenderly enough to have fresh tears seeping from under her closed lids.

"I'm sorry I made you cry." Another kiss. "But you're going to finish telling me the rest of what bothers you."

Her mouth clamped shut…and he chuckled.

"You will. Because I'll push you to the point you'd rather talk than suffer." He slid the glasses back on her face, cutting her tie to the world.

Her skin prickled under the cooling wax—and her arousal had

disappeared, although her swollen pussy throbbed. When she opened her eyes, he was only a giant shape in her distorted vision. A black body in the darkness.

"Don't worry, baby. I'll take care of you." The rich timbre of Jake's voice gathered her thoughts to him, holding her in his will.

She sighed, comforted.

"Time for something new. Open up." With firm hands, he pulled her buttocks outward slightly.

Buttocks. Wait. "Uhhh." She squeezed her muscles to prevent the intrusion.

"We've done this before, sweetling, and you enjoy it." He held her open, and the feel of his hands on her bottom, the acknowledgment of his complete control, sent a wash of desire through her.

As he pushed the slickened plug against her anus, her rectal muscles fought and lost. In it went, stretching her. Nerves sizzled to life around the anal rim, somehow connecting with her core and sending heat boiling upward.

A second later, the pump ring once again covered her pussy. The suction started, fattening her labia, sucking on her clit. The pressure increased, more and more, higher than before. Her entire lower half grew stretched and throbbingly taut.

The sounds from other scenes in the room drifted to her. Murmurs and groans. The harsh smack of a flogger. The lighter slaps of a cane. Through the dark glasses, she saw Master Jake, taller than trees, and his broad shoulders and chest blocked out the wall behind him.

He flattened his palm on her belly, and his fingers lingered on the bare places between the lines of wax. "Your pussy is getting slick and puffy, sweetling," he said softly. "I plan to take you hard afterward."

A tremor ran through her at the carnal promise in his voice. The air itself had grown smolderingly thick.

The flickering flame of a candle rose like a sunrise into her field of vision. And then the first spatter of wax. A second later, fire blossomed under her skin.

In exquisite slowness, he drizzled more wax over her stomach and upward to her breasts. Her body tensed with the effort of anticipating each new drop, each new fiery stream. Her pussy throbbed; her anus burned.

She was panting, groaning. More wax.

A pause. Her muscles tensed.

More wax. The thick pleasure of the heat.

Up and up, she rose, and somehow, somewhere, something snipped her balloon loose and she floated free. Drifting. The bite of hot wax hitting her skin faded into the sensation of warm rain.

"That's right, baby." The subterranean murmur felt part of her, as if the voice had flowered from the warmth impregnating her skin.

Lips touched hers. The light scent of forest drifted to her, reminding her of safety and strength. A face brushed hers, the beard a scrape against her cheek. "Miss Lily took you in."

Were they talking about something? She tried to think, failed, and her worries slid out from under her reason.

"You said you need to be more. Did Miss Lily tell you that?"

Sweet Miss Lily. *"Watch your posture, Rainie."* Frail Miss Lily sipped her tea, her spine ramrod straight, not touching the back of the chair. *"Knees together."* Rainie carefully crossed her legs, only at the ankles, to form a pleasing line. *"Too much cleavage is for tramps; you are a lady." "Don your jewelry, and then remove a piece." "Act like a lady." "Don't swear. No one loves a trashy woman."*

Rainie heard herself whispering the rules.

The slow slide of a deep voice murmured. "Hell. She thought she was helping—and instead she overdid it, didn't she?"

She got another kiss. So light that her thoughts floated again.

Sweet Miss Lily. She could almost smell the elderly woman's lavender, feel her soft wrinkled cheek. "She loved me." Rainie's lips curved up as she soaked in the memory.

Question. A question hovered in her mind, whispered by a husky voice.

"Answer me, sweetling."

Question. "Geoffrey's family didn't like me. Said I was coarse. And heavy." The hurt dug into her like sharp claws. She pulled in a breath, blinking.

Her world changed, came clear.

Holding the dark glasses, Jake leaned down to her. His eyes were sharper than lasers. The forehead strap kept her from looking away from his hard face. "Abandoned by your parents, attacked in foster care, criticized by your mentor, dumped by your wimpy boyfriend. No wonder your thinking got screwed up."

Her mouth worked, but nothing escaped. She'd…told him that? Fragments of her own words drifted through her memory, leaving her more naked than any lack of clothing would.

"You figure you have to make yourself over in order to be loved?"

He couldn't understand. "I do," she whispered. "I have to be smooth and put together and polished and—"

"Jesus. Sweetheart, you're not expected to change yourself." He cupped his hands on each side of her face. "You're supposed to find someone who likes you as you are." His jaw was so tense he had trouble speaking. "The rest is just…polish…like you said, but not who you really are, Rainie."

Not who she was?

"It's like clothes—sometimes you dress up for an occasion. But, sweetling, friends like you no matter what you wear. The man who loves you will adore you without any polish…or clothes."

She stared at him.

His lips curved. "As it happens, I love you naked."

A second later, he stepped back.

And wax splashed on her stomach, up over a breast and down again. Over and over. The heat flared along her skin and through her, growing, blossoming, until she floated away in a cloud of sensation.

Jake stopped to survey his work. Rainie's body was covered in a light sweat, and the wax glowed in the dungeon lights.

He felt as if he'd been dragged behind a truck for a few miles, yet exhilarated at the progress they'd made. Fuck, she'd had a hell of a childhood. Everyone had let her down. In a way, he'd been part of her trauma. That ugly revelation still grated through his system.

She'd seen him at Jennifer's party.

He'd have been near twenty-one, just starting to explore BDSM with his mentor, and thinking about enlisting. Hell, if only he'd met her that day, what might he have spared her? Regret bit at him.

But if he'd met her then...if she'd managed to avoid the heartbreak and trauma, would she be the same woman?

All her friends and even his clinic clients poured out their life stories…because she listened without judging. Because compassion was a river running through her so strongly that anyone who knew her could feel it.

He had to think destiny had set Rainie's feet on her path. And, being the amazing person she was, she'd climbed higher than anyone could imagine.

Dammit, though… Thinking about what she'd been through made him growl. Even her beloved mentor had messed with her head. With the best of intentions, Miss Lily had tried to redesign a brilliant spirit rather than teaching her the difference between internal and external appearances.

He sighed. One scene wouldn't address those insecurities of hers. They'd have to come back to this often. If fact, he should talk her into some counseling as well.

As he ran his hand through his hair, he decided to sign himself up for a bit of therapy too. Damned if he didn't have a few problems to work through himself.

Heather'd been quite clear. *"If you'd said you needed me…if you'd given the slightest hint that losing me would upset your life, I'd never have been able to leave."* He wouldn't make the same mistake twice.

Jake picked up Rainie's hand. "Sweetling, look at me."

Her eyes had glazed again. Good. She had no defenses to keep his request, his plea, from sliding in deep. She'd hear him true. "Rainie, I love you, just the way you are. Please don't leave me."

"Jake," she whispered. Her hazel eyes started to clear, to focus on his face. "Wh-what?"

"I need you, sweetheart. Stay here. With me." If he could, he'd relocate with her, but he and Saxon owned the clinic together.

"Need me?" Rainie's brow puckered. "No."

His jaw clamped down. Had he been wrong about what she felt?

"I'm not good for you. Hurt your future. When I'm more. Better—"

He had to blink away the tears. Jesus, he'd been an idiot. Not good for him? "You're perfect, sweetling. Everything I need in a woman. I don't want you to change."

And next time he asked her to do a list of her strengths and weaknesses, he'd write out his own…and share.

His words slid between the clouds and streaked down like lightning bolts into Rainie's soul. She blinked, unsure if she was really looking at him. But he stood beside her, his eyes brilliantly green. And then he kissed her.

Oh yes, it was Jake.

When he lifted his head, she blinked as the world and the evening spun into focus. The dungeon. Her bet. His vow.

"Rainie, I love you, just the way you are. Please don't leave me." He'd said he loved her.

Oh. My. God.

Her breasts were prickling as the wax cooled. Her skin was tingling and throbbing with heat, as if someone had turned the thermostat of her sensations up to the top.

"Do you trust me, baby?" he asked.

"Yes." She did. She really did.

He grinned and put the dark glasses on her. And lifted something long and shiny from the table.

It wavered, ballooned, curved in the distorting glasses—but she knew he held a *knife.*

Her insides wanted to flinch, but she breathed out and closed her eyes. He'd never hurt her. Not Jake.

The blade burned as it touched her upper breast—and she stiffened with a surge of panic. He was burning her, branding her, cutting her.

He wouldn't. He *wouldn't.* A second later, she realized the burn was…cold. The knife was cold. And wet. "You sadistic jerk." Her voice came out hoarse.

The sound of his easy laugh was like sunlight breaking through a morning fog.

Piece by piece, he pried the wax off her, forming small piles to the sides, and the slow scrape of the knife was incredibly erotic.

The glasses and straps came off. He disengaged the pussy pump and removed the anal plug. Every cell in her body, inside and out, was exquisitely sensitive and quivering.

"Up you come." Without any sign of effort, he carried her to a couch in the dim dungeon corner.

Sprawled on top of him, she relaxed into his embrace. God, she'd missed him so, so much. His arms were hard, safe. When she rubbed her cheek against his shoulder, his scent pulled at her as if she were coming home—coming home in a way she'd not ever had.

"Rainie."

She lifted her head.

"I love you, Rainie. Don't leave me."

How could she leave him? But, she couldn't stay. She wasn't good enough—no, she was. He didn't want someone else. Just her. And she loved him—completely. Her voice cracked as she reached out for what life held. "I-I want to stay with you."

The happiness lightened his eyes. Her tears started again. He really did need her.

He kissed her, a velvety brush of his lips. "I'll assist you with your *polish*, if that's what you want. As long as you don't change the wonderful person you are inside."

A sob broke free.

His thumb wiped her tears away. "I can help you find a fancy corporate job here—although losing you will devastate our staff and clients."

"I love your clinic," she whispered.

"Then stay. Stay at the clinic. And stay with me, Rainie."

Her heart kept expanding faster than she could tolerate, pushing on her ribs and filling her with joy. Her words bubbled up and out. "I love you, Jake."

The pleasure hit his eyes first, then his lips curved. "I've waited a long time to hear that." He kissed her, slowly, possessively, and staked his claim thoroughly.

"Now, for something else I've been anticipating." His gaze heated as he leaned back on the arm of the couch and positioned her to straddle his groin.

Every wiggle rubbed her acutely swollen pussy against him. He urged her to kneel up as he undid his pants and sheathed himself with a condom.

Holding her gaze with his, he put his cock between her puffy labia. Although she was slickly wet, the pressure of his iron-hard erection on her abused, suction-distended tissues made her hiss.

"Yes, this'll be fun," he murmured, a wicked glint in his eyes. "You're going to be even tighter than normal." He gripped her hips, firmly pulling her down onto his thick cock.

As he entered her, all steel and velvet and heat, the sensations swamped her mind, arched her back. With a merciless grip, he prevented her instinctive attempt to push away.

His added demonstration of control sent another surge of heat to her center. Slowly, inexorably, he sheathed himself completely.

"Uuuuhh." The moan escaped, the penetration through her tender labia almost more than she could take. His fingers tightened on her ass, holding his throbbing length inside her.

She leaned forward, her palms on his chest, looking down at his wonderful face as gradually the discomfort transformed into a wonderful, dawning hunger. She squirmed uncontrollably, straining against his hold…and realizing that her extremely swollen clit rubbed wonderfully on his groin.

"Say this to me, Rainie: 'I'm perfect just as I am. I don't need to change to be loved.'"

"What?" She stared at him in disbelief and increasing frustration. "Dude, this is sex, not psychotherapy."

His deep, hearty laughter was the most gorgeous sound in the world, filling the hollows in her soul to overflowing. "You're the one who likes efficiency, baby." His chin lifted, and his compelling gaze melted her objections faster than the wax had dripped from the candle. *"Say. It."*

The words slid from her. "I'm perfect just as I am. I don't need to change to be loved." Then she wiggled her hips, making him laugh again. "Now let's—"

"Again."

"I'm perfect just as I am. I don't need to change to be loved." She huffed out a breath. "I'm beginning to have doubts about *your* perfection, though."

Grinning, he let her struggle to pull herself up. Her eyes half-closed at the hot slide of his cock. Thighs straining, she stopped near the top, quivering with him barely inside her.

And then he yanked her down so rough and fast, a mini-climax pulsed through her, leaving her surging with need.

"Say it again."

"Jaaake." Was that whine hers? Her skin was searing hot, sending off heat waves into the room. Her clit throbbed, her insides burned, and— "I'm perfect just as I am. I don't need to change to be loved." And then she added two more of the damned affirmations for extra measure.

"Good girl." Chuckling, he gave her three magnificent thrusts that almost sent her over.

"Please…" At his raised eyebrows, she chanted, "I'm perfect just as I am. I don't need to change to be loved." Over and over.

"Louder." He lifted her slightly.

"I'm perfect just as I am. I don't need to change to be loved. I *do* need to hit my Master really hard. I'm perfect just as I am."

His laugh made her insides quiver.

He moved, finally, *finally*. Up, down.

A coil of pressure grew inside her, a burgeoning upsurge of release rushing toward the beach. The tsunami of sensation was terrifying in its size and strength—and his thrusts quickened.

God, God, God.

Just as the tidal wave rose and rose, he gripped her hips and pushed her up off his erection. Holding her there on the peak. "Look at me."

Her eyes opened. Every muscle in her body was rigid.

"Rainie, I love you. I love you just the way you are." His lips curved, and he jerked her down on his cock, burying himself so deeply she felt possessed by infinity.

And the climax slammed into her and through her and around her in such a massive fireworks of exquisite sensation that even her cries of pleasure held her answer, "I love you, love you, love you."

* * * *

Eyes closed, Jake lay on the dungeon room couch with the softest, roundest woman in the world on top of him. Satiation radiated through him like a Florida sun in July. Eventually—perhaps sometime tonight—he planned to stand up. Clean the equipment. Get his woman home.

Right now, he was disinclined to budge.

From somewhere nearby, a sound drifted to him.

The noise repeated and settled into something recognizable. A man was courteously clearing his throat.

Jake opened his eyes.

Z stood near the couch, a faint smile on his face as he gazed at Rainie's immobile form.

Politely, he handed Jake a bottle of water before draping a fluffy blanket over Rainie's bare back and butt. "Peggy will clean up the equipment," he said. "No need to move anytime soon."

The Dom was a saint.

"Thanks, Z." Jake ran his hand through Rainie's silky hair and let his fingers curve around her nape. The surge of possessiveness was disconcerting…but fucking nice. "By the way, I appreciate the talk we had…and the bet."

"My pleasure." Z tilted his head slightly. "Should I assume I lost another trainee from the program?"

Rainie lifted up, her gaze on Jake's face.

"I'm afraid so, Z." He touched her cheek and smiled into her joyful eyes. "This submissive is *mine*."

Chapter Fourteen

"I'm sure Jake is here somewhere."

At the sound of his mother's voice, Jake grunted and looked up from the paperwork on his desk. "It can't be seven already."

She strolled into his clinic office, attired in tan casual slacks and a tailored silk top. "I'm afraid so, my darling."

His father and Jennifer filled the doorway.

"Hurry up, J. I'm starving," his sister announced.

He grinned at the nickname they'd shared through childhood and tossed his pen on the desk. "Me, too, J. Did Rainie let you in?"

"Ceecee did. She was on her way out," his father said. His gaze took in the papers neatly stacked in the inbox and the pile of stamped envelopes with letters awaiting his signature. Approval accompanied his nod. "Very tidy."

"Rainie's work." Jake rose. "She must be in the back. If you wait here, I'll grab her and we can go."

In the hallway, he heard footsteps trailing him, and he grinned. Of course, they wouldn't wait. His mother's curiosity about Rainie had peaked—thus the maternal directive that they all go out for dinner.

He passed the feline room and entered the larger room containing the dog kennels.

Empty.

To his surprise, raised voices—Rainie's and one of the new kennel attendants—came from the small supply room.

Rainie stood in the doorway, her back to Jake. "Dr. Sheffield pays the staff to care for the animals. That means the cages are kept clean, the food and water dishes full." Her hands braced on her hips. "I don't know what you've been doing, Duke, but it sure isn't your job."

"Aw, c'mon, Rainie. So I slipped up a little."

"The dogs are sick. Their recovery depends on them getting the basics. Food, clean kennels, water—attention. That's not much to ask. Because of you, we let them down."

"Fuck, cut me a break. It won't happen again."

She sighed. "If you screw-off during the honeymoon period of a new job, you'll be a total loss later. I'm afraid this is a difficult way to learn about consequences, but you're done here."

Jake's mom whispered, "Now there's a natural mother." His father rumbled his agreement.

Despite his anger at the asshole attendant, Jake smothered a grin. *Way to go, sweetling.*

"Jesus Christ, you can't fire me," Duke sputtered.

"I can. I did." When she shook her head, her previously French-braided hair spilled down her back…because she'd spent her break playing with a litter of kittens. "None of us have time to monitor you constantly. Head on out."

"You can't afford to sack me. Hell, this place never has adequate staff—you going to shovel shit yourself?"

"That's why Jake and Saxon hired me. Because I'm good enough to have on hand half-a-dozen workers eager to fill in." She glanced at her watch. "Your position will be filled five minutes after you're gone."

She motioned toward the employee lockers. "Collect your things and meet me at the front. I'll write out your check."

"Bitch. Just because you fuck the boss, you figure he won't dump you when he finds someone prettier?"

She paused in the act of turning. "Actually, I don't think he will. He loves me." Her voice softened. "And I love him—enough to fire your worthless ass."

Now that last sounded like his woman. Jake grinned…and blinked his eyes. A guy didn't tear up in front of a younger sister.

Mouth set in anger, Rainie had taken four steps when she spotted Jake…and the people behind him. *Oh no, no, no.* She stopped dead. Jake's family couldn't have missed hearing her argument with Duke.

Not fair. Totally not fair. Rainie glanced around. No escape route in sight. Where was a good hole in the floor when a girl needed one?

A quick glance told her life could truly get worse. Jake's sister was beautiful, and his mother was one of those women who always looked perfectly put together.

Rainie's slacks bore muddy tracks from a Jack Russell that liked to jump. A huge mottled print decorated her left thigh where a Great Dane'd planted a paw to remind her to pet him. Her hair was straggling down her shoulders. A scratch had bloodied one sleeve of her white shirt.

She cleared her throat. "Did you all just arrive?" *Please, let them have just walked into the kennel area.*

Laughter filled Jake's eyes. "I think we caught most of the show."

Footsteps sounded behind her, and Duke appeared.

"Duke." Jake's voice chilled. "Go out the back. Your rudeness to Ms. Kuras eradicated the courtesy of a quick paycheck. It will be mailed."

Duke opened his mouth, thought twice, and left.

Rainie gazed at her lover. Was it tacky that she found Jake's anger—at someone else—to be totally hot? *Stop. Stop now.* Jake's mom stood right there, observing how Rainie was perving on her son.

Rainie flushed. As the door slammed behind Duke, she straightened her shoulders. Hopefully Jake's parents wouldn't be rude to her in front of him. She no longer thought he'd dump her if they disapproved—he had too much character for that—and he loved her. He showed her that every single day.

But she'd hate to cause friction between him and his family. "Mr. and Mrs. Sheffield, I'm sorry you had to witness that unpleasantness. If you'll excuse me, I must arrange for another attendant to cover tonight."

And Jake could leave with his family, and—

"We're here to take you two out to eat, honey." Jake's mother linked arms with her. "I'm Elaine, and I'm so happy to finally meet you. I can see you're just as wonderful as told."

Rainie stopped dead in the hallway, pulling Elaine off stride. "What?"

Jake's mother burst into laughter. "Oh, everyone has been telling us about the woman our son's fallen for. Madeline Grayson. Zachary and his Jessica. Saxon. Such glowing reports."

Glowing reports? But…

But if these people discovered who Rainie was, what she came from, they wouldn't be so nice. And Rainie couldn't deal with waiting for them to be disillusioned.

She gritted her teeth and manned up. Jake had taught her that hiding her past from loved ones was a mistake. "Mrs. Sheffield, you should know, my parents abandoned me. I ran away from foster care. I'm not—"

"Jake told us." Jennifer stepped forward to take Rainie's free hand and squeeze. "But, hey, we were in school together, remember? I just wish… Back in the day, I'd kinda hoped to be friends. Maybe we can now?"

"But…" Jake's family knew? And still, they came here, wanting to go out to eat. Wanting to be friends. Despite the radiance filling her, she made one final try. "I-I have a bad background. On the streets and—"

"Yeah, I bet that's why you could stand up to the dumbass back there." The sister linked arms with Rainie on the other side and started them walking down the hall. "I would've wussed out. You were awesome."

"She was, wasn't she?" Elaine sounded…proud.

Rainie's breathing hitched, and she stopped dead, frantically blinking back tears.

"Whoa." Hard hands closed on her shoulders, and Jake pulled her away from the women and into his arms. "She's the toughest woman I know, but she falls apart if you're too nice to her. Be warned."

"Got it," Elaine said. She smiled at both Rainie and Jake, gathered her husband and daughter with a glance. "We'll wait for you in the front."

And as the footsteps retreated, Rainie heard Elaine whispering, "She's a total keeper, all right. Saxon was correct."

"You suppose Jake'd let me borrow her?" Mr. Sheffield asked. "That new secretary of mine could use some mentoring and—"

She was getting Jake's shirt wet, she realized, about the time she felt his chest shaking. He was laughing.

Laughing.

She pulled back to glare at him.

"Fuck, you have the cutest mean look," he said, kissing it right off her face. "You know, if you show me you love me, baby, I might—*might*—let you eat supper with us tonight." His grin flashed white in his tanned face; his hands were strong on her shoulders, his eyes filled with his love.

She had to clear her throat before she reached up and held his face in her hands. "I love you so, so much. More than I ever can tell you." She pulled his head down to hers.

And she knew, through all the years they would live, the kiss she shared with him then would rate as one of the most loving of all kisses…ever.

His smile lit her heart like a candle tucked inside.

"Mmmhmm." He pulled her tighter into his arms, as if he couldn't bear the few inches separating them. "That works, buttercup. That definitely works."

The End

Sign up for the 1001 Dark Nights Newsletter
and be entered to win a Tiffany Key necklace.

There's a contest every month!

Go to http://www.1001darknights.com to subscribe.

As a bonus, all subscribers will receive a free
1001 Dark Nights story on 1/1/15.
The First Night
by Shayla Black, Lexi Blake & M.J. Rose

Turn the page for a full list of the
1001 Dark Nights fabulous novellas...

1001 Dark Nights

FOREVER WICKED
A Wicked Lovers Novella
by Shayla Black

CRIMSON TWILIGHT
A Krewe of Hunters Novella
by Heather Graham

CAPTURED IN SURRENDER
A MacKenzie Family Novella
by Liliana Hart

SILENT BITE: A SCANGUARDS WEDDING
A Scanguards Vampire Novella
by Tina Folsom

DUNGEON GAMES
A Masters and Mercenaries Novella
by Lexi Blake

AZAGOTH
A Demonica Novella
by Larissa Ione

NEED YOU NOW
by Lisa Renee Jones

SHOW ME, BABY
A Masters of the Shadowlands Novella
by Cherise Sinclair

ROPED IN
A Blacktop Cowboys ® Novella
by Lorelei James

TEMPTED BY MIDNIGHT
A Midnight Breed Novella
by Lara Adrian

THE FLAME
by Christopher Rice

CARESS OF DARKNESS
A Phoenix Brotherhood Novella
by Julie Kenner

Also from Evil Eye Concepts:
TAME ME
A Stark International Novella
by J. Kenner

Acknowledgments from the Author

Thanks to Liz Berry and M.J. Rose for inviting me to be part of the 1001 Dark Nights project. A big *mwah* to Liz who insisted Rainie needed a story and chose Master Jake to be the hero. *He says *thank you.**

Hugs to the October Beach Babes for their sheer insanity. Note to the world: Lexi Blake, shooters, and an interpretive reading of dinosaur-porn—not to be missed.

Many thanks to my amazing crit partners: Bianca Sommerland, Fiona Archer, and Monette Michaels for their diverse talents and enthusiasm in helping bring a story together.

Kisses to my sweet, sexy Shadowkittens for the pimpage of my books, and to Leagh Christensen and her cohort Lisa Simo-Kinzer for their superb Facebook-flogging abilities.

And giant, squishy hugs to all of you who love to read. I never forget that I'm writing the stories for *you*.

About Cherise Sinclair

Authors often say their characters argue with them. Unfortunately, since Cherise Sinclair's heroes are Doms, she never, ever wins.

A *USA Today* Bestselling Author, she's renowned for writing heart-wrenching romances with laugh-out-loud dialogue, devastating Dominants, and absolutely sizzling sex. Some of her many awards include a National Leather Award, *Romantic Times* Reviewer's Choice nomination, and Best Author of the Year from the Goodreads BDSM group.

Fledglings having flown the nest, Cherise, her beloved husband, and one fussy feline are experimenting with apartment living. Suffering from gardening withdrawals, Cherise has filled their minuscule balcony with plants, plants…and more plants.

Connect with Cherise in the following places:

Website: www.CheriseSinclair.com
Facebook: https://www.facebook.com/CheriseSinclairAuthor

Want to be notified of the next release?

Sent only on release day, Cherise's newsletters contain freebies, excerpts, upcoming events, and articles.

Sign up here: http://eepurl.com/bpKan

Club Shadowlands

Masters of the Shadowlands: Book 1

By Cherise Sinclair

*Club Shadowlands is a breathtaking BDSM that held my attention till I turned the last page. In one word...*POWERFUL. *Recommended Read* ~ Blackraven Reviews

Her car disabled during a tropical storm, Jessica Randall discovers the isolated house where she's sheltering is a private bondage club. At first shocked, she soon becomes aroused watching the interactions between the Doms and their subs. But she's a professional woman—an accountant—and surely isn't a submissive ...is she?

Master Z hasn't been so attracted to a woman in years. But the little sub who has wandered into his club intrigues him. She's intelligent. Reserved. Conservative. After he discovers her interest in BDSM, he can't resist tying her up and unleashing the passion she hides within.

* * * *

Shivering hard, she brushed at the dirt and grimaced as it only streaked worse. She stared up at the huge oak doors guarding the entrance. A small doorbell in the shape of a dragon glowed on the side panel, and she pushed it.

Seconds later, the doors opened. A man, oversized and ugly as a battle-scarred Rottweiler, looked down at her. "I'm sorry, miss, you're too late. The doors are locked."

What the heck did that mean?

"P-please," she said, stuttering with the cold. "My car's in a ditch, and I'm soaked, and I need a place to dry out and call for help." But did she really want to go inside with this scary-looking guy? Then she shivered so hard her teeth clattered together, and her mind was made up. "Can I come in? Please?"

He scowled at her, his big-boned face brutish in the yellow entry light. "I'll have to ask Master Z. Wait here." And the bastard shut the door, leaving her in the cold and dark.

Jessica wrapped her arms around herself, standing miserably, and finally the door opened again. Again the brute. "Okay, come on in."

Relief brought tears to her eyes. "Thank you, oh, thank you." Stepping around him before he could change his mind, she barreled into a small entry room and slammed into a solid body. "Oomph," she huffed.

Firm hands gripped her shoulders. She shook her wet hair out of her eyes and looked up. And up. The guy was big, a good six feet, his shoulders wide enough to block the room beyond.

He chuckled, his hands gentling their grasp on her arms. "She's freezing, Ben. Molly left some clothing in the blue room; send one of the subs."

"Okay, boss." The brute—Ben—disappeared.

"What is your name?" Her new host's voice was deep, dark as the night outside.

"Jessica." She stepped back from his grip to get a better look at her savior. Smooth black hair, silvering at the temples, just touching his collar. Dark gray eyes with laugh lines at the corners. A lean, hard face with the shadow of a beard adding a hint of roughness. He wore tailored black slacks and a black silk shirt that outlined hard muscles underneath. If Ben was a Rottweiler, this guy was a jaguar, sleek and deadly.

"I'm sorry to have bothered—" she started.

Ben reappeared with a handful of golden clothing that he thrust at her. "Here you go."

She took the garments, holding them out to keep from getting the fabric wet. "Thank you."

A faint smile creased the manager's cheek. "Your gratitude is premature, I fear. This is a private club."

"Oh. I'm sorry." Now what was she going to do?

"You have two choices. You may sit out here in the entryway with Ben until the storm passes. The forecast stated the winds and rain would die down around six or so in the morning, and you won't get a tow truck out on these country roads until then. Or you may sign papers and join the party for the night."

She looked around. The entry was a tiny room with a desk and one chair. Not heated. Ben gave her a dour look.

Sign something? She frowned. Then again, in this lawsuit-happy world, every place made a person sign releases, even to visit a fitness center. So she could sit here all night. Or...be with happy people and be warm. *No-brainer.* "I'd love to join the party."

"So impetuous," the manager murmured. "Ben, give her the paperwork. Once she signs—or not—she may use the dressing room to dry off and change."

"Yes, sir." Ben rummaged in a file box on the desk, pulled out some papers.

The manager tilted his head at Jessica. "I will see you later then."

Ben shoved three pages of papers at her and a pen. "Read the rules. Sign at the bottom." He scowled at her. "I'll get you a towel and clothes."

She started reading. *Rules of the Shadowlands.*

"Shadowlands. That's an unusual na—" she said, looking up. Both men had disappeared. Huh. She returned to reading, trying to focus her eyes. Such tiny print. Still, she never signed anything without reading it.

Doors will open at...

Water pooled around her feet, and her teeth chattered so hard she had to clench her jaw. There was a dress code. Something about cleaning the equipment after use. Halfway down the second page, her eyes blurred. Her brain felt like icy slush. *Too cold—I can't do this.* This was just a club, after all; it wasn't like she was signing mortgage papers.

Turning to the last page, she scrawled her name and wrapped her arms around herself. *Can't get warm.*

Ben returned with some clothing and towels, then showed her into an opulent restroom off the entry. Glass-doored stalls along one side faced a mirrored wall with sinks and counters.

After dropping the borrowed clothing on the marble counter, she kicked her shoes off and tried to unbutton her shirt. Something moved on the wall. Startled, Jessica looked up and saw a short, pudgy woman with straggly blonde hair and a pale complexion blue with cold. After a second, she recognized herself. *Ew.* Surprising they'd even let her in the door.

In a horrible contrast with Jessica's appearance, a tall, slender, absolutely gorgeous woman walked into the restroom and gave her a scowl. "I'm supposed to help you with a shower."

Get naked in front of Miss Perfection? Not going to happen. "Thanks, b-b-b-but I'm all right." She forced the words past her chattering teeth. "I don't need help."

"Well!" With an annoyed huff, the woman left.

I was rude. Shouldn't have been rude. If only her brain would kick back into gear, she'd do better. She'd have to apologize. Later. If she ever got dried off and warm. She needed dry clothes. But, her hands were numb, shaking uncontrollably, and time after time, the buttons slipped from her stiff fingers. She couldn't even get her slacks off, and she was shuddering so hard her bones hurt.

"Dammit," she muttered and tried again.

The door opened. "Jessica, are you all right? Vanessa said—" The manager. "No, you are obviously not all right." He stepped inside, a dark figure wavering in her blurry vision.

"Go away."

"And find you dead on the floor in an hour? I think not." Without waiting for her answer, he stripped her out of her clothes as one would a two-year-old, even peeling off her sodden bra and panties. His hands were hot, almost burning, against her chilled skin.

She was naked. As the thought percolated through her numb brain, she jerked away and grabbed at the dry clothing. His hand intercepted hers.

"No, pet." He plucked something from her hair, opening his hand to show muddy leaves. "You need to warm up and clean up. Shower."

He wrapped a hard arm around her waist and moved her into one of the glass-fronted stalls behind where she'd been standing. With his free hand, he turned on the water, and heavenly warm steam billowed up. He adjusted the temperature.

"In you go," he ordered. A hand on her bottom, he nudged her into the shower.

The water felt scalding hot against her frigid skin, and she gasped, then shivered, over and over, until her bones hurt. Finally, the heat began to penetrate, and the relief was so intense, she almost cried.

Some time after the last shuddering spasm, she realized the door of the stall was open. Arms crossed, the man leaned against the door frame, watching her with a slight smile on his lean face.

"I'm fine," she muttered, turning so her back was to him. "I can manage by myself."

"No, you obviously cannot," he said evenly.

Also from Cherise Sinclair

Masters of the Shadowlands (contemporary)
Club Shadowlands
Dark Citadel
Breaking Free
Lean on Me
Make Me, Sir
To Command and Collar
This Is Who I Am
If Only
Show Me, Baby

Mountain Masters and Dark Haven (contemporary)
Master of the Mountain
Doms of Dark Haven 1 (anthology)
Master of the Abyss
Doms of Dark Haven 2: Western Night (anthology)
My Liege of Dark Haven
Edge of the Enforcer

The Wild Hunt Legacy (paranormal)
Hour of the Lion
Winter of the Wolf

Standalone books
The Starlight Rite (Sci-Fi Romance)
The Dom's Dungeon (contemporary)

On behalf of 1001 Dark Nights,
Liz Berry and M.J. Rose would like to thank ~

Doug Scofield
Steve Berry
Richard Blake
Dan Slater
Asha Hossain
Chris Graham
Kim Guidroz
BookTrib After Dark
Jillian Stein
and Simon Lipskar

Made in the USA
Lexington, KY
08 July 2015